ANOTHER DAY IN BIRMINGHAM

TOM HARDING SERIES - BOOK 2

TONY KNIGHT

DEDICATIONS:

To my Wife, Linda, for her 'always there' love, support and encouragement in my writing.

Also, to the real Agnes Clarke, my Great, Great Aunt, stabbed to death by her husband, the real Joseph Clarke who was once described in a family history interview with a relative as 'a vile and horrible man'. He clearly lives up to this reputation in real life as well as this fictional version.

ACKNOWLEDGEMENTS:

FRONT COVER PICTURES (left to right and top to bottom)

Canal boats at Stoke Bruerne – c. 2015, credit and copyright, Tony Knight,

Birmingham Policemen in Calthorpe Park – c.1900, with kind permission of the Library of Birmingham. Catalogue reference - Birmingham Parks Album, (Acc. 2012/146),

Hurst Street, Back-To-Back houses – c.1930, credit, unknown original photographer,

Steam Train – At Tyseley, Birmingham – c.1900's, credit, unknown original photographer,

Aldersley Junction, canal near Wolverhampton – c.1910, credit, unknown original photographer,

EVERY EFFORT HAS BEEN MADE TO TRACE COPYRIGHT OWNERS AND SEEK PERMISSION TO REPRODUCE. OUR GRATEFUL THANKS TO THE ORIGINAL CREATORS.

CHAPTER 1 - A POLICEMAN CALLS

Annie Kane looked round the kitchen of the Emerald Drive house on the Key Royale neighbourhood in Holmes Beach, Florida.

It seemed like ages to her, but in reality, it was still less than 24 hours since the culmination of the terrifying ordeal in which her one time english professional genealogist researcher but now new boyfriend, Tom Harding had nearly perished at the hands of her demented but now deceased brother, David. He had previously confessed to murdering Annie's birth mother in England, as well as her step-parents, Bill and Amy Kane in Manatee County after tampering with the brakes on her car that they were driving at the time.

An additional murder of a girlfriend seemed almost academic, but Annie was still struggling to come to terms with the fact that she had shot her brother to prevent him from shooting Tom.

The sound of the door being knocked loudly at the porch on the side of the house woke her from her mental re-assessment of the situation. Could she, or should she, have done things differently?

Tom was also in the kitchen area, drinking his coffee and glanced through the side window which afforded a good view of the paved footpath leading from the roadway to the house. 'Annie, it is the Police,' he said.

'Oh yes, so it is' was her response. 'Looks like Chief Tusker and one of his female Deputies from the Holmes Beach Police Dept. He has been the Chief here for years. He used to go fishing off the pier with my dad on occasions.'

She opened the door and said 'Good morning, Chief. How are you? I have been expecting you. Are you here to take a statement?'

'Good morning, Miss Kane. Can I introduce Deputy Gregson, also from HBPD? May we come in?'

'Yes, of course,' replied Annie, noting the use of her formal name but stepping back to open the door wider to allow the two cops to enter the house. 'Come through to the kitchen. Would you like coffee?'

She introduced Tom to the two police officers and gestured for them to take a seat.

'No thank you Miss Kane. I am afraid this is an official visit to complete the investigation into the death of David Brown aka James Taylor who you will be aware died from gunshot wounds in the next-door property yesterday.'

'Oh!' exclaimed Annie. 'I assumed this would all be pretty informal given the facts of the case?'

The Chief responded to the effect that it was the facts of the events the previous day that they were indeed there to learn. 'At the end of the day, a man died and I believe he was shot by you?'

'Whoa!' cried Annie 'Whoa! Are you about to read me my *Miranda* rights?'

Annie, a lawyer herself albeit a family law specialist and a partner in the Sarasota law firm of Stringer & Geist, knew all about the so-called *Miranda* rights – named after the result of the landmark 1966 US Supreme Court case *Miranda v Arizona* which established the rights of suspects being questioned for alleged crimes, to be given the benefit of certain procedural safeguards.

'I'm sorry, but I have no option as we are dealing with the death of a man whilst on a property that you and Mr Harding were renting. I do not believe these facts are in dispute as it was you, Miss Kane, who made the 911 call yesterday, requesting both Police and Paramedic attendance?'

'I understand, Chief,' Annie said slightly dazed by this unexpected turn of events. 'Let's get on with it, then.'

The female officer took a notebook out of her pocket and waited with her pen poised so that she could record any comments made.

'Right,' acknowledged Chief Tusker. 'Miss Kane, you have the right to remain silent and refuse to answer questions. Anything you say may be used against you in a court of law. You have the right to consult an attorney before speaking to the police and to have an attorney present during questioning now or in the future. If you cannot afford an attorney, one will be appointed for you before any questioning if you wish. If you decide to answer questions now without an attorney present, you will still have the right to stop answering at any time until you talk to an attorney. Knowing and understanding your rights as I have explained them to you, are you willing to answer my questions without an attorney present?' the words of the formal caution rolled off his tongue from memory, given the many times he had used them before with other suspects.

Annie paused, thinking before replying calmly, 'Chief, I actually would like to consult with an Attorney and also to have a representative with me when you question me. I think it is for the best and until that time, I do not wish to answer any questions.'

'That is your absolute right, Miss Kane' responded the Chief, still maintaining the formal tone. 'It does mean however that I must take you downtown to the County Headquarters in Bradenton. Given the seriousness of the alleged offence, I have to treat this as an arrest and I also have no option but to handcuff you. As I am sure you are aware from your own legal background, I do not need an arrest warrant at this stage, as the shooting that I referred to earlier, may be considered a felony and this may result in some serious charges being levelled at you.'

Tom was looking on absolutely bewildered at these developments but realised that the Police Chief was talking to him now. 'Mr Harding, I understand that you were a witness to the events yesterday and so we will need to take a statement from you also. I will arrange for one of my officers to call by this morning to do this.'

Turning to Tom, Annie said 'My business cards are in a small box on the top of my nightstand in the bedroom. Please can you ring my firm immediately and ask to speak to my partner, Patrick Stringer and tell him what has happened this morning. Please ask him to get down to Bradenton Police Headquarters so that he can represent me.'

Tom looked on, stunned as he watched Annie being cuffed by Deputy Gregson before being led to the police car parked on the road outside. He waited until the car had pulled away from the kerb before rushing into the bedroom to make the call to Annie's partner and soon to be Attorney.

With only light traffic along the SR64, the police car soon arrived at headquarters and Annie was escorted into the impressive, glazed building although at the time, she had a little more than architectural design on her mind.

She was taken to the custody desk to be booked in, where she dutifully gave her name and address in response to the questioning from the duty sergeant. After the routine photograph taking and fingerprinting, she declined the option of the three additional free telephone calls as she knew that Patrick Stringer was on his way to represent her and to attend her imminent police interview.

As if by some psychic power, Patrick, one of her partners at Stringer & Geist and a long-time friend, appeared in the corridor and immediately addressed the duty sergeant. 'I need to discuss the situation with my client immediately. Please can you allocate us an interview room where we can talk in private?'

'Yes, of course, Mr Stringer. This deputy will show you to Room 54. We would however like to begin the interview with your client at the earliest opportunity. It is a little after 10am now. Will you be ready for, say, 10.45?'

'I'll be ready when I'm ready' snapped the Attorney. Please can you remove the handcuffs from Miss Kane? I would appreciate it as my client is hardly a flight risk.'

The handcuffs were duly removed and Annie gently rubbed her wrists to reduce the aching sensation and to restore circulation. The deputy showed them to the windowless interview room, unlocked the door and stood back to allow them to enter, before locking the room and returning to his post at the desk.

The décor was plain off-white walls with the room containing basic furnishings including just a table and four wooden chairs, supplemented with two brown sofas, the upholstery of which had clearly seen better days.

Annie and Patrick chose the sofas and after sitting down and removing a notebook from his laptop case, Patrick suggested that Annie had better bring him up to speed with all that had happened that had led to today's events.

Annie knew that her attorney was already aware of her recent trip to England to try to solve the mystery surrounding her birth and how Tom Harding had not only solved her genealogical secrets but had also returned with her to Florida. She now knew where she had come from even if she wasn't who she originally thought she was! She had made her partners at the firm aware of her intended return to the office only the previous day……. 'Wow, was that only yesterday?'

She explained what she had discovered on her return to the house and how it had come about that she had come to shoot and kill her brother David as he, in turn, was about to end Tom's life.

Patrick listened intently whilst, at the same time, making copious notes and occasionally interrupting her with questions so that he could clarify specific points.

He turned to her and said 'Annie, I won't beat around the bush. We don't know what charges the Police intend to bring, if any. It won't be murder as there was no malice aforethought but clearly, it could be manslaughter. As you are not a criminal lawyer and even though you may know this already, I will explain that there are different degrees of manslaughter which can either be a first degree or a second degree felony.'

Annie nodded in acknowledgement as her attorney continued 'First degree manslaughter occurs when someone intends to injure someone severely and instead of just hurting them, the injuries actually cause death. On the other hand, second degree manslaughter occurs when someone acts recklessly and despite being aware of the outcome being potentially fatal does not stop, resulting in another person's death. Manslaughter is also broken up into two major categories which are voluntary and involuntary.'

Annie looked confused and said quietly with a nervous giggle, 'it's complicated, isn't it? Sometimes I'm glad I chose to specialise in family law!'

'It surely is', confirmed Patrick 'but that's what I am here for. To clarify, voluntary manslaughter is when someone intends to commit an act that is neither excusable or justified and which results in another person's death. If an accused person commits the act themselves, this is called Manslaughter by Act which is also known as voluntary manslaughter. There are multiple elements to the crime and a person cannot be convicted if those elements are not met.'

'So, what are these three elements that you refer to, Patrick?' asked Annie.

Her attorney responded quickly saying, 'Firstly, there must be a sudden, unexpected event that serves as provocation with the second element being anger or emotion that results in an action being taken. Finally, the third element is that the action I just referred to, must be the cause of another person's death.'

'From what you just described then', replied Annie, 'is that I could be charged with voluntary manslaughter? If that is the case, what sort of sentence could I be looking at, if I am found guilty?'

Patrick paused, thinking and replied gently 'Annie, I think you are right. I don't believe the Police have any option but to look at a manslaughter charge. If guilty, there would be a prison sentence and possibly a fine in addition. Minimum prison time is laid down as 9 ¼ years with a maximum of 15 years. However, my job is to get you off. From how you have described events, including the facts that your genealogist discovered in England, I think we have a reasonable chance – no, make that a good chance, of getting you off on the grounds of self defense as I will be claiming justifiable use of force, which would be termed involuntary manslaughter. Florida law allows the use of force, even deadly force to protect yourself, your property or even another person, so long as the force is proportionate to the threat. What further helps is that originally, the law said that a person had to firstly try to retreat before engaging with the aggressor to claim self defense and then this could only be raised at a trial. However, in a 2005 amendment known as the *Stand Your Ground Law,* the duty of retreat was withdrawn and replaced with the right to not only stand your ground but introduced a permit to meet force with force, even if that included deadly force. That force has to be essential to prevent death or severe bodily harm or any other forcible felony and is aided particularly if the aggressor is unlawfully in your residence.'

For the first time, Annie allowed herself a little smile and asked her attorney to continue with his briefing.

Patrick blinked his eyes, before adding, 'There's actually more good news. *The Stand Your Ground Law* now allows us to raise the issue of self defense not only at pre-trial but also at trial if it goes that far. However, if the District Attorney or the Judge agrees that your actions were justified, he or she must dismiss the charges and the case will not go to trial. If it does however go past pre-trial, the same defence can still be presented to the jury and they can independently decide whether your actions were justified. If you're ready Annie, let's get the Chief back in here and get this show on the road! Above all, don't worry – I've got this!'

CHAPTER 2 - INTERROGATION

Patrick and Annie were on one side of the table, facing the Chief and one of his Deputies who were both seated opposite.

Chief Tusker opened the questioning by stating that while it was not mandatory in Manatee County to video record all interrogations, it was practice to do so when interviews in respect of the more serious felonies, such as murder or manslaughter were being conducted.

Annie visibly paled at the mention of the word murder.

'Would you have any objection to a full recording being made of our interview?', the Chief asked, turning directly to Annie. She glanced in Patrick's direction and after an almost imperceptible nod from the attorney, she replied 'No, Chief, that would not be a problem.'

At that, the deputy reached over and turned on both the camera and the audio equipment, following which the Chief introduced himself and the deputy before asking Annie and Patrick to identify themselves.

'Right, let's make a start. As you have your attorney present now, I will assume that you will have no objection to this interview proceeding?'

'No objection.' confirmed Annie after an encouraging smile from Patrick.

The Chief continued 'We are investigating the fatal shooting of a UK citizen by the name of David Brown, who also identified as James Taylor. The shooting occurred yesterday at a rental property in Emerald Drive, Key Royale which, Miss Kane, we understand that you were residing at on a temporary basis with a Mr Thomas Harding – also a UK Citizen?'

'Er - yeah, that's right,' replied Annie. I was still clearing out my deceased parent's house next door and wasn't ready to move back immediately after my return from my recent trip to the UK. I still had to clear out some of their effects and had taken some clothing to the goodwill store.'

The Chief studied his notes and paused before responding. 'We just need to establish the facts to decide whether we should issue a warrant and formally arrest you or not. Now, you told my officers attending the scene directly after the shooting yesterday, that Mr Brown whom by your own admission, you fired a fatal shot at, was the same Mr Brown whom you had discovered was your own brother whilst on the recent trip to England that you just mentioned? The same Mr Brown who apparently was also responsible for your parents' deaths a while ago in an auto accident.

The attorney cut in 'Chief, I think you should be careful not to put words into my client's head or in any way imply that the incident was in any way pre-meditated. Whilst Miss Kane did admit to the shooting yesterday, she was also the person who called 911 to get the first responders to the scene.'

The Officer held up his hands in mock surrender. 'Not implying or accusing, Mr Stringer, I am just trying to ascertain the facts. We are also taking a detailed statement from Thomas Harding and hopefully, his version of events will corroborate with yours, Miss Kane. Now,' he said turning to Annie, 'in your own words, please can you just summarise everything you know about this Mr Brown, from when you first became aware of him, right up to yesterday and how it came about that he ended up dead on your rental kitchen floor?'

Annie was flustered but settled quickly with her own legal instincts kicking in as she began the long story recounting how she had hired Tom Harding as a professional genealogist in Southampton, England, to research the facts relating to her birth parentage. She listed each of the discoveries during his diligent research. She added in the names of the detectives in the UK police that had become involved in her case and who had been trying to locate David on suspicion of further murders on his home soil.

The Chief and Deputy listened intently to all that she said, interrupting occasionally to ask for more information on some of her answers in her statement.

Annie finished off by explaining how she and Tom had crossed the line of a professional/client relationship, becoming first friends, then quickly lovers and how after solving the mysteries of her early life in England, they had returned to Florida to work out if they had a future together.

She explained 'We didn't know that my brother was in the local area or for that matter, anywhere in the USA, believing that as he was a fugitive, the TSA would have him picked up if he tried to enter the country. We were clueless to the fact that he had changed his name, then stolen someone else's identity and travelled on a false passport with the intention of killing me to claim my share of our birth mother's estate.'

Annie finished her statement by confirming that after she had returned to the rental from an office visit, in which she was discussing her return to work, she had walked in on David confessing his crimes to Tom, making it quite clear that he was about to kill the genealogist. 'It was the first time I had seen David in person, but I recognised him from photographs I had been shown by the family solicitor and the police in the UK.'

She added 'I had previously found an ex-service revolver whilst clearing my parents' house. I had put it inside one of the pouches in my laptop bag as I had planned to hand it in at the HBPD. There was no doubt in my mind that my brother was about to kill Tom Harding as I heard him say so. To prevent that happening, I was on auto-pilot and instinctively took the revolver out of the bag and I...I..shot him.' Tears welled in her eyes and she held her head in her hands and sobbed repeatedly.

Patrick intervened again 'So you see Chief, I am sure you will agree that Miss Kane was acting in self-defence by preventing harm to another person. There was no pre-meditation as you may have been implying.'

The Chief realised that he was cornered but hit back with a curt response 'I am going to meet with the DA later this afternoon and I will present my full report and recommendations to her. At present, the Assistant DA is taking the time out to interview various witnesses in the hope of evidencing the circumstances one way or the other. Then we will see if it is agreed whether there is probable cause for a homicide charge. If so, a first appearance in Court will be arranged to see what the Judge has to say. Shouldn't take more than a couple of days to set up.'

'One step ahead of you, Chief' came back Annie's Attorney with a glint in his eye.

'Anticipating the direction this might take, before I left my office this morning, I got my paralegal to contact the County Clerk of the Manatee Circuit Court seeking an urgent first hearing if it was required. I am sure you will agree, that Miss Kane does not present any risk to the public or any flight risk and is herself well known in this community for both her legal and charitable work. It's a useful network I have but as a result, we have a provisional hearing set for 4pm today in front of Judge Dean. I have a bondsman ready to act if he is needed but hopefully, we won't get as far as a pre-trial request!

'Got it all worked out, eh?' spluttered the Chief.

'I think so,' came the cool response. 'I have also had confirmation from my Office that we have received copy documents emailed from the firm of lawyers across the pond that were dealing with the affairs of Miss Kane's family after the death of her birth mother, confirming certain facts. Now I would like to spend some more time with my client to discuss strategy. See you later, Chief!'

The Officers left the interrogation room, leaving a colleague on duty outside the door, where Patrick and Annie could see his outline through the opaque door panel.

Patrick turned to Annie to explain that at the moment, she was not under arrest and so would be free to leave. 'Once law enforcement has gathered sufficient evidence through investigation, the case is given to the District Attorney who is effectively, the lawyer for the State responsible for bringing charges against a defendant. The Police refer the investigation to the County DA who goes through the file to determine if there is sufficient probable cause for referring the case to a Judge to issue an arrest warrant and to ensure that probable cause exists. The DA has an alternative to finding if probable cause exists and that is the ability to completely forego criminal charges. This is one peculiar aspect of the American criminal justice system called 'discretion to file' meaning that she has sole discretion to determine whom to charge, what charges to file and pursue, and what punishment to seek.'

Patrick added that the preliminary hearing was regarded as the most critical parts of the Florida criminal process, but a defendant and their attorney can begin building the defense, adding 'but if sufficient evidence is introduced, then there is potential for the case to be thrown out or dismissed altogether, especially if there is no probable cause.'

Annie responded with a question 'Patrick, I am used to family cases and civil law of course but not the criminal side of things, so what do you actually mean by probable cause?'

Patrick answered 'Great question! It's part of a citizen's rights under the 4th amendment. There is no complete definition in Florida law but it is generally accepted that a prosecutor must prove beyond reasonable doubt that a prudent and cautious person would reasonably believe that a crime was being committed and that it was the defendant that likely committed it.

He added 'At the same time, my job is to prove that the evidence does *not* show probable cause or that there are other explanations. Now I suggest you return to Key Royale and change into some slightly more professional looking clothes than those capri pants and tee-shirt that you are currently wearing, just in case! Try not to worry and I will see you here at 3.30pm as I first need to study those papers that were sent from England. If the information is what I expect, I will pass a copy of the file to the Chief to expedite his decision making!'

Annie returned home where Tom was waiting for her and after a fleeting cuddle, she quickly updated him on the morning's events. She went to the bedroom to shower and change and on Patrick's advice to emphasise a professional appearance, she had selected a dark blue skirt and matching jacket, choosing a white blouse to complement.

On returning downstairs, she found that Tom had made up a ham sandwich on white with a few chips on the side. She didn't feel much like eating but realised she was actually more than a little hungry as the Chief had interrupted her first meal earlier in the day, just as she had started to take the first mouthful of her breakfast pancakes.

Tom took the wheel and drove her back to Bradenton for the appointment with Patrick and Chief Tusker. She had asked Tom to stop by the drug store on the way as a headache had started to trouble her but by around 3.20, they had arrived back at the Police HQ and after crossing the sidewalk, climbed the few steps into the lobby where Patrick Stringer was already waiting for them.

'Hi, Patrick', she greeted him and gave him a brief hug.

'Hey Annie, good to see you and you also, Tom. Let's get this over and done with. The Chief is waiting for us and the deputy over there is going to show us to the interview room. Tom, I am afraid that you will need to wait here in the lobby.'

Attorney and client were taken to the same room where that morning's interrogation had taken place and sat themselves down at the table under the watchful eye of the deputy.

At 3.30 on the dot, the door opened and Chief Tusker entered the room with another officer a few steps behind. He nodded to the cop who had shown them in, who then quickly walked back out into the corridor, pulling the door closed behind him.

The Chief had a serious expression on his face as he took his place at the table, facing Annie and Patrick.

'Right' said the Chief, 'I am going to keep this formal.' Annie's face fell and she felt her world closing in around her, such was the grimness of tone. She felt rather than saw, Patrick sitting up straighter in his chair next to hers.

'I had a 2-hour discussion with the DA' continued the Chief 'and I put it to her that there was little doubt in my mind that there was probable cause for a voluntary manslaughter charge. In my view the evidence was there for all to see. Not only were your prints on the revolver that fired the fatal shot at Mr Brown, but you had also admitted to my officers that the gun was in your possession and that it was you, Miss Kane that had pulled the trigger.'

Annie had not been expecting this and could not look the lawman straight in the eye. She stared down at her hands resting flat on the table.

'I also discussed with her the self defense theory that Mr Stringer had so eloquently put to me after you left the Department earlier as well as the extensive data supplied by the firm of lawyers in Southampton, England that had acted for your late family. A Mr Curley was particularly strident in his support for you and has supplied email transcripts of interviews with the UK police during their investigations into the crimes committed by Mr Brown.'

Annie raised her eyes and looked directly at the Chief who added 'The DA felt that whether charges are served on you all hinges on whether she felt that there was premeditation or whether the shooting was a knee jerk reaction with you acting in self defense.'

Annie listening intently, shot a glance to Patrick whose facial expression was very neutral.

The Chief continued 'When the DA considered the premeditation theory, my report emphasised the discovery that the victim had previously been identified by you as the person responsible for your adopted parents' deaths. This gave you a reason to plan to shoot him to avenge them for their demise – clearly premeditated!'

'No!' cried out Annie. Patrick put a hand on her arm and gave her a look which left her in little doubt that he did not want her to react to the allegations.

'If I may continue, please, Miss Kane?' asked Chief Tusker drily. 'Your statement and one from Mr Harding, confirmed each other's versions of events in that although Mr Harding had been in close contact previously with Mr Brown, you had never met him, in person. We also checked the facts with the TSA who confirmed that Brown had entered the United States illegally with a false passport on the pretext of identifying as a James Taylor.'

Patrick intervened 'Chief, we seem to be going round in circles here. You're not telling us any new facts. It's all as per my client's statement!'

'Getting there, Mr Stringer, getting there, 'responded Chief Tusker. 'Just indulge me a while longer, please. As I was saying, it meant that the DA had two possibilities to consider in that both manslaughter and self defense were equally plausible. Considering your impeccable record prior to the event, your community standing and not least, the recent history and the slaying of your adoptive parents, the DA feels that if this went to trial, you would eventually be acquitted and in the circumstances, her decision is one of no probable cause. I don't entirely agree with her but you are free to go, Miss Kane.'

'Whaaaat!' exclaimed Annie, 'Oh my God! That is fantastic' and leaned across to Patrick and hugged him enthusiastically. 'Thank you, Patrick, thank you. I can't believe it. We must go tell Tom straight away!'

They burst from the corridor into the lobby where Tom had been pacing up and down nervously. He turned on hearing the door slam open and rushed toward Annie who had the biggest grin on her face. 'I'm free, Tom! Take me home please. Despite changing earlier, I feel I have stale jail odour on my clothes.' They said their goodbyes to Patrick with a departing promise from Annie to see him at the office on her return to work in a couple of days.

'C'mon Tom, let's get outta here and when we get back, maybe you can help me off with this outfit and scrub my back…….'

CHAPTER 3 - ROOTING 4U

Tom and Annie were in the Emerald Drive back yard lying in a large hammock under the lanai at the side of the pool, watching as the big red sun starting to dip below the rooftops of the houses on the opposite side of the canal. A grey heron was strutting along the dock, checking out the menu for his evening meal.

Annie leaned in towards Tom and stroked him on the cheek. 'An intense couple of days, huh?'

'You can say that, again.' came the reply.

'An intense couple of days, huh?' said Annie collapsing into a fit of giggles. 'You Brits, what are you like?'

Tom grinned back and said 'Annie, can we be serious for a moment? When you left for the office yesterday, I said I was going to give a lot of thought as to our future and whether that future was together. It's just all this stuff with David, the shooting, the Police, well it's all got in the way of telling you how I really feel.'

'Oh shoot.' and then her hand flew to her mouth when she realised the irony of her comment.

'Look, let's put all that behind us for now,' he replied. 'We have options. We can stay as just friends and I can go back to England while you get on with your career and I can come over to visit on holiday……sorry, vacation…… or we make a go at a relationship and see where that takes us. That means staying in Florida as you can't be a partner in a Sarasota law firm while living in England but I think I would be able to undertake genealogy projects from here, maybe take a rental on a small office, if there was enough business around to support it or just work from home?'

'Listen, Tom, 'replied Annie 'I don't want you to feel pressured in any way. It will be a big deal for you, not just moving house but living and working in the United States will be very different.'

'I know that but if we don't try, we'll never know. I really want you to be part of my life and for me to be part of yours. There's nothing to keep me in England. I can let out my flat on a short lease and my only living relation now is my Aunt Jemima in Birmingham. I only usually see her once a year at the moment anyway, but I can always go back and visit. I would love you to meet her as well and we can always Facetime or Zoom with her, which is what I do now.'

'Wow, this is exciting,' responded Annie 'but you don't seem as enthusiastic or at least, if you are, no-one has told your face. Why the frown?'

'Well to be honest, I worry about managing money wise. It took me nearly 3 years to develop the business back in the UK to the point where I could look my bank manager in the eye. In the early days, while I was getting my name known, it was a financial struggle and I worry that it could be the same here? I basically have as my total assets the fee from my last client, a lady by the name of Miss Annie Kane from the USA. The rental income from the Southampton apartment should cover the loan repayments and agency fees, but I will be totally reliant on any genealogy income over here to support myself.'

'Oh Tom, my darling Tom. Please don't worry and also don't get annoyed at what I'm about to say but as you know, I am a relatively wealthy woman. Over the years, my law career has enabled me to put some savings aside and of course, I am the sole heir to Mom and Dad's estate. There is this house and additionally, Dad made some shrewd investments when he was alive. Don't forget also that I am now the sole heir to my birth mother's estate in England. According to the English lawyer, Mr Curley, as David is no longer around, his share transfers to me under the terms of her will. With the value of the Southampton house added in, as that has now had a sale agreed on it, it takes the total to around $1.5M and so I really can help support you. If you had not traced my birth parents as quickly as you did, then David would have inherited the entire estate, before I could have claimed my share within the time limit set in the original will. I know you love your work as much as I love mine. I obviously don't actually need to work any longer but I hope to continue to do so because I love helping families out as much as I love solving their problems. If you live here, as I surely hope you will, the house has no mortgage and so there would only be food and utilities to take care of as far as regular bills are concerned. Let me do this for you, Tom, please.'

Tom interjected 'I don't want to be a kept man and so the sooner I get the Florida branch of *Rooting4U* underway, the better. Have you any thoughts on the best way of marketing the business?'

'Your research on my family and the terrible mysteries you identified and solved means that I now have some closure. Along with the enormous sadness of losing the two wonderful people that I called Mom and Dad, I'm now hoping to find some stability in my life going forward. I am sure that I can help you with introductions to people in my network and in addition, I know my law firm use the services of genealogists for bona vacantia work.'

'Oh,' said Tom 'Do you have bona vacantia over here too? I always thought that was just the british system of tracing people who are entitled to a share of the proceeds of a will?'

'Yes', said Annie 'although it's not a national system as you have in the UK. Here, each individual state maintains its own database and as well as tracing lost heirs, has its own program for dealing with various types of unclaimed property such as insurance funds, shares and that sort of thing. I'm sure I can get you on our firm's list of approved genealogists!

She put on a serious face and added 'there is a stringent approval process of course with lots of paperwork, character references and residential requirements but then there is also the Stringer & Geist fast-track approval system too.'

'OK' said Tom 'what does the fast-track system involve and how can I get on it?'

'Well,' replied Annie 'this involves the applicant taking the interviewer to bed for as long as she demands! Are you ready to start your interview, Mr Harding?'

'Errr, but of course, Miss Kane' laughed Tom, sliding out of the hammock and helped Annie to do the same, standing up together, 'I may need a practice session for the interview, followed by the real thing tomorrow. What do you think?'

'I think Tom,' purred Annie 'you'd better get your pants off and get into the bedroom' Seeing Tom's quizzical eye, she added, laughing 'I am never going to learn to speak UK English. Trousers! – It's your trousers to get rid of, not your pants, although thinking about it, I may have been right first-time round!'

The next morning, Annie announced she was planning to go to the office for a few hours to see the best way that she could ease herself back into her daily routine again.

'Why don't you go up to the AMI Historical Society at the museum complex on Pine and introduce yourself? Mom used to be on the Committee there and so they know me well. I am sure they would try to help you out by passing your contact details to anyone showing an interest.'

'Hey, that's a great idea. Is that the building behind the old jail that you showed me when we came back from your UK visit?' replied Tom.

'That's the one,' responded Annie, 'See if Patty Gee is there. She is the senior docent and will be keen to make some introductions.'

'She is the senior what?' said Tom 'What on earth is a docent?'

'Oh of course,' teased Annie. 'I forgot you Brits don't speak proper English! Basically, a docent is a visitor guide in a museum or a similar visitor attraction.'

'Mmmmm, all right,' grinned Tom 'now, where can I get some business cards printed here on the Island?'

'There is a business center on the parade of shops on East Bay Drive. If you are ready to leave, I can drop you off there and then you can get the trolley back from the stop opposite Publix, the big grocery store.'

Tom watched Annie drive away down Gulf Drive as she headed for the Cortez Bridge on her way to downtown Bradenton and to the offices of Stringer and Geist. He turned and walked towards the store to start the process of becoming a businessman again, without realising he was being watched.

Once inside the store, he showed the clerk one of his existing business cards and ordered a print run of 500 with revised contact details. With the memories of David tracking him down and twice being at the wrong end of a loaded revolver, he also took out a three-month subscription on a private mailbox at the center, so the address could be printed on the cards. Also, any letters would be redirected to him there, rather than to Annie's house. Most of his mail was electronic anyway and so other than sending for certificates and other family history documents, there would be little demand for a physical mailbox. Even the General Register Office in the UK could now send pdf copies of birth and death certificates by email. With his access to most of the major genealogy and ancestral websites, he would be able to download them to his laptop.

The man behind the counter had a large name badge clipped to his shirt, announcing that his name was Brad and he said to Tom 'We're quiet presently and so if you give me 30 minutes or so, the cards will be ready for collection.'

'That's great Brad, thank you,' replied Tom. 'I'll go grab a coffee up the mall.' he said slipping into American mode, 'and I'll be back in half an hour.'

Tom strolled up the mall peering into the windows of the various outlets. A hardware store, Dunkin Donuts and The Dollar Tree, which Tom decided was the equivalent of Poundland back home. He sat at a small table after ordering a coffee and bagel to do some serious people watching, without realising that someone conspicuous but unnoticed was watching him in full view and and blending into his background.

Tom picked up a free paper from a stack by the door and looked at the small, classified ads amongst the many properties for sale, letting and short-term holiday rentals placed by a multitude of realty companies.

There were no ads for genealogists and Tom thought he might try and advertise amongst the locals, drafting the ad in his notebook trying to follow the style of the other contractors offering air conditioning, remodelling, pest control and various other services. He made a mental note to drop into the newspaper office later that day spotting that the address was quite close to the location of the museum where he was due to go later.

After finishing his coffee and scooping up the last few crumbs of the bagel, he walked quickly back to collect the business cards which, as

Brad had promised, were now ready for him. 'I have taken one of them, hope you don't mind?' said the sales assistant, 'I have pinned it to the business card display over by the cash register. I do that for all of my business card clients, and you never know who might see it and be interested.'

'Well thanks Brad,' added Tom 'I appreciate that. Have a good day.'

After hopping aboard the free trolleybus up to the top end of the Island, Tom entered the museum building to be accosted by a lady, probably no taller than five feet with curly grey hair. 'You must be Mr Harding!', she exclaimed, 'I saw you yesterday stepping out with young Annie. I recognised you as soon as you came through the door! I was expecting you.'

'Then you must be Patty Gee?' he enquired 'and please just call me Tom. I am really pleased to have the chance of a guided tour. Perhaps we can talk whilst you show me round? Here,' he added 'let me also give you one of my new business cards,' handing one to Patty.

Tom spent a very enjoyable hour being shown the various exhibits and learning a little about the history of Anna Maria Island from the time of the original discovery by Spanish sailors and some facts about the modern settlers in the 1920's. He explained a little about his business plans and Patty immediately offered to spread the word amongst her many local social contacts.

Walking up Pine Avenue, he noticed the seeming greater affluence in the area with higher price tickets in the shops there, particularly in the boutiques compared to similar outlets lower down the Island. The area seemed more affluent and sophisticated and less tourist orientated. Taking a left and tuuollllllllllllllllllllllllllllllllllllllllllllnurning onto Gulf Drive, it was just a short walk to the editorial offices where $30 later, he had secured an ad in the next four editions of the local newspaper, advertising the services of *Rooting4U* to the residents of Bradenton Beach, Holmes Beach and Anna Maria City, although he still found it difficult to come to terms as to how an Island which was only 7 miles long, could have three cities in such a small area?

He was at home on his laptop, perched on a stool sitting at the breakfast bar when Annie returned from the office. 'What are you doing, Hun?' she asked.

'Just some research, checking up on the sort of rates that other professional genealogists charge in Florida so that I can make sure I am competitive in price terms.' he replied.

Over supper, he told her about his day, his visit to the museum and some of his plans for the future, not realising that someone locally already had plans for him.

CHAPTER 4 – WALES, UK, 1871

Joseph Clarke was not a happy man but then he rarely was, unless he was inflicting grief on someone else. His own family had been often heard to describe him as a vile, horrible man and perhaps they had good reason.

Nothing was beyond his imagination in the field of causing pain to others but this time, even Joseph had surpassed himself and this was the reason that he was on the run from his hometown of Birmingham and currently hiding out in lodgings in the little village of Ogmore, close to the town of Porthcawl on the Welsh coast.

Three nights earlier, he had returned home from work seething with anger. The foreman, Albert Fellows, had pulled him to one side as the men were leaving Josiah Mason's pen factory in Birmingham's Jewellery Quarter. 'Clarke', he shouted above the noise of the furnace being operated by the night-time workforce. 'Clarke', he repeated loudly and then in his broad black country accent, 'Yow're finished 'ere now. Yow waste far too much time gawping at the women and flirting with Enid Murphy, that oirish wench. The girls are there to make pens for Mr Mason, not spend time in idle chit chat with yow. Them talking and singing is forbidden and so you'll be pleased to know I've let 'er go too so 'er family going hungry is all your fault too. 'ope you're pleased with yourself?'

A familiar red mist descended in Joseph's eyes and he pushed the foreman so hard that after stumbling a couple of paces, the white-haired man staggered backwards and fell, his shoulder smacking into one of the stanchions of the turning machine. He tried to get up but Joseph was on him and kicked him on his other arm as he stayed on the floor, followed by a fist in the face. Watching the blood pouring from the man's nose gave Joseph a great deal of satisfaction and he turned on his heel and walked out of the door to the cheers and whistles of his ex-colleagues, happy to see the jobsworth foreman on the receiving end for once.

Joseph walked out of the huge iron gates of the factory, where the air was much cooler, compared to the overpowering heat generated by the furnaces inside the factory.

He had a few coins jingling in his pocket and so instead of going straight home, decided to drown his sorrows at The Jewellers Arms in nearby Hockley Street. He downed three pints of Holt's Mild in rapid succession and became even more argumentative with some of the other customers who were doing their best to ignore his abusive ramblings. He kept one eye on the door in case the police came in, possibly called by Albert Fellows. One man who he simply knew as Bill came up to him and handed him another glass of ale. 'Ee-yar, mate, get this down yer neck for dropping one on old Albert, 'Bout time 'e was taught a lesson.'

'Ta, Bill' replied Joseph 'I'll be off 'ome after this one though and see what swill Agnes 'as dished up for me dinner tonight.'

He left the pub and weaved his way through the crowded pavements until he reached the place that he called home, which was a back-to-back house in Court 3, back of 24 Vittoria Street where he lived with his wife, Agnes. Their son, also called Joseph and their daughter in law, Eliza lived two streets away. These houses had originally been built some 30 years earlier and with next door, as four back-to-back houses, two faced the street and two looked towards the courtyard to the rear.

Although originally designed for single families, the back to backs had quickly become hopelessly overcrowded. Next door to the Clarkes lived a widow by the name of Sally Hudson, together with her five children. The house at the front of Joseph and Agnes was occupied by Hubert Newman, who made glass eyes in his sitting room workshop, sharing the very cramped accommodation with his wife and their eight children. Another large family lived next door to the Newman's. This was the cheapest possible housing for the poverty-stricken working-class families and had come to represent sub-standard construction, inadequate ventilation as well as some of the worst sanitation possible. The shared water supplies meant that the multiple households residing within the enclosed courtyards in the Vittoria Street properties, suffered appalling living conditions. It was little wonder then that these hovel-like conditions had turned Joseph into the angry man he was, given the poor levels of health and hygiene that all of the residents experienced.

Joseph was feeling the effects of the beer as he approached the entry tunnel into the back yard and unable to wait any longer, relieved himself there and then. The stream of urine trickled away adding to the already unpleasant stench from the one toilet shared by around twenty-five people, both adults and children.

He buttoned himself up and then opened the door to his home. Standing there with arms folded was his wife, Agnes and at the table, seated were his son and daughter in law.

'Oh, so yow 'ave decided to grace us with your presence, then, Joseph?' demanded Agnes in an aggressive tone of voice. 'About blurry time. We've bin waiting to dish up dinner an' all yow can do is drink yer wages away!'

'Oh, give over, woman!' Joseph shouted back at her. 'Oi had a swift beer on the way 'ome after a hard day's graft, Surely, nothin' wrong with that or do yow begrudge a man a quick drink?'

Agnes was ready for his lies and argued straight back 'Not according to Lily who works on the pickling line at the factory! She told Sally next door that yow had been let go again... and that means we'll only get a couple of coppers each week while yow be doing labouring at the Wharf, because that's the only work going around here, especially as people know about your violent nature!'

Joseph responded aggressively 'Oi told yow to give over. What violence? Oi be as calm as a millpond on a sunny day!'

Agnes wasn't going to lose this one 'Oh, so decking old Fellows is being calm as a millpond, is it? Yes, Lily told Sally about that too.'

'Now look 'ere,' responded her husband ' yow don't know what yow be blatherin' about. E's always 'ad it in for me, 'e as. Got what 'e deserved. Anyways, there's another job lined up for me and not down the Corporation Wharf, neither' he lied. 'Now, nuff of this claptrap, my sweet. Where's my blurry dinner, eh?'

Joseph senior sat down at the table, pulling his chair out with a racket as it scraped on the wooden floor. Nodding in turn to his son and daughter in law, he sat down and started banging his knife and fork on the tabletop.

Agnes put four plates down, all of which had seen better days with cracks of varying sizes and the pattern nearly worn away. She spooned out a grey-looking stew like mixture to each of them.

Joseph stared at the offering in front of him 'What the... and what the hell is this supposed to be? Looks like the devil's own work!' and he grabbed the loaf of bread and the serrated breadknife next to it on the chopping board and proceeded to gouge a large slice off the end.

Joseph junior and his wife looked on bemused but Agnes exploded 'How dare yow, Joseph Clarke? How dare you? Yow're nowt but a nasty, ignorant, lazy good for nothing who spends more on beer than 'e does on 'is family! 'May the good Lord forgive me for the thoughts I am having about yow, roight now!'

Joseph snapped and not for the first time that night, lost his ability to think straight, no doubt aided and abetted by the beer in his system. He threw the lump of bread towards Agnes meaning to scare her and quickly followed this with the sharp knife thrown in her general direction. He didn't intend to harm her, but Agnes moved to her right to avoid the chunk of bread and in doing so, moved into the path of the knife which lodged in her side, penetrating just under the ribs. She gasped as blood started spurting from the newly inflicted wound and soaked into her once white apron.

Everyone in the room seemed to be watching in slow motion as she clutched her side and then collapsed in a heap on the floor, seemingly unconscious. It was their son who leapt to her aid and raised her head where she lay but she was unresponsive, with her eyes open wide staring back at him.

'She's dead,' he exclaimed 'and yow killed her.' he added accusingly, turning towards his father.

'What? No! No! It can't be,' shouted Joseph. 'I didn't mean it. The silly cow shouldn't have got in the way! I only meant to stop her moaning on and on! Look, we can sort this out, I'll run and get a copper and if we tell the story as it was as to 'ow she was getting in a bit of a strop and went for me and so I used the knife in self-defence, it'll be awlroight.'

'Ok', he added as an afterthought and dashed out of the house, leaving his son and daughter in law to deal with the situation.

In truth, Joseph Clarke had no intention whatever of fetching a policeman. He knew that his reputation preceded him and that as sure as eggs were eggs, there would be a murder charge. The last thing he wanted to feel before he departed this world was the hangman's noose around his neck and the blindfold over his head.

CHAPTER 5 - THE ASSIGNMENT

The next morning, he had no sooner watched Annie reverse off the driveway in her yellow sports car when Tom heard the ping on his laptop, announcing the arrival of a new email. He read the message which was from a Barbara Flynn:

Dear Mr Harding – I saw your advertisement and wondered if you could assist me?

My father always talked about his own grandfather being a soldier in the Civil War and while I always meant to ask him for the details, sadly he suffered a heart attack and passed away a few months ago before I could find out more. I wonder if I could hire your services?

If you can please call me on 941-778-4695, I would appreciate it.

Sincerely

Barbara Flynn

Tom let out a little whoop of celebration at the thought of his second American client, realising from the 778 in the phone no. that this was a person that lived locally. He called the number, omitting the regional 941 and after a couple of rings, someone picked up at the other end, 'Hi, this is Barbara,'

'Oh, hi', answered Tom, before introducing himself and quickly arranging to call on his new client at 10am. He noted down the address and realised that her house on Concord Lane was only two roads up from Annie's house in Emerald and so he could easily walk there. Glancing at his watch, he saw the time was already 9.30 and he quickly gathered his laptop, mini-recorder, notebook and pens and stepped out in the already warm sunshine, quickly reaching the junction with Key Royale Drive.

As he walked along the pavement, not sure that he would ever get used to saying sidewalk, a police car that had been parked further down Emerald Lane passed by, heading for the main canal bridge at the entrance to the Key Royale neighbourhood.

Barbara Flynn welcomed him into her home and suggested they sat in the caged pool area at the back where the sun's rays had not yet reached and so would be cooler for them. He accepted her offer of a coffee and he jotted down the bare facts as she answered his questions about that part of her family history that she did know, including her parents and their birth dates but she didn't have any details of her grandparents as they had passed away before Barbara was born. She told Tom that as far as she knew, her family had always lived in Florida moving from the centre of the State to the Gulf Coast around 50 years before.

'OK' said Tom, 'I'll can start work on your assignment straight away. I would suggest a flat fee of $250 which will give you 5 hours of research time. At that point, I will contact you to present an update and then agree either extra research hours or to terminate at that stage. Any expenses will be additional,' he added.

'That is wonderful!' exclaimed his new client 'I am so excited and look forward to hearing from you just as soon as you can.'

Tom hurried back to the Emerald Lane house that was currently his home and perched in his favourite breakfast bar location, he fired up the laptop to research some basic civil war facts to try and prepare a timeline rationale that supported the possibility that Barbara Flynn had indeed had a military ancestor. He already knew that the civil war had taken place between 1861 to 1865 when government troops, known as the Union Army, fought against confederate soldiers who represented some breakaway Southern States seeking independence.

This was very much relatively simple, bread and butter family history research. He had the names and dates of birth of Barbara Flynn's parents and it should be a straightforward task to track the family back via the USA census returns as they were readily available online as late as 1940. Tom reflected on the fact that the USA did not have the same attitude to privacy as was the case in the UK, where a 100-year closure period applied to most public records.

He started to draw a basic family tree diagram with Barbara's name at the bottom and showing her birth year as 1961. Above that, he wrote the names of her parents, Hank Flynn and Grace Timmins recording their marriage year as being 1958 and their respective birth dates as 1935 and 1937.

Tom quickly logged on to his Ancestry account and after finding both Hank and Grace as small children in the 1940 census return, he soon also had the names of all four of Barbara's grandparents. He was on a roll now and quickly followed the family backwards through the various US census returns until he reached 1860, the year before the American Civil War had started.

The draft tree that he had set out as a chart, now had five generations starting with Barbara's parents. Barbara had insisted that her family were all long-term Florida residents and indeed, her grandfather Charles Walter Flynn was living with his wife Sandra, with Hank as an only child in Orange County just outside the Orlando city limits. Tom murmured to himself 'Ah, that's interesting,' and duly noted the facts that sprang off the page that Charles had been born in November 1909 but in fact, came from Baltimore, Maryland. After locating their marriage, Tom mentally thanked her grandparents for helpfully just making it into the 1910 census return, carefully cross checking as he moved through the years. Genealogists were perhaps the only professionals it was thought that taking more steps backwards, rather than forwards was considered a good thing!

He poured himself another cup of coffee and after adding some half and half to the beverage, he continued with the research. He soon had a great deal of information on Barbara's family lines.

He thought it a tad inconsiderate that the war had started in 1861 and ended four years later so that neither the 1860 nor the 1870 census returns gave away any information as to a military background of any of Barbara's ancestors, instead showing a heavy agricultural influence and a not insubstantial involvement with the slave trade, one of the major factors in the start of the civil war, as the abolitionists in the more industrial northern states were applying pressure on their southern counterparts to cease their inhuman labour activities .

Tom switched to checking the Civil War Muster Roll Abstracts and he found what he was looking for in one of those eureka moments that all genealogists experience occasionally. The name of Captain Frank Flynn lay before him. Captain Flynn, the record told him, had blue eyes, brown hair and a light complexion. Clearly a small man at just 5ft 4 inches, Frank, whom he had already identified as Barbara's 3 x great grandfather, had been shot leading a confederate attack on a union brigade in the battle of Olustee in February 1864. Although removed to a nearby military hospital, Frank had died from his wounds a few weeks later but not before he had been recognised for his bravery with a posthumous award of the *Roll of Honor.*

So, here was the very man that Barbara had heard family myths about and unusually, a true story unlike many of the hand me down myths that were a regular feature of some family trees through generations. One such piece of research Tom had completed last year was where an alleged Ghurkha captain in World War One had turned out to be a 2nd Lieutenant in the rifle brigade Ghurkha reservists.

Back to the present and having found Frank previously on the 1860 census owning a large farm, he had already discovered that the man had been born in Ireland in 1821 and was not a native of the United States. He knew that Barbara was going to be really excited as the fantasy of Irish ancestors did appeal to the vast majority of US citizens. Tom could hopefully imagine Barbara's words when he delivered his report, 'Tom, I need you to carry on with the research and find out everything about my Irish pedigree!'

He had been sitting at the laptop for a couple of hours and so Tom decided to stretch his legs and take a walk along Key Royale Drive and down to the golf course. One of his watcher's assistants picked up his cell phone and reported into his boss.

It was Saturday morning, Tom and Annie had enjoyed a lazy morning over a leisurely breakfast. Barbara Flynn's reaction to Tom's news had been exactly as anticipated and she had asked Tom to continue his research but to concentrate on her Irish roots.

Annie had been given a difficult case to get her teeth into on her return to the office involving an acrimonious divorce between a very wealthy local businessman and his wife. She said to Tom 'Fortunately, there are no children involved to squabble over, just the settlement to negotiate. It's going to keep me busy for a while! To be honest though, my heart isn't in it. The business over David is still unsettling me.'

'What about you?' she added, 'anything else lined up?'

'A couple of very straight forward enquiries in addition to Barbara's research. Having said that, a lot of Irish records were destroyed when Government offices were destroyed in the 1922 uprising and so it's not so straightforward. I have warned Barbara of that, and it may take a while. I don't imagine she will be keen to fund my expenses for a trip to Dublin.' he replied.

'I was going to suggest that you try some business networking. Did you do any formal networking in the UK?' she asked.

'I did go to a meeting once, but I was a financial adviser then, not a genealogist, but I guess that's not a bad shout. What local groups are there? I imagine that if it's anything like the UK, where there has been an explosion of networking groups setting up that there will be plenty to choose from.' he replied,

'Well, one of my clients, Angela Loach, is the area organiser for the Manatee Networking Group, or MNG for short and I am sure there is a group that meets in Bradenton. You should visit. Even if you decided not to join, there's a good chance you could make some useful contacts from other local businesses. I'll text her now and ask her.'

Annie tapped away on her cell and sent the message. Within a few minutes, her device pinged to confirm a response. 'It's Angela,' she told him 'Yes, not a problem and she's going to book you in for a visit to the Cutting-Edge Group, over breakfast next Tuesday at 7.00 am. They meet just off 39th Street. I'm planning to work from home that day so you can borrow my car as long as you don't wake me up too early!'

Tom checked the website for directions and noted that the structure of the meeting was very similar to the group he had attended back in the UK meaning that he had to give a 60 second pitch about his business. The rationale was that each member looked for business opportunities for the other members, advising on the sort of business that they were each looking for.

'It's called an elevator pitch over here,' advised Annie 'on the basis that any business owner should be able to deliver a pitch in the time it takes to ascend 20 floors in an elevator.'

It was still dark when he left the house the following Tuesday as he wanted to leave plenty of time to find the venue, which was actually very straightforward. A not unattractive lady was at the door to greet him. She introduced herself as Carrie and said, 'I will be your host this morning, anything you need to know, just ask!'

'I will, thank you, Carrie.' replied Tom, as he collected some breakfast from the buffet and sat down with three other men of varying ages. Introductions were made with the usual excitement over Tom's English accent. The inevitable 'I have a friend in Manchester. Maybe you know him?' question but Tom was getting used to the locals thinking that the UK was such a tiny place!

He chatted over breakfast to his new acquaintances, learning about their businesses and telling them about genealogy and how he was now in Florida as a result of Annie hiring him in the UK, having discovered she had been adopted in England as a baby.

The meeting started and the captain as he was referred to, made the introductions and explained the agenda for the benefit of the visitors. Tom listened intently to the pitches from the members and made a note of people who could be useful to him such as the printer who might be able to produce family tree charts for him. He would start off with a self-made website but there was a marketing consultant who could probably help with search engine optimisation as the business developed. One woman stood up and said she wanted an introduction to family lawyers and so later, Tom told her that he would introduce her to Annie. All in all, it was quite a positive experience and Tom was told that he could visit again the following week if he wanted to. He was very impressed as to how friendly everyone was and how much they wanted to help each other. A lot of people asked him for his card as he left and so he walked back to the car with a very positive feeling.

It was just after 9.30 am and the traffic was heavier as he drove back to the Island, crossing the drawbridge where Annie's stepparents had perished just a few months before. He knew that Annie always avoided the SR64, preferring to take the Cortez Bridge route to Bradenton, to avoid passing the scene daily on her way to the Bradenton office where she headed up the family law division, having moved from a similar role in the firm's smaller branch in Sarasota.

Two lanes had merged into the one about a mile before the bridge and so the 45-speed limit reduced to a maximum of 35 on the approach. Traffic was inevitably heavier in the one lane single file road, but he was enjoying the view across the Intracoastal Waterway which separated Anna Maria Island from the mainland.

Tom had assumed that it was just a local feature given the frequent use by pleasure boaters, but Annie had told him that although there were gaps, the waterway actually ran from Boston on the East Coast of America down the Florida coastline with a few breaks, before passing round the tip of the State and returning up the Gulf Coast as far as Tarpon Springs which was around 60 miles north of Bradenton. Annie had teased Tom when he had stifled a pretend yawn 'It's what you used to do to me in Southampton, doing the tour guide bit when I was in England, showing me this important Fleming building or the Civic Centre that won an architectural prize, so don't accuse me of being boring, Mr Harding!' she responded.

He continued the drive home, unknowing that someone had just reported on his cell phone to his superior as to Tom's whereabouts. Parking the bright yellow sports car in front of the double garage that seemed to be a feature of many of the homes in the neighbourhood, Annie had seen him approach and met him just inside the doorway. He noted she was still in nightwear and said 'Err, I thought you were having a working from home day and not a lazing around in the home day?'

Her response was to grab his arm and steer him towards the bedroom. 'Just because you got up early for your meeting, there's no reason why you're not going to get up again for an appointment with your favorite lawyer!' she said playfully pushing him onto the bed and shedding her nightdress in one movement.

CHAPTER 6 – SNOW HILL STATION

Joseph Clarke ran until his lungs felt as if they were about to burst. Years of beer and cigarettes had rendered him quite unfit. His house wasn't too far from Snow Hill Station which just that year, had opened as a permanent building replacing the original 1850's wooden structure. Trains went from Snow Hill regularly to London, Liverpool, Wolverhampton, and Wales but Joseph didn't know, nor indeed did he care where he was going. He just knew he had to put some distance very quickly between him and Birmingham.

He had now slowed down to a rapid walk through the station concourse, partly as he was out of breath and partly because he didn't want to draw too much attention to himself.

He had no ticket, nor did he have money to buy one as he had spent his last few coppers down the pub. He waited by the ticket office until a well-dressed man with a flustered look about him, turned away from the small glass window, trying to balance his wallet and train ticket in one hand, a suitcase and overcoat in the other. Joseph seized the opportunity and bumped into the man while practising his pick pocketing skills learned several years earlier, 'Oh, sorry me ol' mucker,' he said apologising profusely, seemingly helping his victim to recover his belongings, but he was soon in possession of a ticket to freedom as well as a small brown leather wallet which he had quickly stuffed into his pockets.

Wanting to avoid any suspicion being drawn to himself, he waited until the ticket collector had finished assisting an elderly couple and as Joseph flashed his ticket at him and sidled past him, the GWR official pointed in the direction of platform one, where a green steam engine was hissing and puffing to get up a head of steam as it prepared to start its journey. As he walked down the platform, he noticed a man deep in conversation with a well-dressed lady and unnoticed by either of them, he picked up a small suitcase which was standing on the floor behind them. So now he had a ticket, money from the stolen wallet and luggage to his, as yet unknown, destination.

Joseph opened the door to the second-class carriage tipping his forefinger to his head. 'Good evening' he said to a fellow passenger as he sat down on the wooden bench, receiving a 'good evening' in response. He had only been on a train once before in his life several years ago and he looked round, taking in his surroundings. The brown and white carriage was a single compartment with a long wooden seat on each side. There was no corridor and no way of changing carriages unless a passenger changed places at one of the frequent station stops.

Almost immediately, the guard gave a long blast on his whistle and the steam from the engine enveloped the carriage momentarily before it turned into flying white breath as it chugged away on its journey.

The light was poor with the only illumination provided by a dripping smelly oil lamp swinging to the motion of the train as they picked up speed. 'I say, old chap, where are you travelling to?' asked Joseph's new companion. Joseph was nonplussed because he simply didn't know, having placed the ticket and the contents of the stolen wallet into his pocket without examining them. He had disposed of the wallet in a nearby litter bin prior to boarding the train. He thought quickly 'I'm on a journey to God's own country, and you?'

The man replied 'Ah, so you're off to Cardiff too. Good man! I'm Henry, by the by.'

'Err, James,' lied Joseph with a nod, not wishing to reveal his true identity or to be particularly friendly. 'Now if you'll forgive me, I am somewhat fatigued and propose to take a nap.'

'Of course, old chap, might have a snooze myself. It's going to be at least five hours before we reach the terminus, I imagine.' replied Henry.

Joseph had no idea how long the journey would take. He was not an educated man. He had overheard conversation in the past about Cardiff and as far as he could recollect, it was a town in South Wales, but if Henry was right, it would be the early hours of the morning before they would be disembarking.

As he slept, the stations flashed by – the train passed the jewellery quarter where, until very recently, he had lived and worked. Then in turn, Smethwick, Kidderminster, and Cheltenham were behind them as they chugged onwards towards their final destination.

Joseph woke with his back aching caused by being slumped in a cramped position on the wooden bench. He was cold because the carriage windows were open to the night air, as glass was only a benefit for the wealthier passengers in the first-class compartment to the front of them. He so wished he had pinched the overcoat from his earlier victim too as he pulled his jacket tighter around him, to try and fend off the cold air that swirled around.

He looked across at Henry who grunted in his sleep with his head at what looked an awkward angle across the back of the bench. There was a bump as the train went over some points and Henry opened his eyes taking a minute or two to get accustomed to the dim light.

The Welshman looked across at Joseph and asked him if he had slept. It was the fugitives turn to grunt 'Yeh, a bit' and noted the first glimmer of light filtering through the cloud as dawn approached.

'Well, another thirty minutes or so and we should be there,' said Henry after consulting his watch, fastened into his waistcoat pocket via a half albert gold chain.

Joseph had a plan 'Where are you going onto afterwards or are you staying in Cardiff? he asked. Another of his skills was mimicking accents and he knew it was time to limit the use of his Birmingham vocals.

'Oh, I'm off to Porthcawl where I have business with a supplier later.' was the response.

'Well, that is an amazing coincidence! 'replied Joseph, 'Porthcawl is my destination too. I have an aunt who lives there and as she is sick, I said I would visit her. Perhaps we can take a hansom cab together?' he added, wondering where Porthcawl actually was, but deciding that anywhere was a safer destination than Birmingham.

'Actually James, that won't be necessary as my colleague has arranged for a carriage to be waiting for my arrival, but I am sure that there would be room for you too and we can drop you off in the town.'

'That would be absolutely splendid,' answered Joseph 'you are most kind, Sir.'

After they had descended onto the platform and had walked just a few steps, Joseph was alarmed to hear the guard call him back 'Sir, Sir!' was the shout, 'you have left your suitcase in the carriage!'

Joseph smiled and thanked the railway official and thinking that he should be forgiven for forgetting a suitcase that didn't even belong to him! He retrieved the luggage and caught up with his newly made acquaintance in Henry. After exiting the station, the pair were soon on their way to Porthcawl in a small carriage pulled by two large black horses, gently carrying them on the 25-mile trip from Cardiff.

CHAPTER 7 – THE CHIEF IS BACK

After their intimate spell, Annie was working on her laptop preparing a document for the court on behalf of a client, while Tom was sending an email to request a quote for some leaflets from the printer whom he had met at the networking meeting earlier that morning. He planned to distribute the flyers to some of the more wealthy residential areas of the Island, figuring that these were residents who may have some sufficient disposable income to enable the hiring of his services.

They were both engrossed in what they were each doing and startled, looked up at the sound of the doorbell, neither of them having seen their visitor park on the roadway outside, twisting the revolver into its holster to assist his exit from the car and walk up their driveway.

'Heck, it's Chief Tusker. What can he possibly want with me now?' questioned Annie 'Surely, all that shooting business is behind us now? He did say the DA wouldn't be proceeding with any charges!'

'I'll go,' offered Tom 'He's seen us through the window anyway, so we can't exactly pretend that we're not in!'

He opened the twin paned frosted glass panelled door 'Good morning, Chief. How can we help? Annie is in the living room.'

'Thank you,' replied the Chief stepping into the house 'but it's actually you that I have come to visit.'

'Me and what have I done? Did I drive at 26 in the Key Royale Drive 25 miles an hour zone?' he added with more than a touch of sarcasm.

'No, I'm not actually here on police business, it's a personal mission. Look, I'm sorry I had to get tough last week with you, Annie but it's my job. Tom…….is it ok to call you Tom? I'm Bob by the way. I want to talk to you about your job.'

Nonplussed, Tom said 'Yes fine, err Bob. What do you mean?'

The Chief looked sheepish and hesitated for a couple of seconds 'Well, you have just completed a genealogy assignment for Barbara Flynn?'

Tom's eyebrows knitted together, puzzled 'Sorry, I can't comment on that. Client confidentiality, Chief, I'm afraid.'

'Darn it, you'll find if you live around here for more than a short while, that we are a small community and that everyone knows everyone else's business. Besides, what you don't know is that Barbara and I are good friends, an ex-neighbor of mine, when I lived on Gull drive. So, she told me how impressed she was at the detail in your research and since then, I have been keeping an eye on you and talking to people you have talked to, including Patty Gee over at the museum and young Brad, the clerk down at the office supply store on the East Bay Drive Mall, who was happy to talk about your plans.'

Annie interjected with a smirk on her face 'Look Bob! Is it ok to call you Bob? This is all very interesting but if you're not here on police business, get to the point. It's not like you're reading a deposition in Court!' her eyes twinkling as she saw the humour in her own joke.

'No ok, I get it,' came the response. 'You obviously know what you are doing from the things people have told me. From what I read, you also handled Annie well... umm, professionally speaking of course,' he spluttered, colouring up but recovering well from his verbal faux pas.

'Well, the thing is, I would like to hire you to try and solve a family mystery in my own line.' He continued 'You see, when I was a boy, my daddy told me that his family came from England and that there was a bit of a strange rumour that they were not the most honest members of society. When I was older and was applying to join the police, he told me that I would not be accepted, if they found out about his ancestor's past. Once I was in the police, I thought they had either not found out or more likely that there was nothing to find out. I preferred the second option and forgot about it until you came to the Island and showed that you are pretty good as an investigator in your own right.'

'Do you know which part of England that your family were supposed to have come from?' asked Tom 'it's a bigger place than most of you seem to think.'

'Hell yes,' came the reply, when I was tiny, I always thought that it was a funny name for a town because it kept me thinking about a pan of overcooked bacon. It was quite a few years later I discovered that Daddy wasn't talking about a place called Burning Ham, but he was referring to Birmingham, the same as in Alabama!' he laughed and then added 'Do you know it, Tom?

Tom was astounded and said, smiling 'Yes, I know it well. One of my family lines came from there too and I still have an Aunt Jemima living on the outskirts of the city. I would be more than happy to take on your assignment. I will email you my fees for standard online research but will warn you that if I found it necessary to travel back home to England, I would be looking to be reimbursed my travel, food and other incidental costs. It all depends on how far I can get working remotely. Don't worry, I would travel cattle class and I might be able to stay with my aunt, if I give her some notice, so as to keep the expenses down.'

'Ok,' said Bob Tusker 'consider yourself hired. What's the first step? he enquired.

'So, as I said, I'll send you the fees and a draft contract to sign and return, please. Then what I will need from you is a document either handwritten or in a Word file noting down as much as you know about your family. I would like the names of your parents, grandparents, great grandparents, if you know them, as well as any aunties and uncles, brothers, sisters, their birthdays, marriage and death dates. Just any facts whatever that you can remember. If you have any other living relatives, ask them too. If you are unsure or if it's a guess, then tell me that also so that I can treat that aspect with caution.' Tom instructed.

'I can do that and I'll let you have the information back by the weekend if that is ok with you?' asked the Chief. 'I mean, with the exception of the nagging doubt based on Daddy's story, I always thought my family came from Florida and Georgia as my mom told me that she spent her childhood in a township called Byron. But I am certain that I have a 100% USA pedigree anyway.'

'That'll be fine' responded Tom 'but there may be some surprises on the way. Genealogists have a bit of a tagline which basically says that a person doesn't know where he or she's going until they know where they came from. What that means is that learning about the past can help explain traits, interests as well as likes and dislikes and indeed, their current personality. For instance, one client of mine in England loves eating black walnuts. He didn't know why, but his father and grandfather also had the same unusual taste and would often spend a lot of money sourcing a supply to snack on.'

The Chief went to interrupt, but Tom held up his hand to stop him and continued 'When I did some family research for him, he had specifically requested that I should include information on the houses that they had lived in and to provide as much detail as possible. I found myself researching title deeds, old maps and newspapers. What I found and it came as a bit of a surprise to him, was that some of his long-time deceased ancestors back in the 19th century, used to own a walnut orchard in a little village on the east coast of England. Apparently, black walnuts were introduced into Europe in the mid 1600's and were reputed to have herbal medicinal properties. This was based on reports that the population of the villages near the main black walnut growing centres apparently suffered far fewer heart issues. Modern research proved that black walnuts lower cholesterol levels in the body and so it is likely that there was some truth in the myth. My client had no idea why he liked black walnuts, but my research showed that nuts were in his DNA!'

'Mmmm,' cut in Annie 'and there was me thinking that a man's DNA was controlled by his nuts.' she added mischievously.

The weekend following the Chief's unexpected visit, Tom was reviewing the notes that Bob Tusker had sent round to the house. In his usual fashion, he began every research project by drawing up a simple line chart mapping out the generations to see if there were any gaps.

'This is very strange,' he said to Annie, herself engrossed in the pages of the Bradenton Herald. 'I've got the Chief, his parents and grandparents as well as his great grandparents listed and validated back to the 1900 USA census and then……. nothing! Although the ancestral line starting with his grandparents shows they were born in Georgia and Florida respectively as he suspected, the census states that his great grandparents were English, both born in England with his great grandfather having naturalised as a US citizen in 1895, two years after the family had arrived in the country.'

'So, what's strange about that?' questioned Annie, absent mindedly. 'Surely you can pick them up on the passenger list records or on the Ellis Island immigration database, arriving in America?'

'Well spotted, apprentice Kane,' responded Tom with a touch of irony. 'I can see that my hours of careful tutoring in England haven't been a total waste of time.'

'In fairness, it wasn't just family history in which you were giving me the benefit of your expertise,' she said, winking at him. 'So, what's your problem, Professor Harding?' the sarcastic tone being returned in Tom's direction.

'Well, they're not on the Ellis Island website listings but in fairness, they could have arrived at any one of the Eastern seaboard ports. Alternatively, the data could have been mis-transcribed or simply lost by the State concerned. I have found some passengers with the family name of Tusker arriving in Boston in 1893 with the right first names but they're not quite the right age. If I return to the census, the couple who were the Chief's great grandparents, Theodore and Lilian, should have been aged 43 and 42 respectively in 1893. The two passengers on the manifest are both shown as being 39 years old.'

'Nothing really strange about that though, is there? You are always telling me that mistakes are made particularly with people's ages because someone had copied it down wrong or misheard what they were being told in the first place?'

'No, no – its stranger than that! As I said, assuming it is them on the passenger list and I have reasonable confidence in that, then the manifest shows that the ship had left Liverpool three weeks earlier, but prior to their departure, there is absolutely no trace of them in any of the British online records!'

Annie was listening intently and nodding her encouragement, silently urging him to continue.

'Well, the Chief's great grandparents are not on the 1881 or 1891 UK census where I would expect to find them. I have tried the English and Welsh census records as well as the databases on Scotland's People. I have tried the various different spellings of Tusker and I have even tried wild cards in the search engine. Zilch, nothing, nil, nowt and sweet FA.'

'Sweet FA?' I've not heard you mention that phrase before. I remember when we were living in the Southampton apartment, the local soccer team were playing Portsmouth in the FA competition or something and you told me then that FA stood for Football Association?'

'Mmmmm, well yes.' mused Tom, 'It also has another more very basic definition as a synonym for nothing. The A stands for all and as for the letter F…. well, I'll leave that to your imagination.'

Annie looked puzzled and then almost instantly, realised what he meant and frowned 'Tom Harding, you are a potty mouth. Where has my very polite Englishman gone to?'

'Sorry, my love' apologised Tom. 'It's just so frustrating. It's not often that I hit a brick wall this early in a research project. I can usually get back to the 1830's very quickly but to get blocked off in the 1890's is not only very unusual, it's downright annoying! I'll have to ask the Chief whether he's ever taken a genealogical DNA test. Maybe that will throw some light on things? I'll email him now. Hey, do you think I should call him Bob or just Chief? It still feels odd being on first name terms with someone who was trying to hook you up with a homicide charge just a week or so ago!'

'Yeh, I know what you mean, even though he used to occasionally go fishing with my dad, I've always known him and traditionally referred to him as Chief, as have most Islanders in fairness. I'll carry on calling him by rank but it's not a problem with me how you choose to address him. He's your client, after all!'

'Yes,' said Tom 'and we know what happened last time I crossed the line between a professional genealogist/client relationship to a personal one,' he added with a grin on his face. I think for now, I'll follow your lead and he can be Chief to me too.'

He picked up his Samsung phone off the table and punched in the Chief's personal cell phone number that he had been given earlier. 'Oh, hi…err, Chief. It's Tom Harding here. I have been looking through the family notes that you gave me, trying to make some sense of them and I was just wondering if you had ever taken a DNA test on any of the genealogy sites?'

Annie could only hear one side of the conversation but heard Tom reply to the Chief's answer by saying 'You have? Ok, would you be happy to let me have your log in details and then I can look into that side of things for you? Great, well if you can email it across to the address on my card, that would be great.' and added almost as an afterthought 'It could be useful in the long term.'

He ended the call and returned the phone to the side of the chart. He turned towards Annie and said 'Yes, apparently he did do a test earlier in the year and he's patching the details across so I can log in when I have some spare time. Of course, we could also get you to take a test. Who knows, it might throw up some additional relations if your father had siblings for instance. We didn't have time to research that side of things as David's involvement sort of distracted us!'

'Sure,' came back the reply, 'I'll spit in a tube for you as long as we don't unearth another David!'

Tom twisted back in his seat and said 'Well, I'll try a few more sites for the elusive Tuskers but as well as that, as it's an unusual name, perhaps I'll research the origin of the name and find out in which regions in the UK the highest density of Tuskers come from. Again, it might help to pinpoint the research.'

Annie interrupted 'What was that site you told me about, Tom? You know where people research a specific name and put the data online?'

'Now that's a good call,' he replied 'you mean the *Guild of One Name Studies*. No time like the present' and logged in quickly but to his disappointment found that no-one to date had researched the Tusker dynasty.

The email pinged on Tom's laptop, and he found the Chief had been as good as his word and that his Ancestry DNA details had arrived. He told Annie he would check it out later.

He added 'usually following a DNA trail is extremely frustrating trying to work out how the various subscribers were connected and trying to interpret some terrible errors in some of the family trees.'

Annie chimed in 'I remember you saying that a large number of so-called researchers simply copy the incorrect work of someone else without checking it out and then others plagiarise and compound those errors. To me, that would take the fun out of the whole thing!'

Annie then put on her serious face and turned to Tom 'I've been thinking,' she said, 'I really enjoy helping you with your research and the last few days have only helped me to decide that I am not yet ready to return to the legal practice on a full-time basis. I had a long chat with Patrick yesterday and told him how I felt. He thought it was likely that I hadn't been able to grieve properly over the loss of Mom and Dad but also that the stress over the shooting, the arrest and all that followed were still affecting me and probably will do, while the memories were still raw.'

'Ok, I get that,' answered Tom. 'What's the answer, do you think? Is there one?'

'Well, Patrick offered me a 6-month sabbatical from the office or leave of absence, call it what you will. He knows that if I am not in the right state of mind to concentrate on my work, the clients are not likely to get the best outcomes either. It might also reflect badly on the firm.'

'And?' asked Tom.

'And I'm going to say yes, of course. Tom, I have a proposal for you. Don't worry, not a marriage proposal!' seeing the shocked look on Tom's face. 'If you'll have me, can I be your assistant at Rooting4U? I'd like to learn more about the genealogy business and research techniques. What do you think?' What are your thoughts?

Tom's face lit up at the thought of working closely with Annie again. During her time in England, researching her family history, their relationship had developed, and it had also helped him to have someone to bounce ideas off.

Annie watched him anxiously as he looked pensively at her for a few moments, before he replied with a huge grin on his face, 'Well, I will have to interview you of course, to check your suitability, qualifications and experience but I think I may have a position for you....' he added as they headed off to the bedroom to start her induction.

CHAPTER 8 - TUSKER

After alighting from the carriage and bidding Henry a good day, Joseph walked into the town centre to explore his new surroundings. He realised that he would need to find some accommodation for a few days at least, to give him time to think as well as making some plans for his future.

There were two hostelries that caught his eye which might be suitable for him. After all, he just needed a small room to rest up. He saw the *Seabank Hotel* overlooking the Bristol Channel but decided it looked too expensive. He approached the door of the *Jolly Sailor* adjacent to the village green in Church Street, more of a pub than a hotel but definitely more within his means and an establishment in which he might blend in more with the other customers. He observed a sign in the downstairs window, advertising beer, wines, hot food and rooms. The inn did not open until 11am and although it seemed an age ago since his hurried exit and the overnight journey from Birmingham, it was still almost two hours until opening time.

Joseph was tired as he had worked at the factory for the whole of the previous day, stopped off at the pub on the way home before the unfortunate incident with his wife and then he had only slept fitfully on the train journey. He continued walking down Church Street, still carrying the small but as yet, unopened suitcase and came to the cliff top, overlooking the sea. He dropped wearily onto a wooden bench. It was an exceptionally clear day and as he watched, some boats bobbed along the estuary with what seemed to be a large rock promontory in the distance. An old man with a long white beard and wearing a tweed suit that had seen better days, shuffled up to him and sat down at the end of the bench.

'Watching old Tusker, be thee?' enquired the new companion.

'Eh, you what?' demanded Joseph, not having the faintest idea who or what a tusker was or what on earth the old man was gabbing on about.

'Old Tusker.' replied the old man 'That lump of rock you be staring at over yonder.' came the response. Eventually, after several more strands of conversation between the two men, Joseph learned that the Tusker Rock, allegedly named after a Viking king rumoured to be responsible for marauding in the Welsh valleys. The rock was only visible at low tide and was effectively a ships' graveyard with many a casualty over the years. Only the previous Christmas, Dasher, ironically a Cardiff based pilot boat, had foundered on the rock but thankfully, the Porthcawl lifeboat *The Good Deliverance* had been launched in a timely fashion and as a result, the pilot and the whole crew of three men had been saved from a watery grave, even though the cutter itself was lost.

At this point, the old man got up from the bench and after wishing Joseph the best of luck, he shuffled off in the direction from which he had come, leaving the runaway alone with his thoughts once again.

Joseph mused for a while, enjoying the sea air and the calling of the gulls flying overhead. He looked at the half albert watch which was now adorning his waistcoat pocket and wondered if Henry had missed it yet. Careless Henry, not even noticing Joseph's sleight of hand as he had alighted from the horse drawn carriage as he had been dropped off at Porthcawl, earlier that morning.

He decided that as it would now be fast approaching opening time at the *Jolly Sailor* and picked up the suitcase before heading back the way he had come earlier. The smell of stale beer hit his nostrils as soon as he walked into the bar. The landlord was a jovial rotund chap, whom Joseph guessed, was aged about sixty and who soon confirmed that there was indeed a room that Joseph could rent for a few nights, payable in advance. The publican led the way up some rickety, creaky wooden stairs protesting under the man's weight, before he opened the door which had peeling blue paint on the outside.

The room could only be described as basic, furnished with a single bed and small cupboard with a washstand standing atop of walnut legs. The walls were nicotine-stained and there were distinct signs of woodworm having been the previous or possibly even the current residents. The washstand contained an enamel bowl with chips in the rim, confirming that it too had seen better days. Next to the washstand on the floor stood a metal bucket, which the landlord told him was there for the purposes of the allowance to have the bucket filled once a day with cold water from the downstairs tap at whatever time of day that Joseph chose to fetch it.

The landlord had earlier introduced himself as Joshua Jones and had told him that the toilet was the third door down on the opposite side of the landing and then gave Joseph the details of the times that meals would be served, making it clear that if guests chose not to attend in the dining room at the specified times, there would be no second sitting……and no refund either.

'I'll leave you to settle in then sir, I hope you have a comfortable stay,' he bade Joseph who keeping up the pretence of being James, thanked him and said he would come down to the bar shortly to partake of one of Joshua's fine ales, likely a Buckleys, a sign for which Joseph had noticed was displayed on one of the hand pumps downstairs.

Once his host had departed, Joseph sat down and picked the suitcase up before placing it next to him on the bed. His fingers flicked the twin latches but to no avail as the fastenings were locked tight. He cursed and looked round the room but then grunted as he remembered his own keychain with the switchblade knife attached. He pressed the button on the handle and out flicked the evil looking blade. The locks stood no chance and soon he was eagerly lifting the lid to see if there was anything of value inside.

Yesterday's newspaper lay on top and noting it was the *Birmingham Post,* he put it to one side to read later. Next, he picked up a small wooden box and excitedly saw that it contained a gold ring with what looked like diamonds inlaid and accompanied by a matching pendant necklace. A label inside the box proclaimed *'Baleny, St Pauls Square, Birmingham'* and underneath he read the words *'By Royal*

Appointment' confirming that this was indeed a quality set and should fetch a few bob when Joseph contacted one of his less law-abiding friends in Birmingham.

He returned his attention to the remaining contents of the case and realised quite quickly that all that was left were items of wearing apparel, which would have been far too large for him to wear. Disillusioned, he was about to return them to the case for later disposal when he caught sight of the corner of a manilla envelope poking out of the lining of the suitcase lid. He quickly retrieved it and slit it open with a grubby forefinger before peering inside. A grin lit up his face when he pulled out banknotes to the value of £30, which would keep him in bed, board, beer and maybe even the company of a local nymph of the pavement if he played his cards right. He secreted some of the money behind the lining again as it seemed that this was a good hiding place. After all, he himself had nearly missed it and he was sure that Joshua would be searching through his effects, given half of a chance. He then put a few pounds inside his shoe and a gold sovereign in his jacket pocket to give him some immediate spending power.

He decided that it was nearly Buckleys o'clock and that he was thirsty. He realised that he had not had a beer for the better part of 24 hours…. was that all it had been since his fight with the works foreman and the fatal stabbing of his own wife?

It seemed longer but never mind; life goes on. His own late father had often told him 'Look after yourself, son because no other buggar will!' Picking up the copy of the *Birmingham Post* off the bed and tucking it under his arm, he made his way down to the bar, whistling tunelessly to himself.

After ordering and paying for a pint of Buckley's bitter, he carried the foaming glass over to a table by the window which overlooked the green. He took a sip of the amber liquid, wiping the froth from his lips with the cuff of his shirt sleeve. 'By 'eck, that tastes good.'

He unfolded the newspaper and started to read the main story lines. The Franco Prussian war had ended a month or so before and there were a couple of stories relating to Bismarck's victory parade in Paris and the Prussian troop withdrawal, under the terms of the armistice agreement with the French Government.

Turning to the local news section, there were reports from the Birmingham Police Court which reported on a prostitute by the name of Fanny Prosser who had been charged with passing a counterfeit florin in a shop in Balsall Heath. Joseph noted that one of his ex-neighbours in Vittoria Street had donated some jewellery to help raise funds for the building of the new St Marks school.

He supped some more of his ale and after turning to the next page in the newspaper, his eyes glanced over a story of a railway tragedy and was just about to move to the sports section to read about the annual display of the Birmingham Athletic Club in St Alfred's Place when something dragged his eyes back to the railway story that he had just glanced at. He read the article again but this time with a little more concentration.

The Fatal Collision on the Birmingham and Stourbridge Railway. — *The coroner's inquiry into the death of Charles Tusker, who was killed by the accident to the South Wales express on February 8, was resumed yesterday afternoon at Cradley, by the Coroner, Captain Tyler. The accident in reference was a very serious one. The fireman, Tusker, was killed on the spot, the engine-driver was seriously injured while several of the passengers travelling on the express were much bruised and shaken. It was reported that a goods train, which had been improperly drawn out onto the main line just as the express train was due, was the cause of the disaster.*

After the examination of several witnesses yesterday, a lengthy report was handed in by the Government inspector. Having fully reviewed the causes leading up to the accident, Captain Tyler pointed out that the rule requiring the keys of the switches to be in the signalman's possession before any train was allowed to leave or pass through the station, had not been adhered to. The siding points were 376 yards from the signal box, and it could hardly be expected that the keys be carried backwards and forwards over that distance, whenever a train was due to pass the station. Rules which were difficult or impossible to obey were by human nature, generally more or less disregarded. The foreman and the signalman had instead got into the habit of exchanging hand signals in regard to the main line being clear or obstructed and the signalman assumed responsibility for the safety of the main line in connection with the sidings. The yard foreman went a step further leaving the stop blocks and switches unlocked while the sidings were occupied by a shunting train and while other trains were passing on the main line. There was some excuse for the men in the general laxity of discipline consequent upon their working under the disadvantage of a rule which it was hardly possible to carry out.

The remedy which was required in the opinion of the coroner with a view to the proper working of these sidings for the future, was obvious. In addition, should be installed a siding signal, worked by a wire from the signal cabin and this siding signal should be interlocked with the main signal line signals with stop blocks or safety points on the sidings. The coroner summed up at great length. The jury returned a verdict of unintentional manslaughter against Daniel Porter, the guard of the goods train who was the person who gave orders for his train to be moved out onto the main line. They also censured both the signalman and the yard foreman while recommending that the company should erect a siding signal worked by a wire from the signal- box.

Joseph read the article twice more, digesting every word. He guessed it was the name Tusker that had caught his eye. Having been observing Tusker Rock that very morning whilst in conversation with the elderly gentleman on the bench overlooking the sea, here was the same name!

Joseph thought to himself, 'This must be an omen; The fates are trying to tell me something.' He knew he couldn't risk returning to his beloved Birmingham as Joseph Clarke, even when the fuss at home had died down. However, if he adopted a false identity by taking the name of Charles Tusker whilst at the same time changing his appearance, he might, just might get away with it, aided and abetted by family and friends. The real advantage of this was that the real Charles Tusker was unlikely to be protesting at his subterfuge any time soon, given his very recent demise.

Joseph's blonde curly hair had at times often been the subject of ribbing and good-natured ridicule amongst both workmates and drinking friends and he resolved straight away that he would either dye his hair black or perhaps even buy a wig. On reflection, he favoured the dye option as he would worry that he would either not put on the wig straight or even forget to put it on at all. If all else fails, he could always shave his head completely, he suggested to himself, very much as an afterthought.

'What a brilliant plan!' he congratulated himself. 'Joshua, another pint please' he called across the bar, adding 'and have one yourself, my man?'

CHAPTER 9 - ENGLAND'S GREEN AND PLEASANT LAND

The next few days were a whirl of activity for Tom and Annie. Having completed the agreement with the partners at the law firm for Annie's leave of absence, they had made plans for a return to England partly by way of an extended holiday and partly to continue with the Chief's genealogy research.

Even though Tom's preferred airline was Virgin Atlantic, they managed to secure earlier flights on British Airways from Tampa Airport and seemingly in no time at all, the couple were taking off and in Tom's case at least, were heading home.

The plan was to land at London Heathrow and as it was an overnight flight, they had also booked a day room at one of the airport hotels so that they could freshen up and rest for a few hours before continuing the journey. Tom's apartment in Southampton was currently being let and so this was not an option for them to stay. He had loaned his car to Colin who was a good friend of his from his youth when he had played football.

Tom had told Annie that he had booked them into a hotel in the centre of Birmingham for the first week 'It's near the Birmingham Central Library which has a big genealogy department. Most of the parish registers recording the area's baptisms, marriages and burials as opposed to just the limited selection available on the net can be found there' and added 'as can be the electoral registers and other more obscure records that are simply not available online at all.'

'I am really looking forward to it, Tom' replied Annie, 'are we also going to meet up with your Aunt Jemima?'

'Oh yes, without a doubt. In fact, that is arranged for our first full day in Birmingham. When I phoned her to tell her we were coming to England, she insisted that we visit as soon as we had settled in.'

Annie responded 'Do you know what? I am really looking forward to meeting her. From what you have said, she is really fond of you as well as being a member of your family too!'

'Well, it's going to be my privilege to introduce you to her. I'm sure you will like her. She's always going on about my settling down, so you may be in for an interrogation!'

Soon they had passed through immigration at Heathrow, meeting up again after Annie had been directed to a separate line to show her USA passport, whereas Tom was fast tracked along with the other UK passport holders from their flight. After collecting their luggage, they were soon checking in at the reception desk at the Marriott hotel within the airport before taking the lift to their day room on the second floor.

There was a small coffee machine standing on top of the cupboard. 'Would you like a cup?' offered Tom.

'I sure would,' came the prompt answer, 'I didn't sleep very well during the flight. I'm bushed. I'm going to have the coffee and then grab a couple of hours of shut eye.'

'Sounds like a plan,' said Tom 'I'll do the same, so I won't be too tired to drive to Birmingham later. We can pick up a car from one of the hire firms afterwards.'

After grabbing a sandwich in the hotel bar at lunch time, the couple were soon on their way in the hired Volvo XC40 and were on the M40 motorway heading north in no time. The traffic was kind and the weather dry and so they made good progress.

'Let's take a break at the Cherwell Service area,' said Tom. 'We can stretch our legs and grab a drink if you like?'

'Sounds good,' replied Annie 'I could do with the rest room, anyway.'

Tom pulled into the car park and parked in a quiet area, slightly paranoid at scratching the paintwork on the hire car and wanting to avoid ending up with an extortionate bill. Half an hour later, they were back on the M40 before later switching to the M42. Opting to leave the motorway at the Solihull exit, Annie woke up from her doze. Tom pointed out the town centre on the left. 'This is where I was brought up until I was 14,' he reminded Annie.

'Uh-oh, I sense Tom Harding's Tour Guide is about to make another appearance,' she joshed good naturedly, referring to his detailed explanations of the history of Southampton during their recent adventure there.

'Well after Annie's Information Service on the entire population of Anna Maria Island, it's only fair.' he bantered back.

'I'm only joking, Tom, as you well know it,' she countered 'I am actually interested in history generally as you well know!'

By this time, they had passed through Solihull and Tom commented, 'It's quite a wealthy town nowadays but despite it being an affluent area nowadays, it was actually built on effluent.'

Annie looked puzzled but Tom went on to explain that the hill where the church of St Alphege sits atop, was actually created by pig farmers in mediaeval times who used to take their animal waste and tip it there. What originally was a pit, became a mound and eventually turned into a hill known as Sill Hill and then some historians argue, it became Soily Hill. From that derived the current name of Solihull but ex-pupils from the independent school based nearby are still known today as Old Silhillians!'

Annie mused this snippet of information but before long, they had left suburbia behind them and the trees had been replaced by grimy, dirty bricked terraced houses as they reached the more industrial area of Tyseley, famous for its railway history where the Great

Western Railway had built a depot at the start of the 20th century. 'The railway still runs through Tyseley from Birmingham today,' he informed her without knowing the relevance that railway history would bear to their current investigation.

They soon arrived in the City Centre and Tom had no option but to slow down in the much heavier traffic, before he turned into Broad Street. He had arranged the option of underground car parking at the Hyatt Hotel and after parking in an allocated bay, they went to check in. Once in the room, he phoned Aunt Jemima and agreed to go over to her house in Elmdon Heath the following day.

'Right, apprentice,' he said addressing Annie, 'let's crack on, shall we?' He pulled open the briefcase, put the laptop onto the desk, plugging in the mains adapter to charge it up before spreading the Tusker timeline chart that he had started to prepare back in Florida. Annie pulled up the spare chair and sat beside him. 'So, show me the chart and let's have a refresh as to what we have so far,' she asked.

'Ok,' came the answer. 'We have the Chief here at the bottom of the page and immediately above are his parents, Brandon and Shelley, born Florida 1922 and 1924 respectively.

I have just concentrated on his father's line as he is only interested in the Tusker name right now and above his parents are their parents, who are obviously the Chief's grandparents, who went by the names of Joseph Charles Tusker and his first wife, Ruth. Finally, we get to Theodore and Lilian who you will recall I mentioned before, were the couple who immigrated into the USA in 1893 with Theodore becoming a naturalised US citizen two years later. He was born in Birmingham in a run-down area called Aston but his wife reportedly came from Liverpool. All this information is based on data from the 1900 American census. The naturalisation papers may mention their actual birthplaces, whereas the passenger list only shows their last known UK address, which unhelpfully is listed as The Mercantile

Hotel in Liverpool. The 1900 census that I mentioned only states the cities where the pair of them were each born in England.' as Tom continued to reel off the dynasty to date.

Presumably their son, Joseph wasn't with them when they came to America?' questioned Annie 'and so he presumably must have been first generation in the United States?'

'Spot on,' Tom answered 'Joseph Charles Tusker was born in Byron, Georgia in January 1894 so it seems that Theodore and Lilian must have moved south from where they landed in Boston so that they could find work, before they then moved onto Florida. According to the 1900 census where Joseph appears for the first time, Theodore is a steerer but doesn't say what sort of thing he steered. It could be a horse and carriage, a boat of some sort or possibly, he worked in some capacity on the railways. It's likely that he may have used experience that he gained in his job back in England though and so it might help us track them down as we try and locate them over here.'

'So, where do we start, Tom?' Annie asked, 'presumably we can add to the US information by checking births, marriages, deaths and the later census returns?'

'Well, yes, we can and that will help build up the bigger picture for the Chief. By the way, that will be your task when we get time but tomorrow, we go and call on my aunt,' came the reply 'and I think our first visit after that, should be to the library to ask the archivist if there is any local knowledge of the surname. I'm quite tired still with the jet lag and the driving today and so an early night could be called for.'

'Mm mm,' said Annie after considering the situation, 'an early night does have its appeal,' she said, 'I might do some research myself.....'

They slept soundly but were awoken a little after 6.30 am the next day with the hotel becoming a hive of activity. Doors were banging as other guests let them slam shut behind them and additionally, there was the rumble of traffic noise outside as early morning commuters arrived in town with engines idling in the early morning congestion, adding to the general city centre din.

After showering and dressing, Tom and Annie went down to the restaurant for breakfast and agreed to go for a walk around the city centre afterwards. They weren't due to see Aunt Jemima until 11.30 and so had some time to kill but not enough in which to do any serious research. Walking along Broad Street from the hotel, Tom took Annie first to Gas Street Basin and then along the Grand Union canal towpath, talking a little about some of the history. They left the towpath at The Mailbox which is a small but upmarket shopping arcade on the site of what was originally the Post Office sorting facility. Tom then took them past New Street Station and pointed out the Rotunda building adjacent to the Bullring shopping centre. 'Now that brings back some memories,' he said 'I used to work there for an insurance company after I left school and one day, we were working extra hours on a Saturday morning. I was planning on going to a soccer match in the afternoon' he told her, briefly reverting to American terminology, 'but I discovered that I had been locked in as the security man had gone home. To make matters worse, while I was coming down the stairs, I had accidentally set the intruder alarm off and the Police were called. It was ok because I must have looked trustworthy as when I explained what had happened, he obtained the key and happily, because he was also a Birmingham City supporter, he gave me a lift to the ground in his police car. Good job he didn't support one of the other Birmingham teams though, as I would probably have been locked up and still be there today!' he laughed.

Annie said 'Why is it called the Bull Ring, Tom? I thought that was a Spanish attraction?'

'Yes, it is' came the answer 'but this place has been a big market trading area for hundreds of years and just down there, in front of St Martin's,' he said pointing to the nearby church 'was a circular area where they used to chain the bulls prior to slaughter and because of its shape, it became known as the Bull Ring.' Tom explained.

They continued their walk along New Street and back into Broad Street, with Tom indicating the library building where they planned to begin their research the following day. Briefly returning to their room to freshen up, they set out in the car heading for the Elmdon Heath home of his Aunt Jemima.

CHAPTER 10 - MR C TUSKER

The recently dyed and now black-haired Charles Tusker, aka Joseph Clarke, stared back at himself in the mirror. Since leaving the Porthcawl pub, he had made his way back to Cardiff and taken board in a common lodging house there. Conditions were poor but no questions were asked of the residents, which meant he had been able to stay there for a few days while he completed his transformation with his unshaven face now sporting a beard and moustache, also suitably dyed.

'Not bad, Jos…..' he stopped. 'Not bad Charles, I mean' he corrected himself. He needed to get used to his new name especially as he intended to return to Birmingham shortly. Earlier that day, he had sent a telegraph to his son, Joseph, to see how the land lay after his sudden exit from his hometown.

The pair had always been close 'or as thick as thieves' as Agnes had preferred to describe her husband and son. Joseph Jnr had telegraphed him back almost immediately and told him all was quiet as it seemed that although the police were still looking for him, they had better things to do with their time. Even though Agnes was dead, the impression that they were giving was that they were regarding it as a domestic incident especially as Joseph Jnr. had embellished the truth and given a statement that Agnes had accidentally stabbed herself brandishing a kitchen knife in an argument over his fathers' drinking and womanising habits.

Charles sent a further telegraph 'Am now Charles STOP Meet me tomorrow 7pm STOP By cemetery, corner of Vyse St and Warstone Lane STOP jc'

He didn't return to the lodging house as he had no need to collect any possessions because he knew that anything of value was likely to have been already stolen as soon as his back was turned. Instead, he had earlier placed the money and his spare clothing inside the small, purloined suitcase in a safety deposit box at Cardiff Station in Central Square. He borrowed another battered black leather bag from a distracted customer bartering with the stallholder at the fishmongers in the marketplace. Charles quickly scurried back to his safety deposit and noting nothing of value in his new baggage, switched the contents between the two bags, leaving the old suitcase to be found by some lucky or unlucky person later.

'A 1st class ticket to Birmingham, please' he said to the clerk behind the window, feeling he could afford a much more comfortable return journey, thanks to the generosity of the previous owners of the suitcase.

'Certainly, Sir. Do you have any additional luggage so that I can arrange for the porter to board it for you?' was the response.

No, thank you, my man,' came Charles' response. 'I just have my Gladstone bag so that I can attend a business meeting later' he added, mimicking the Welsh accent which he found quite easy to replicate. Picking up his change from the purchase of his ticket, he quickly made his way to the platform and climbed into the assigned carriage, a much more comfortable affair than his journey down. 'My, it even has a water closet.' he noted with satisfaction.

This time he was alone in the carriage which suited him fine. The less attention he drew to himself the better. The train was due to arrive in Birmingham around 6pm, which would leave him plenty of time to walk cautiously to the planned rendezvous with his son outside the cemetery, later in the evening.

The journey was almost pleasant with the daylight warmth a pleasing contrast to the night-time temperature that he had experienced a couple of weeks previously. The trip seemed to pass by quite quickly and he spent the time alternating between looking out of the window and reading a newspaper that a previous passenger had discarded.

The train slowed and he realised that he was pulling into Snow Hill. Glancing at the half albert adorning his waistcoat, he observed with satisfaction that it was five minutes before six pm. He waited until the carriage had come to a complete halt and tipped a threepenny bit to the guard who had opened the door for him to enable Charles to alight on to the platform. 'Thank you, Sir. Very kind of you.' said the railway employee, touching his hand to the shiny peak of his uniform cap.

Charles was wary and took a circuitous route out of the station, particularly when he espied a police constable walking in his general direction. He knew he would not be recognised with his black curls and newly acquired facial hair but better to be safe than sorry, he thought to himself.

He walked up Livery Street away from the station and after sidling down a few smaller roads, turned into Newhall Street, approaching Vyse Street. Although he trusted his son implicitly, he knew that he could at times be gullible and might easily be followed without him realising. So, he took an additional detour via Hockley Street and then walked down Pitsford Street, cutting across the cemetery and hiding in the shelter provided by the catacombs, the final resting place of some of the impoverished people of Birmingham who had been given a public grave along with many others of their era.

Charles was a little out of breath after the exertions of his walk and watched the arranged meeting place, having moved a little nearer but still concealing himself behind a large headstone. There were only a few people around as most of the workers were already back in their homes or perhaps quaffing ale in one of the many pubs in the area.

He had an unrestricted view of the corner and watched as his son, Joseph came into view and whilst looking all around him, half sat, and half leaned against the red brick cemetery wall.

Charles noted with satisfaction that his son seemed to be alone and when Joseph was looking in the opposite direction, stayed down low and walked through the iron gateway some 30 yards away. He pretended to be reading the folded newspaper that he had brought off the train and then walked closer to his son, stopping about 10 yards from him. His son looked in his general direction and seeing a bearded man with black curly hair, when he was expecting his father's blonde locks, he turned away again, searching down the street again.

'Hello, Joseph,' said the new Charles Tusker, in a louder than normal voice 'don't look at me or acknowledge me in any way just in case you were being followed. I want you to look like you are fed up with waiting and walk down to the *Golden Lion.* Walk in the front entrance and then straight out of the side door, cross over the road and wait for me out of sight in the porch of St Pauls. I'll stay here for a few minutes more and then make my way to meet you.'

Joseph feigned anger and after theatrically looking at his watch, marched past without a glance in the direction of his father who was still leaning against the wall, pretending to look at his paper.

Charles watched him enter the pub and was pleased to see that no-one was following. After two or three minutes, he sauntered casually towards the church where he was soon reunited with his offspring, each hugging the other. The younger man assured his father that all was well and that the police seemed to have accepted the explanation over the occurrence that had led to the fatal stabbing of

Agnes. 'Yes, that Inspector Dawes was a bit persistent at first with his questions but seemed to give up quite easily!'

'Gawd, did you say Dawes? I could be in trouble here. He is no man's fool and certainly not one to give up easily as you suggest.'

At that moment, they heard the echo of footsteps approaching on the cobblestone pathway that led to the porch where they were concealed and it was the burly shape of Inspector Dawes of the Birmingham Police Force that was blocking out much of the fading light. 'Well, well,' the policeman spoke, 'if it isn't Joseph Clarke senior....and junior. It's jail time for you both, methinks. Like father, like son. I think that you should get a few years for assisting a criminal m'boy, particularly one wanted for questioning over the killing of his wife. The fact you fled the scene afterwards and now appear in some disguise, will make my evidence that bit more believable by the jury. With a bit of luck, it'll be a noose for you, Clarke. I've been after you ever since you made me look a fool all those years ago when I was just a constable and you were part of the gang raking coal off the canal bed. My uniform stank for ages after you and your cronies threw me into the canal and left me for dead. I said I'd get you then and now I have. You're both under arrest!'

Charles moved forward and said, 'I think you are mistaken Sir,' he replied. 'My name is Charles Tusker and I am a respectable businessman. Look let me show you my papers' and his hand went to the inside pocket of his overcoat but instead of any document, he pulled out an object, which although ironically named a life preserver, was actually a weapon of similar appearance to a cudgel, consisting of a stout piece of cane about a foot long, with a five-ounce ball of lead attached firmly to one end by catgut netting. The other end had a strong leather loop which went round Charles' wrist to stop an opponent snatching the weapon from his hand.

The weapon was very effective, very deadly and Charles was an expert in its use having had to defend himself several times in the past when attacked in the night-time streets of Birmingham. Before the policeman could react to protect himself, the lead ball was impacting against the side of his head and he fell immediately to the ground with blood pouring from his left ear. Immediately, Charles launched himself forward and rained blow after blow on to the only man capable of limiting his freedom. His son joined in and started kicking the prone man in the ribs and in the stomach with his steel toe capped boots. Eventually, their victim lay still, no breath left in his body with which to try to defend himself further. Father and son looked at each other, the reality of the situation coming home to them.' It was the older man who spoke 'We are fortunate indeed. Dawes has always acted as a loner and so I doubt that he has anyone with him.'

His son agreed 'I think you're right, Father. He always came to the house unaccompanied, but I think that even though we are out of sight of the passing public in this porch, we should still leave quickly.'
'Well at least, he's already near the churchyard and so they won't have far to carry him,' his father added with a hollow laugh. 'Right, what are you waiting for? Let's get out of here.'

Under cover of darkness, they approached the younger Joseph's house, just round the corner from his parent's previous residence in Vittoria Street. That house had already been re-tenanted by a new family whom the new landlord was hopeful might pay the rent, a novelty for which their predecessors were not renowned. No-one was around and the pair were soon inside the safety of the back-to-back house. Joseph's wife, Eliza, was aghast when she saw the state of her husband and father-in-law, questioning why the latter had dramatically changed his appearance. Some of Dawes' blood had splattered onto their hands as well as their clothing and she demanded to know what was going on.

The men filled her in and emphasised to her that from now on, the older man was not her father-in-law but would be known as Charles Tusker, a businessman who would be lodging with them for a while if any of the nosey neighbours chose to ask, which they surely would if they noticed a stranger in their midst. There was an attic at the house and it was agreed that Charles would sleep up there to avoid too many prying eyes and the possible visit from the constabulary following the exchange of a shilling for information received. There was the thinnest of timber partition walls separating his attic from the one next door and it wasn't a difficult task for Charles to craft an escape route into next door and then into the house adjoining that one, should the need arise.

CHAPTER 11 - AUNT JEMIMA

Tom and Annie collected the hire car from the hotel car park and soon they were bowling along in the moderate traffic. Tom opted for the A45, Coventry Road route, before turning right at the traffic lights next to Birmingham International Airport and heading for Aunt Jemima's Damson Lane home in Elmdon Heath, on the outskirts of Solihull.

He pulled up outside No.148 and as expected, Aunt Jemima was in the front garden of her moderate three-bedroom semi-detached house, eagerly awaiting their arrival. On seeing them, she rushed out and gave Tom a crushing hug, 'Oh Tom, my dear Tom, it is so wonderful to see you again!'

'Yes, Auntie. It has been far too long,' he agreed 'now, can I introduce you to Annie?'

'Ah yes,' replied Tom's Aunt 'I have heard much about you, my dear. My nephew seems quite struck on you, it seems.'

'Likewise, I have heard much about you too and most of it good,' Annie countered with a smile.

A little flustered, Jemima ushered them indoors, 'The kettle is on. Let's go and have a cup of tea, come on in and rest your feet. Oh

Tom, could you nip into the garden and pick me a sprig of mint from the herb bed, please for my usual mint tea?'

After he had left, Jemima turned back to Annie and said 'Tom is my only living relative I have left. I am very fond of him as you will have gathered. All I will say to you is you had better not hurt him as otherwise, you will have me to deal with!'

'I can assure you that……' Annie started to respond but Jemima doubled up, laughing with her whole frame shaking while her tight curly hair seemed to come alive.

'I'm sorry, love. I just couldn't resist it. I'm only teasing. Tom really has told me much about you and his feelings. He kept in touch during the time you were last in England and has also updated me on your family history project. It was me who was responsible for getting him interested in genealogy in the first place, quite a few years ago now.'

'Tom told me that and he also told me about some of your family secrets too. Did you ever find the source of the Bantu speaking people as reported by your DNA test?' she asked innocently.

'Touché. I can see Lass, that you and I are going to get on just fine, so don't worry. Ah there you are, Tom. Come on, your tea is getting cold. Sit down, I want to hear all about your latest investigation, I am sure that it is not just wanting to see me, that brings you back to England.'

Over the next hour or so, they discussed the latest mystery with Aunt Jemima who like the experienced genealogist that she was, made a few suggestions as to possible research angles. 'Tusker, you say. That's an unusual name although I am certain that I was in the same class as a girl of that name at the Tilton Road Board School, after the War! I believe she was an orphan and was being brought up by her grandparents. Now what was her name? Daphne? No, that's not right, Dorothy perhaps? Oh, I'm not sure. It was a long time ago, I'm afraid. I've got some old classroom photos up in the loft along with many of my family history records. I will check them out and let you know if I find any information on her or her family.'

The time sped by and after eating a light lunch that Aunt Jemima had prepared, it was soon time for Tom and Annie to take their leave but with the traffic heavier, it took them about an hour before they were back in Broad Street. They took themselves off to a coffee shop in Brindley Place and sat on an open terrace which overlooked the canal, watching the occasional narrow boat idle by.

'OK,' started Tom, 'let's decide on a plan of campaign. We stayed a bit longer than we intended at Aunt Jemima's and so there's not much research time left today. So, we'll make the library our first call tomorrow and have a chat with the archivist, to see if anything rings a bell with the Tusker surname. In the meantime, I'll check the British Library Newspaper Archive to see if there are any mentions of the name Tusker before 1893.'

'Hey, why limit to prior 1893? I know that's when Chief Tusker's family immigrated to the USA but they may have had relatives who stayed behind so don't you think it would be sensible to search later?'

'It would,' agreed Tom, 'although the amount of later material available in the BNA is still fairly limited, but let's see what we can find', he added optimistically as he logged in to the site.

'Well, there's not much at all,' he said as Annie had left her seat and was looking over his shoulder. 'Quite a few reports on elephant hunting in India as it seems tusker was a nickname for an elephant. There are a number of reports of ships going aground at a place called Tusker Rock off the Welsh coast and there's a short article from 1913 that refers to a police inspector from Stafford called Tusker, so the Chief isn't the first law enforcer by that name. He will be interested in that, I'm sure,' he added as he bookmarked the article from the Birmingham Mail.

'Look, what's that one,' asked Annie, pointing to a headline,' looks like there was a railway accident in 1871?'

'Probably of no real relevance,' replied Tom after scanning the column that carried the article, 'it's a report of a coroner's inquest following the death of a railway worker by the name of Charles Tusker crushed by a train. It happened in Cradley Heath which is only about 12 miles or so southwest of Birmingham. Who knows? Maybe its relevant,' he said, again bookmarking the page for future reference.

'What about Aunt Jemima's school friend?' asked Annie, 'do you think there's anything relevant there?'

'I don't know if I'm totally honest,' Tom replied 'It would be the wrong era for the Tuskers we are initially looking for. If you remember, we had Bob Tusker's earliest ancestors emigrating to America in 1893 and they are traceable in the States after that.'

'Mmmm....they were, let me think,' came the reply, 'Theodore and Lilian, am I right?'

'Absolutely right,' said Tom 'and that is where the problem starts, or at least as far as England is concerned. No trace of Theodore being born nor Theodore Tusker marrying a Lilian anybody. They don't appear on the UK census records in 1871, 1881 or 1891 when at the age that they were in the 1900 USA census, you would most certainly expect to find them. It's almost as if they didn't exist prior to getting off the ship at Boston!'

'What I don't understand' interrupted Annie 'is how someone can just disappear off to another country, without leaving a record. You most likely found the Tusker ancestors arriving in the United States having been listed on the passenger manifest leaving the UK but surely, someone can't just get on a ship without proving their identity or by showing their passport? Are there any passport records that we could search?'

'Yes, we can but the records available, like so many others, are incomplete. Here you are,' he said with a grin, handing her his laptop having removed it from its sleeve, 'show me what you remember by logging into The National Archive website and then search passport records. There will be a downloadable fact sheet on the general availability'

'OK,' came the eager response, rapidly followed by an 'Oh, surely that cannot be right? They are surely not serious. It seems that the only records available are for roughly 40 years between 1851 and 1903. It says that these are FO records. I might regret asking as it's probably a silly question, but what does that mean?'

'No need for regrets as the only silly questions are the ones that aren't asked,' came the response 'FO in this context means Foreign Office. They were responsible for both immigration and emigration records whereas if you see records beginning with BT, that stands for Board of Trade which was the body responsible for maintaining all of the passenger lists, for instance.

'Well, it says here that the records that they do have are actually online on the Find My Past website. So, if I log in there as I know your username and password are automatically saved, displaying an appalling standard of cyber security, I might add,' she smirked, 'I will have a look and just see if on the off chance, there are any Tuskers recorded.'

Tom already knew what she was going to find but said 'Sure, good thinking, student Kane, go for it.'

Annie navigated to the site and soon was querying the passport records, 'Oh shoot, it says no record exists for Tusker!'

'That doesn't surprise me,' said Tom 'but search for Smith and then you will see that what you would have found if there had been any, would have been of little use in any event.'

Annie did as she had been instructed and the expression on her face said it all as she was returned with an index page which just showed the surname and an initial alongside the date of the passport application. 'Not very cool,' she complained, 'what is the point of keeping those records and where are the rest? Surely, there has to be more information and more passports?'

'Oh Annie,' replied Tom, 'I like your logic, if only it were that simple. I can't speak for the system in your country but in the UK, it wasn't compulsory for someone travelling abroad to apply for a passport before the start of the First World War. The vast majority of people travelling overseas had no formal documents and it was mainly merchants and business owners who travelled regularly, that actually bothered with passports.'

Annie was puzzled, 'but I don't get it. Surely some form of ID was needed to get into another country?'

Tom continued 'you're absolutely right and that's the key point. It's emigration versus immigration. Generally speaking, it wasn't a problem to leave a country. Provided a traveller had enough money to buy a ticket to get on board a ship, then they were ok to leave England. It was entirely up to the receiving country whether they let a person in through their front door, so to speak.'

'Oh, I see,' said Annie as the realisation of the situation dawned on her, 'that's why the Tuskers were on the passenger list leaving England because that's actually the record of them going to America in 1893. Then they naturalised and appeared on the 1900 US census and subsequent census returns going forward as my country took over the record keeping of the family.'

'She's got it. By Jove, I think she's got it!' exclaimed Tom 'and if you can tell me where that line comes from, I'll pay for the coffee!' he added, laughing.

'Well, Mr Harding,' answered Annie, I think you will find it's a line spoken by Professor Higgins from *My Fair Lady,* a film and play based on the novel *Pygmalion* by George Bernard Shaw!'

Tom's mouth dropped open 'How on earth do you know that?' he questioned.

'It might actually surprise you Tom, to learn that Americans are educated. I studied Shaw in 8th Grade High School and then when I was 14, I played the part of Eliza Doolittle in the school play at Manatee High. What is it you genealogists say about never assume anything, it's all about the evidence? Now, by Jove, get your wallet out and pay for the coffee!'

CHAPTER 12 - UP THE CUT

Days passed by in Birmingham and all seemed quiet. Charles avoided contact with the neighbours as much as possible, although it was impossible to be completely invisible, given the need to visit the privy to answer nature's calls from time to time. The facilities were shared by the many families living in the courts of the back-to-back houses. Charles couldn't keep count but at a best guess, he thought that one privy could serve over 50 people.

The stench was intolerable and it was no small wonder that anyone spent as little time as possible in occupying the block. It suited Charles though as apart from the occasional mother hanging her washing on the line or clipping a kid round the ear, there weren't many people around in daylight hours. The menfolk would generally be at work and the women inside cleaning, cooking or making pin money, such as undertaking some process in the home-based pearl button industry.

He was still disguised with his tightly curled black hair, beard and moustache which he had to touch up every now and then, but there was little chance of anyone recognising Charles Tusker as Joseph Clarke from a previous life that already seemed a long, long, time ago.

It was nearly two weeks since the national census of 1871 had been taken on 2 April and his own entry had been written for the enumerator's benefit as Charles Tusker, a widowed railway worker aged 39, his age having been adjusted in line with the previous real but now very deceased Charles Tusker. His replacement just happened to be living in the house of Joseph and Eliza Clarke as a male lodger.

'Mornin' Mr Tusker,' he heard a female voice speak to him, interrupting his thoughts as he wandered back to the house, having been for a short walk in the early morning sunshine. He had bought a copy of the *Birmingham Daily Post* so he could work out his next move. 'Oh, er morning, Josie.' he replied to the daughter of Harry and Dolly Wright, the couple who lived next door to his son and daughter in law. 'It's a lovely morning, how are you, today?' he enquired.

She was probably about 19 with light brown hair and he knew that she didn't work in the factories like most of the other girls of her age. She was wearing a blouse with the top buttons undone, leaving him with no doubt as to the pleasures that lay within. Rumour had it that she was a dressmaker, which whilst being a good profession for a decent girl, Charles knew that it was also a euphemism for ladies who plied their trade in other ways, with clientele consisting of only male customers.

'Yes, it is nice and I would say that I could make your day a little nicer if you've got a shilling or two to spare, Mr Tusker,' Josie said, 'My mom and dad are out at work and so we'll 'ave the 'ouse to ourselves, if you'd like a cup of tea or some other form of entertainment perhaps?' she added.

Charles could see that Betty Sweeney from two doors away, was peering at them through her grimy window. The last thing he needed was to be the subject of gossip and speculation in the neighbourhood. Word could spread quickly about the stranger staying in the close community and even if whispers didn't reach the ears of the police, people like Betty Sweeney would make sure that Harry and Dolly Wright did get to hear about the exploits of their daughter and the lodger who lived at Joseph and Eliza Clarke's house.

'Sorry, Josie but I think that would be an expensive cup of tea. Now if you'll excuse me, I have my newspaper to read so that I can look for some business opportunities,' at which point he turned on his heel and walked into the downstairs room that served as the kitchen, sitting room and scullery in the tiny house.

Charles sat down at the table and he poured the remains of the cold stewed tea out of the pot, rather than go to the effort of putting a pan of water on the stove to make fresh. He spread the broadsheet newspaper out and skimmed the pages. He turned from the front page, full of public notices, mainly advertising theatre performances and public auctions. Page 2 was similarly of little interest, dominated by classified adverts for horses, carriages and harnesses as well as properties to let, although he let his mind wander a little at the prospect of renting a 6-bedroom house in Kyricks Lane for an annual rent of just £15. Perhaps he could persuade Josie and some of her less reputable friends to set up in the hospitality business there, in return for a suitable commission perhaps? 'No, you silly old buggar,' he reprimanded himself, 'got to be more responsible now.'

Pages 3 and 4 of the paper were no better, this time given over to situations vacant adverts and he couldn't help but think to himself that the 8-page newspaper was a waste of a penny. Perhaps he should go and find Josie, after all?

He carried on with his reading, turning to page 5 quickly hoping to find some inspiration but instead there was a very long and tedious article relaying the story of the Westminster Abbey funeral of some scientist of whom Charles had never heard.

On to page 6 and finally he found some local news with reports ranging from the story of a newborn baby having been found deserted on the steps of a house in Hospital Street before she had been taken to the workhouse. The irony of an article on a fatal railway accident was not lost on Charles either as he reflected on the rebirth of Charles Tusker, deceased railway worker as a result of a similar incident. Not being remotely interested in the price of corn in markets up and down the country, he moved onto page 7 and then he saw a headline that grabbed his attention straight away and he read avidly the report accompanying the headline:

INQUEST ON MURDERED HERO POLICE INSPECTOR

On Saturday afternoon, an inquest was held at the Golden Eagle Inn, Lodge Road by Mr Aspinall, the Borough Coroner, on the body of Inspector Percy Dawes (44) of the first division of the Birmingham Constabulary who died from the effects of injuries sustained four weeks ago. Chief Inspector Lomax watched the proceedings on behalf of the Police. Selina Dawes, widow of the deceased, told the jury that her husband had served for several years in the Birmingham Force and having initially been appointed as a constable. He had been quickly promoted to the rank of detective, a role at which he had enjoyed considerable success, thanks to his ability at solving crimes. On the evening of his death, he merely told her that he was on night duty and was pursuing a man that he suspected was guilty of the manslaughter or even the murder of his own wife.

The coroner asked whether he had mentioned the name of the quarry but Mrs Dawes replied that he had not. Chief Inspector Lomax added that the Inspector's notebook had not been located either at the scene of his demise or at his residence. Dawes, he added, preferred to work alone and tended to act on his own initiative, preferring not to take others into his confidence.

The coroner called witnesses and firstly Mary Ann Bull said she had been walking along the pavement and had seen Inspector Dawes in Vyse Street, seemingly concealing himself behind a horse trough. He appeared to be watching two men leaning against the cemetery wall some 50 yards distant and when one of them departed the scene, the Inspector waited for two or three minutes before following the second man when he also left his post at the wall. Witness was asked whether she saw the deceased again that night or whether she had recognised either of the men that he had been observing. Witness replied that she had not, in response to both questions.

George Richardson was then called to give his statement. He told the jury that he had been to a public house and was walking home, cutting through St Pauls Churchyard. He admitted to being slightly the worse for wear as he had consumed four pints of ale and tripped over something lying on the pathway. On picking himself up, he realised quickly that it was a person that had caused his fall but the person was quite motionless and seemed to have been bleeding heavily. He ran to the main carriageway where he found Constable Hawkins who then called for help.

The police constable then read his statement to the assembly, confirming the facts thus far narrated.

Dr William Webb had prepared a statement confirming that PC Hawkins had asked him to attend and that he had confirmed that the man in question was indeed dead, undoubtedly as a result of severe injuries to his head and torso. A post-mortem had been carried out at

Dr Webb's premises and concluded that the severe head wound and subsequent loss of blood was the primary cause of death, probably caused by either a cudgel or life preserver style of weapon. Further bruising was noted on his chest, back and groin area.

The jury retired for just a few minutes before unanimously returning a verdict of unlawful killing. The coroner thanked the jury for their diligence and expressed his deepest sympathies to the deceased's widow, Mrs Dawes. He added that he hoped that Inspector Lomax would leave no stone unturned to find the perpetrators of this terrible crime.

Charles sat back and reflected on what he had read. It was now nearly five weeks since the murderous churchyard incident – or accident as he preferred to think of it as after all, he had not gone to the church with the intention of killing anyone. It seemed that neither he nor his son had been identified by the witness who had seen Dawes watching them. Later, on the night of the attack and under cover of darkness, Eliza, who was very loyal to her husband, had collected up their bloodstained clothing and disposed of the garments by dumping them in a nearby rag and bone man's yard. No-one had so far come knocking on their door brandishing a warrant and so it was reasonable indeed to think that they were now safe.

His eyes returned to the newspaper and he re-read the inquest details again, absorbing the information in greater detail. Deciding he had done enough reading and that there would be little more in the publication of interest to him, he was just about to fold the paper up on the table when his eyes were drawn to a small, classified advertisement at the foot of the same page as the inquest report that he had just finished reading. As was his habit, he read the details out loud to himself, almost as if this helped to concentrate his mind and focus on the matter in hand.

CANAL BOAT FOR SALE For sale, a canal boat in thorough repair, a large sum having been expended on her in the beginning of the season. Capable of carrying 30 tons, fitted with moveable hatches, also included are a complete set of tarpaulins, harness and ropes. Horse included. Quick sale required in view of ill health. For further particulars and price, contact Mr John Kelly at King Edwards Wharf, Oozells Street, Birmingham

Charles reflected on this for a short while. When he had been in his early 20's, which seemed a lifetime ago now, he had worked as a canal labourer aboard a narrowboat, running from Camp Hill Locks taking coal up to the Potteries at Stoke on Trent and then fertilisers and lime back down as far as Stoke Bruerne. Sometimes a longer trip to London, which was far more profitable, would be offered to him. It was a life he enjoyed with the lack of regulation and the camaraderie amongst fellow boatmen. He had only changed careers and start work in a factory at the behest of Agnes, his long-suffering former wife.

Some of his comrades on the boats were rough and ready and even criminal but then that is where he had learned half and possibly three quarters of the mental and physical skills that he used now on an almost daily basis. He recalled the farmer who once had described him as being "a man of moral and intellectual darkness." Charles thought this harsh at the time, although as he had just stolen two of the man's sheep, it was probably not completely unfair.

He had kept it a secret from his son and daughter in law that he had the proceeds of his brief one-man crime wave in Cardiff upstairs, still concealed in the little suitcase. He had over £70 in Bank of England banknotes rolled up inside a pair of socks.

He decided to stretch his legs and take a walk to Oozells Street to see a man about a boat. Walking at a quick pace along Vyse Street, past the cemetery and then on to the Birmingham and Fazeley canal towpath at Farmers Bridge Lock 3, he then turned under the Sheepcote Street bridge. His pace was slower now as he reminisced about some of the happier memories of his time aboard a narrowboat, so called because of its maximum 7ft beam, as opposed to a barge which had a minimum width of 11ft.

One of the advantages of canal life was that a man could appear and disappear quite easily from under the eyes of the authorities, as the network of waterways could take a boat in any direction that was chosen, whether that was north to Wolverhampton or Stoke, south to London via Banbury and Oxford or west on the Worcester links to Gloucester. It was a hard life on the canals, as boatmen worked in all weathers – rain or shine, snow, sleet as well as fog because if they didn't work, they didn't get paid.

As he walked out from under cover of the bridge, he saw that a narrowboat was tied up some 30 paces down the towpath. He recognised it straight away as the "Lottie", operated by a seasoned canalboatman who was only known to most folk in the community as Curly but who also happened to be one of Charles' previous drinking companions and a regular law-breaker. Curly lived with his family in Watery Lane where they operated a coal yard off Glover Street. Curly's exploits were legendary, allegedly a bare-knuckle fighter on a Saturday night, where the winner would take the purse, but the loser would then be thrown into the canal with his hands tied behind his back and made to swim to the next bridge, some 100 yards away. Rumour had it that Curly had never had to swim the swim of shame. No-one in living memory could recall Curly as having a single hair on his head as he was bald as a coot. One unlucky punter in the pub had asked Curly why he had that nickname and allegedly had ended up on the canal bed tied up in a sack weighed down by bricks. No-one had asked a second time.

He could see that Curly was on the deck of the boat, a cigarette hanging from his lips. Charles could see the wisps of blue smoke, dispersing in the light breeze. He had to get past "Lottie" to reach the wharf, but would Curly recognise him? Charles regularly topped up the black hair dye and trimmed his beard and moustache. He sauntered along the towpath and was nearly past the moored boat when Curly's voice boomed out, 'Oi you, come 'ere.'

He turned and faced Curly who had himself stepped down from the boat and onto the towpath. Curly stared back at him 'You dropped your paper, me old mucker,' he said, pointing to Charles' copy of the *Birmingham Daily Post* where it had fallen out of his pocket onto the towpath.

Charles quickly bent down to retrieve it and said 'Ta, mate,' in a fake Irish accent to throw Curly off the scent before wheeling round to continue on his way to the King Edward Wharf, leaving a bemused Curly staring after him.

Having walked another 100 yards or so along the towpath, Charles reached the wharf, passing several brightly decorated narrowboats all tied up in a neat line. 'I'm looking for Mr Kelly?' he said to a woman on board one of the boats who was busy sweeping the deck clear of debris.

'That's 'im over yonder, on board 'is boat' she replied, nodding towards a narrowboat moored in the next berth. Charles thanked her and walked towards the boat that he could see went by the name of *Bessie*. After introducing himself to the man who confirmed he was indeed John Kelly and that this was the boat that had been advertised for sale, he accepted the offer to be shown around. Not that the tour would take long as he saw that the cabin was the usual 6ft 6in by about 4ft 6in, with a height that did not reach 5ft, Charles estimated. He knew also that in this typical space would live the canal boatman, his wife and sometimes up to six children. Organised was one word that entered his mind, whilst filthy and cramped were others. In reality though, the *Bessie* was quite clean. John Kelly, who was in his late 60's, informed Charles that his wife had become ill and that as a result, she was unable to work the canal any longer. The arduous day was not just a case of cooking and cleaning. Mrs Kelly, like any other narrowboat wife would be operating locks and helping to load and unload cargo as required.

Charles asked how old the boat was and some general questions relating to the horse and the routes that Kelly and his wife operated.

'Your advertisement said you were looking for a quick sale, Mr Kelly. How quick and importantly, what sort of price are you looking for?'

'T'is true I want to get it sold,' came the reply, 'but not at silly money! I reckon it is worth £45 including the horse.'

'Ha, that old nag.' Responded Charles, 'I've seen more flesh on a butcher's slab. The knacker's yard is likely where he'll be heading soon. No, £30 is all I am offering and all it's worth. I'll take the horse off yer 'ands to help you out, like.'

Kelly's face went a funny shade of puce and Charles thought he was going to have a fit of some sort. 'You, sir, are a scoundrel, offering that sort of money to a man in distress. How dare you try to take advantage of my circumstances? I'll not take a penny under £40!'

Charles went on the charm offensive 'not wishing to upset you, sir' he replied ' but I would be happy to split the difference at £35. I have the money in cash and we can complete the transaction now…… if that's a quick enough sale for you?'

The boatman spat on his hand and the two men shook on the deal. Kelly said to Charles, 'I will take all of my personal effects off the boat and if you return at 3pm today, I will hand over the keys and *Bessie* will be yours. Good luck and look after her, won't you?'

CHAPTER 13 - BROAD STREET

The next day saw Tom and Annie striding out along Broad Street, heading for Centenary Square. Tom had suggested that they both ate a hearty breakfast, before their stint at the library. 'Why? I thought a hearty breakfast was just for condemned men,' she said.

'Oh, very funny, came the response, 'no, it also applies equally to genealogy researchers so that they don't feel the need to interrupt their research for such a mundane thing as lunch or a snack!'

They reached the library building and were soon accelerating up in the lift to level 4 which housed the Archive, Heritage and Photography section. 'I guess we will need a CARN card like we did when we were in Southampton?' asked Annie.

'You guess partly right, then. I'm beginning to think that all that I taught you is beginning to have an effect!' Tom grinned at her. 'I take it you have the necessary ID to get you registered?'

'Of course, all ready. What do you mean by partly right, anyway?' Annie asked.

'Well, the CARN system is being gradually phased out and replaced with Archive Cards which are issued by the Archives and Records Association. So, my CARN card is still valid until expiry next year but I'm afraid that you will have to apply for the new card. Don't worry, it's a very similar application process. I would suggest you apply for a longer-term card, this time rather than a visitor's pass,' he added.

Tom had made an appointment with one of the archivists and soon they were sitting in front of the lady in question, who had introduced herself as Isabelle Brown and who quickly arranged the issue of Annie's Archive Card.

Tom had emailed ahead to advise that they were undertaking a professional genealogy research project and were searching for any Birmingham connections to the Tusker surname.

After checking Tom's card, Isabelle updated them on their quest, 'When I received your email, I did some initial research but from personal experience, I already knew that this was not particularly a name of local origin. However, there are several examples of families who have migrated to the area, probably tempted by the bright lights and work prospects of Birmingham,' she informed them with a grin, adding in an almost scathing tone of voice, 'Obviously, we have a lot more records available here than are generally accessible on the various online commercial websites and then of course, we have all of the original records in the Wolfson Centre reading rooms.'

'What is the Wolfson Centre? asked Annie.

Isabelle smiled at her and replied 'The Wolfson Centre is a dedicated reading room on the upper floors of the library with fantastic views across Birmingham! Researchers into Birmingham's past often tell us what a pleasant and relaxing working environment we have created. So, I am sure we can sniff out your Tusker family if they're from around here. We have a lot of original records that are simply not available elsewhere, such as Birmingham wills up to quite recent times as well as access to coroners' reports that are over 75 years old.'

Tom quickly summarised what they knew so far, ending with the mystery of the allegedly Birmingham born Theodore Tusker and his wife, Lilian, neither of whom appeared in any UK census record, birth, or marriage searches.

'You are an experienced genealogist I understand, Mr Harding?' queried Isabelle 'and so I imagine you have already looked at name variations.'

'I have or rather Miss Kane here has, but we found nothing using either slightly different spelling or by using the Soundex system for similar sounding names,' Tom replied.

'That's right,' added Annie, 'I tried Tucker, Tacker, Tasker as well as using some wild cards in the searches, but nothing of interest, I'm afraid. Theodore and Lilian just don't seem to have ever existed, 'she said with a forlorn expression on her face.

'Well, I suggest making a start with our electoral roll collection. It's far more extensive than the partial online offering as we have 1832 to 2001 available,' the scathing tone having momentarily returned to the Archivist's voice. She continued 'we have many more years available in book format and these are all indexed. You do need to know the address or the voting ward that people lived in. Obviously, if you can't find them yet, that might be a tad more difficult', she added drily and perhaps a little unnecessarily.

'I think that where we'll start will be by using the online Archive index to find any instances of the Tusker name as well as any mentions of Theodore. After all, it's not a very common name. If I do that,' he said turning to face Annie 'then at the same time, you can conduct the same exercise but searching the index for each of the censuses from 1841 to 1911 in detail. Last time we just skimmed over them just specifically looking for mentions of Tusker.'

'Ok,' came the reply, 'That sounds like a plan. We can work separately and then compare notes later?'

The Archivist got up from her seat, signalling that their meeting had come to an end. 'The other dataset to perhaps also consider would be our collection of Directories which include trade and residential entries. Might be worth a shot?'

Tom and Annie both nodded their thanks to Isabelle who responded, 'Just let me know if you need any further assistance or if there are any questions,' before turning away and walking back to her glass partitioned office.

They both powered up their laptops and logged on. Using their own private mi-fi had become a habit given the huge increase in hacking attacks recently, with a lot of incidents attributed to public internet connections. Tom first navigated to the Birmingham Library website which held a full index of all of their various holdings. Annie in the meantime went to Ancestry and first called up the 1841 census, intending to search each return methodically, rather than interrogating the UK census collection in one go. Hopefully, she thought this would result in there being fewer hits on each search and she would be able to follow potential leads through the years. Rather than flick from one tab to another, she had an A4 notepad at the side of her laptop to jot down any results.

Every now and then, either Tom or Annie would glance up at the other and if simultaneously, they would smile at each other and continue with their individual research.

Annie's process was simple. First, she searched for the surname of Tusker although there were many more hits nationwide than she had anticipated. She amended the search and restricted the results to Warwickshire which was the County that Birmingham was originally part of. Her plan was to repeat each census year using "T**er as a wildcard entry but then she remembered that if she didn't tick the "exact name only", the programme automatically gave her similar names such as Tasker and Tacker and this would cost her a huge amount of time. However, as she explained later to Tom, there were over 1600 hits returned just in the 1841 census alone. Following a hunch, she then limited a second search to the exact spelling of Tusker and felt much happier that only 26 names were returned, but her elation was short lived when she realised that none of them were born in county and so had not originated from the Midlands.

Before she had embarked on the exercise, Tom had said 'Keep an eye out for Theodore, just in case. The one we want should have been born in the 1850's if the estimated ages on both the passenger manifest and the USA censuses were correct, but you might strike lucky and find an earlier Theodore whose name may have been passed down the generations.'

Annie's eyes returned to her screen but there were no Theodore results on either the exact or the wider name search. She made brief notes on the notepad but then abandoning her handwritten jottings, she opened a word document, cutting and pasting the results so they could refer to them at a later date, if it was felt necessary. She repeated this for both searches noting that while there were over 1600 names returned, there were some variations born in Birmingham. She further amended the search so that the name variation option was restricted to Warwickshire and adjacent counties and then cut and pasted that list into her word document, which she had carefully headed up 1841 census.

Tom had spent his time searching the Birmingham Archives and Heritage online catalogue looking for anything that might give them a lead in their complicated project. As expected, there were only a few hits for anything related to Tusker, other than a coroner's report under the records of the Birmingham and Stourbridge Railway Co following the fatal accident to a Charles Tusker in late 1870. This seemed familiar to Tom but after checking previously recorded rough notes that he had made, he was reminded of the newspaper article that they had found before, telling the story of the railway worker crushed to death. However, he made a note of this second mention of the incident and the reference no. in the catalogue, joining the facts relating to the celebrated Inspector Tusker of the Stafford police force.

His attention was drawn to some police records from 1892, fascinated to see that there was a file on a Charles Tusker relating to court proceedings but the catalogue entry did not give any further information. He quickly noted down the reference no. L42/021/794376 to order from the archive for later viewing. Police records were one of Tom's particular interests and he always happily allowed himself to be distracted by catalogue entries in the crimes, offences and misdemeanours sub-class.

He searched for name variations and found several references to 19th century land transactions involving a Mr Tasker and several property transactions in partnership with two other men, but quickly dismissed these as irrelevant. He rubbed his eyes, still tired after the rigours of the trans-Atlantic flight and the resultant jet lag. He looked across at Annie who was frantically tapping out notes on her keypad with a very concentrated expression on her face.

He closed his laptop down and walked across to her table. She looked up as he said in a very English accent 'How's things going, Sherlock?'

Annie smiled and said, 'Just bad–ass, man,' over emphasising her American accent. In response to his puzzled look, she laughed and added 'Good, Tom, it means good, really good. Seriously, I have quite a few possibilities to work on.'

'Well, I suggest we take a short break, grab a coffee and compare notes.'

Annie logged out, packed her stuff into her bag and they walked out of the library into the bright sunlight of Centenary Square where they found a table outside a small café and ordered a sandwich and coffee each.

They chatted about their discoveries to date with the conversation commandeered by Annie. She excitedly described the summary of her census findings which was that although so far between 1841 and 1861, there quite a few Tuskers in Birmingham, there was absolutely no mention of any carrying the first name of Theodore. 'That's a bit unusual, isn't it? We would have expected that if our man was around 40 when he arrived in America, based on his age in the 1900 census, he may have been on the 1851 UK census, depending on the accuracy of his age but he should definitely have been on each of the UK censuses between 1861 and 1891. So where is he?' she asked, theatrically slapping her hand to her forehead.

'The simple answer is we don't know!' Tom replied, 'he could have been out of the country or managed somehow to avoid the enumerator. It's possible he was in a workhouse, prison or asylum and shown by his initials only….or of course, Theodore may not have been his correct name, whether that was by accident or design.'

'When you say accident or design,' questioned Annie, 'you mean a mis-transcription or a false name, presumably?'

'Exactly,' came the answer, Now, if you've finished lunch, let's get back to the library. We have lots of work to do!'

CHAPTER 14 - CRIME ON THE CANAL

Nearly five years had elapsed since Charles had purchased *The Bessie*. Joseph and Eliza also now lived with him on the narrowboat, having vacated their back-to-back tenement house with its cramped conditions and swapping it for shared quarters which possibly offered even more cramped conditions. A typical boat cabin measured 6 ft by 7 ft 6 by 4 ft 6 and in this space, a family would cook, eat, sleep and live.

The work was hard and boats could take up to seven days to travel from Birmingham to London with boatmen having to work up to 20 hours a day. Although the winters were cold and demanding, the summer months were by contrast, relatively pleasant.

Charles remembered very well the winter of 1871 which was their first winter aboard. It was the year that would probably go down in waterways history as the year that the canal froze over. The boats were unable to move as they were locked in the ice, resulting in the crews being unable to ply their trade. This in turn meant no money in the pocket and no food on the table. Employed boatmen enjoyed a slightly better life than the own account boat owners as often they were able to get an advance on their wages from their respective employers.

However, the crew of *The Bessie* used their initiative and as a result, fared somewhat better. The ice was often six inches thick and while the other boatmen went about organising working parties to smash the frozen waterways, Charles and Joseph with Eliza acting as lookout, used to pay clandestine visits to the other unattended vessels and steal anything of value. Canny boatmen with full loads were in the habit of mooring in the canal on the opposite side to the towpath, if loaded so that the risk of thieves undertaking illegal unloading was reduced. However, as Charles said to Joseph 'It's not the load of coal or lime we're after and if it was, mooring on the opposite side of the cut won't stop us.

'No,' agreed Joseph, 'all we've got to do is walk across the ice,' he added, laughing.

Sometimes items of jewellery would find their way to the pawn shop, while on other occasions there would be money heading directly into their pockets or food to put onto their own table.

The other boatmen had their suspicions of course but there was never any proof. One silver sixpence looked just like another and there were no distinguishing marks on a pot of vegetable broth.

On occasions though, their luck ran out and they found themselves on the wrong side of the law. August 1875 was one of those occasions when *The Bessie* was moored at Camp Hill Locks on the outskirts of Birmingham. Having carefully noted the habits of other canal boatmen in the vicinity, Eliza had walked 50 yards further along the towpath and seated herself on the lock gate, from which viewpoint she had a clear unobstructed view of the entrance door of the *Wellington Inn,* where the boatmen from the narrowboat moored at the next berth, had gone to sink a few beers.

Charles and Joseph had taken advantage of the situation and removed two windlasses as well as a large bag of horse feed from the neighbouring vessel. Eliza signalled that the crew of the boat were on their way back from the pub and so Charles had sent Joseph back to *The Bessie* with the horse feed to deposit it in their own feed barrel, hidden in plain sight as it were.

Meantime, Charles had walked to a nearby dilapidated store to hide the stolen windlasses until such time as he could safely retrieve them, with a view to selling them on to an acquaintance who had a marine store near to Gas Street Basin.

Unfortunately for Charles, he was observed by Constable Nevill from the Aston Division, who promptly arrested the hapless boatman. He was held in custody, as it was thought that being a boatman with a waterborne mode of transport, the chances of him absconding were high.

The next day at Aston Petty Sessions, the court building was packed with no less than twenty-three different hearings scheduled. At a little after 10.45am, Charles was brought up from the cells and stood in the dock, flanked by two police constables. The court was instructed to be upstanding for the bench which on that particular day, consisted of John Mottram QC, William Stone, Thomas Hill and with Tobias Ansell JP, chairing the proceedings.

'What is your name and your occupation?' asked the Chairman, Mr Ansell.

'Charles Tusker, Sir,' came the reply in a firm voice and without any hesitation, added 'and I am a boatman, the owner of *The Bessie*, Sir.'

'*The Bessie* is a canalboat, one assumes?' questioned the Magistrate and added 'do you live on the boat alone or do you have a crew with you?'

'Well sir, I now have my son Joseph T Clarke and his wife Eliza living aboard with me and we operate as a common carrier service from Wolverhampton and the Potteries in the north and down to London in the south.'

'Yes, man get on with it. I do know whereabouts in the country Wolverhampton and London are. I don't need a Bradshaw's Guide or an explanation from you.' Tobias Ansell responded sternly but after thinking for a moment, added 'You say that your name is Tusker and yet you just told the court that your son and his wife take the name of Clarke, didn't you? Would you care to elaborate for the benefit of the Bench?'

Charles was flustered and angry with himself for slipping up so easily, 'Yes sir, well sir, it's a bit embarrassing but my mother's name was Mary Ann Tusker and she was a servant girl living in a house next to a coal yard in Sandy Lane. She became acquainted with and began stepping out with my father who was a canal boatman, originally from Banbury, but who moved to Birmingham and settled there many years ago, sir.'

'That doesn't explain why you carry the name Tusker and your son goes by the name of Clarke?' interjected the Magistrate.

'Well sir, that's the thing. My father and mother were not married and I was born a bast....sorry sir, I was born illegitimate,' he corrected himself quickly. So, when I found out several years later, which was after I got married to my Agnes, I decided out of respect for my old ma to change my name back to her surname and so I became a Tusker again. You see sir, it was the name by which I was officially registered. By that time, my son had been born and registered under the name of Clarke and so we let things be, so to speak,' he explained, the plausible sounding lies tripping easily off his tongue.

'Mmmm very well,' replied the Chairman 'let's continue. You may be seated and we can hear the charges against you.'

Police Constable Nevill was called to give his evidence and he turned to the bench, 'I was on duty yesterday afternoon, observing a number of canal boats moored at Camp Hill on the Birmingham and Fazeley Canal. There has been a considerable amount of thieving reported recently and Sergeant Siviter, accompanied by myself, were despatched by the Inspector to keep a watch in the hope of catching the petty criminals responsible for this nuisance, sir.'

The Chairman asked for a detailed report on what he had seen and PC Nevill continued after consulting his notebook, 'If it pleases you, sir, I saw the defendant carrying two windlasses along the towpath and looked to have the intention of concealing same in a disused store house, next to the lock keeper's cottage. Sergeant Siviter had received a complaint relating to the theft of two windlasses and a quantity of feed from the owner of a narrowboat by the name of *Dudley,* which had been also moored at Camp Hill for three days. The defendant's boat, which bears the name *The Bessie,* was moored at the adjacent berth yesterday morning and is owned by the defendant.'

The Chairman thought for a moment or two and then asked the policeman, 'Constable, did you actually see the defendant either on board *The Dudley* or removing the said items from that vessel?'

'No sir, but the defendant is not of good character, being of the canal boat fraternity and we have already heard of the poor moral character of his family. I did apprehend him with the said windlasses in his possession, sir' came the reply.

The Chairman turned to Charles who was now standing in the dock and had been listening intently to the policeman's statement. 'What do you have to say for yourself, Tusker? You were caught in possession of stolen goods, were you not?'

Charles looked at him 'It is true, sir, although I was unaware that the windlasses were stolen property at the time. I had been taking the air and was returning to my own boat, when I saw a somewhat rough looking man running towards me. He spotted me when he was about 70 yards away and he dropped some items he was carrying onto the towpath, before he then ran away in the opposite direction. I watched him until he crossed over the canal at the lock gate and then he ran up the hill in the direction of Holy Trinity Church, sir,' and hesitated.

'Go on, man, please continue,' instructed Mr Ansell.

'Yes sir, thank you sir. Well, I walked along and carefully examined the items that he had abandoned and noted that there were two windlasses of the type commonly used on narrowboats. Not knowing as to where they had come from, or indeed to whom they belonged,

I decided I would put them into the old storehouse, thinking they would be more secure there, while I made enquiries as to the owner of the equipment in question. It was then, sir, that the policeman accosted me and accused me of stealing! I may be an illegitimate boatman, sir, but I am an honest boatman and I have never been in trouble before, sir.'

'Thank you, Tusker, you may be seated.' advised the Chairman and the bench conferred amongst themselves. After several minutes of discussion, Tobias Ansell sat up straight, turned to the front and addressed Charles, 'Tusker, it seems that the evidence against you is somewhat flimsy, given that there are no witnesses to larceny on your part nor any evidence that at any time places you on board the prosecutor's boat. However, when you made reference to being an honest boatman, it is apparent that your propensity for the truth may be a little questionable, as of course, there is no such human creature as an honest boatman. This court knows from experience that the canalboat community have a long history of undertaking nefarious activities but on this occasion, you are free to go. I will leave you however with my promise that if you appear in my court again, you will not be enjoying this same degree of leniency. I hope that this has been a warning to you and that you will take heed of my words?'

'Yes sir, I will indeed, thank you, sir,' and turning away as he was let through the door of the dock, he winked mockingly at the now fuming PC Nevill.

Charles joined Joseph and Eliza and they made their way back to *The Bessie* with plans for an immediate departure from Birmingham to continue their activities further down the line.

The family did indeed take heed of the Magistrate's warning after that incident and although they carried on with their thieving, they did exercise a little caution, if only not to be caught within the area covered by the Aston Court. They had no wish to meet up with Tobias Ansell again or indeed, with PC Nevill or Sergeant Siviter, neither of whom took kindly to have been made a fool of in the public eye. The local paper *'The Birmingham Daily Post'* had carried a report on the court case on the same page as the local football results, under the headline 'Canal Boatmen 1-0 Coppers'. PC Nevill resolved there and then to score an equaliser.

CHAPTER 15 - WHERE IS THEODORE?

Tom and Annie had returned to the research room at the library to continue with the Tusker investigation. Tom was truly puzzled as to the absence of Theodore and Lilian from any of the search results so far.

'Neither of us have found any trace of the couple that travelled across the Atlantic in 1893,' he said with a glum look on his face.

'Hey, c'mon Hun, it's not like you to be defeatist,' queried Annie, trying to cheer him up, 'they must have come from somewhere or had an alternative identity. They can't just have appeared out of thin air.'

'It seems on this occasion, that is exactly what has happened,' argued Tom, 'they are not on the 1891 census, no birth of a Theodore Tusker nor a marriage record between him and Lilian.'

'I remember you saying that there is no such thing as wasted research though,' replied Annie 'wasn't it along the lines of elimination is just as much a part of genealogical research as a positive identification?'

'You are right, of course,' said Tom, pulling Annie towards him for a close embrace much to the disapproval of other nearby library users, 'let's compare notes and come up with a strategy, over and above the strategy I have for you when we get back to the hotel!' he added with a wink.

Annie blushed at the prospect and wagging a finger playfully at Tom, said 'Enough, Mr Harding! For now, we have research to concentrate on.'

They sat down at one of the research desks and Tom pulled over a spare chair from the next table so that they could sit alongside each other. 'Right, show me what you've got,' he said and seeing the expression on Annie's face, added innocently, 'from a research perspective, of course.'

With a look that suggested she would give him the benefit of the doubt this time, she powered up her laptop and then opened the word document that she had prepared showing the results of her morning's research.

'As you will see, I have a separate page for each of the UK census returns for Warwickshire and additionally, one each for baptisms, marriages and burials, concentrating on Birmingham but extending into adjoining Counties such as Worcestershire and Staffordshire as I remember you telling me that the County boundaries have changed fairly dramatically over the years?'

'Well done,' commented Tom 'and you're right about boundary changes. For instance, a place called Yardley which is now firmly within the Birmingham city boundary was originally in Worcestershire and so if you had limited yourself to Birmingham or Warwickshire, you would have potentially missed out on search returns that could have been quite valid.'

'Ok, so as I said earlier, the fact is I could not find any mention of a Theodore Tusker in any census return nor does it seem that he got baptised, married or buried which flies in the face of the Chief's family myth that his family came from Birmingham. It seems they just arrived on the gangplank of the ship, without being anywhere first!'

Tom was pensive 'there's one thing that contradicts that though and the only thing that made me think that finding Theodore and Lilian would not be particularly difficult was the fact that on the 1900 and 1910 USA census, the birthplace for both of them was shown as *Birmingham, England.*'

'Well Tom, as we know that they were there in 1893 for the Atlantic crossing, it would make more sense to start at that end of the timeline, wouldn't it? Maybe the 1891 census and then work backwards? she suggested.

'Sounds logical to me,' Tom replied, 'so who do we start with?'

Annie countered with 'Before we do that though, what about you? Did your research throw anything up of interest?'

'To be honest, no it didn't,' Tom answered. 'Apparently, there's a great big lump of rock off the Welsh coast which has been responsible for some fairly spectacular shipwrecks over the years. It's called Tusker Rock after some marauding Viking, but obviously a bit too much of a tenuous link, even for us,' he laughed.

'Anything else?' Annie enquired.

'Well, Tusker is mentioned on more than a few occasions in articles in the British Library Newspaper Archive, but like you, I found no mention of anyone called Theodore, with or without a wife called Lilian. There were several articles covering criminal activities, train crashes, inquests and that sort of thing but nothing I could really shake a stick at. So, let's go through your results, one Tusker at a time.'

They spent the next 3 hours or so comparing each Tusker person and cross referencing them through births, baptisms, marriages, deaths and burials as well as the various census returns from 1891 back to 1851, quietly eliminating several of the candidates especially as and when some of the female Tuskers married and changed their name. Tom and Annie would then methodically pick up the relevant couples on subsequent census returns and cross them off the list.

It was a similar process for each of the variously named Mr Tuskers and in some cases, Master and Miss Tuskers for the children recorded in the family entries. Tom had suggested that they looked at each of the online results and move to the offline parish register entries on microfilm where there were gaps in the digital records or where there was some doubt on the accuracy of the transcriptions.

'Tom, did you ever check the Chief's DNA? He sent you his log in details, didn't he?'

'I'd totally forgotten about that. Let's have a look, now,' he suggested.

Soon, they were poring over the Chief's ethnicity results on Ancestry but surprisingly, there were relatively few connections apart from the usual array of very distant cousins but all seemed to be American citizens many with just a handful of centimorgans between them.

The closest relative was a Tim Clarke and when the pair clicked on his profile, it showed that he hailed from the English West Midlands from where he derived 79% of his ethnicity.

'The Chief's results show a West Midlands connection,' said Tom, 'although only 18%, so our Birmingham research suggests we are on the right track at least!'

'Five minutes to closing. Please return any documents to the counter as quickly as possible.' announced the stern looking archivist and frowned in the general direction of Tom and Annie, or at least so it seemed to the pair of researchers.

'Thank you, Isabelle, for all of your help earlier,' said Tom with what he thought was a winning smile on his face, 'We really appreciate it and we'll be back tomorrow to carry on if you can reserve us the same table, please.'

He picked up the laptop off the table and linking arms with Annie, they made for the exit and the pair were soon walking back along Broad Street to their hotel, talking as they went, enjoying the freedom to speak at normal volumes instead of the enforced low volumes in the research room.

'So, what next?' asked Annie, 'We've made some progress today, I think.'

'Yes, we have,' replied Tom 'we have a whole batch of potential Tuskers who could be related to our elusive targets. I think we will take Isabelle's suggestion tomorrow and compare the families for whom we have addresses against the electoral registers.'

By now, they had reached their hotel room and Tom had filled the kettle with water from the tap in the bathroom and plugged it in to make a hot drink. He knew that Annie would have coffee as he had not quite converted her to become an english tea drinker yet.

'So that way, we start to build up a picture of the different families and see if there are any anomalies? Gee, it really is a case of elimination, isn't it?' responded Annie 'and by the way, have you got the hots for our archivist, Isabelle?' she demanded 'I saw the smile you gave her at the end!'

'Oooh, do I detect a streak of jealousy with a slight tinge of green?' laughed Tom, 'No, on the contrary, one basic rule about archivists is always keep them onside as they have all of the answers to all of a genealogist's questions, even if they don't know what those questions are.'

Noticing the part puzzled, part infuriated look on Annie's face, he continued, 'remember that they are the keyholders to the past. I have known records suddenly become unavailable or allegedly go out on loan, simply because someone has got stroppy or has been rude to someone behind the desk.'

'Oh, ok then,' replied Annie in a more conciliatory tone, 'just wanted to check. Anyway, forget the coffee as I have research ideas of my own and I definitely have all of the answers!' she grinned, pushing Tom back onto the bed.

CHAPTER 16 - SOMEWHERE ON A CANAL, 1878

'He's got a bloody cheek, that man,' shouted Charles.

'Who's he moaning about now? Eliza whispered to her husband, Joseph.

'Oh, it's that Primitive Methodist Minister who's caused such a stir, demanding that Government pass new laws to clean up the canals and the people on it,' replied Joseph, 'and now he's finally got his way with this new act of parliament that came in to force last January,'

'I can hear you talking about me, you know,' said Charles who was standing in the stern, steering the boat towards the towpath as they made their way slowly en route along the Grand Union, somewhere between Banbury and Birmingham. He then moored up expertly a short distance from the next lock gate in order that they would be able to take a short break and rest the horse for a little while.

'But yes, you're right, it is that damn George Smith I'm complaining about! Why couldn't he have stayed at home in Coalville sorting out the employment conditions at the brickworks? No, instead, he's poking his nose into us hard working, ordinary canalboat people,' Charles continued with his tirade, but seeing Joseph and Eliza exchange glances, corrected himself 'all right then, ordinary canalboat people. I mean, he complains of people on canalboats carrying smallpox, disease and filth from town to town but he seems to forget about the useful stuff we carry such as wheat, coal and pottery.'

'Mind you, I agree with you,' weighed in Joseph, 'it was in the paper yesterday as to how he's telling stories about drunkenness, filthy conditions, immorality with co-habiting taking place between unmarried crew members. I mean, chance would be a fine thing for you wouldn't it, Father?' he added glancing in Charles' direction.

'I'll have you know, I've had offers any road,' came the reply from Charles, 'Only last week, there was that Mary woman down at the pub at Napton bottom lock, making it quite clear that she would bed me if I asked!'

'Oh yes,' chimed in Eliza, 'you mean Merry Mary? If you remember, she did want a shilling for her trouble? She is known locally as the towpath tart. You'd probably also get a dose of the clap from her for your shilling!'

Joseph, probably a little concerned that his father might mention an indiscretion or two of his own decided to change the subject 'The whole point is that we have to register the *Bessie* when we get up to Birmingham and then be inspected, for heaven's sake.'

'Well, that just goes to show how stupid that man is then. We have to register at a place where there's a school so that the non- existent children on board this boat can get an education.' argued Charles and getting his own back on Eliza, 'It's also about sanitation on board so you'd better get the carbolic out and get scrubbing, woman!'

After the break, with their horse fed, watered and seeming to have a spring in his step again, they continued on their way with the intention of reaching Camp Hill locks on the edge of Birmingham before darkness the following day.

They made good time and were lucky to find most of the locks on their route empty and so didn't have to wait for other boats coming the other way to clear the waterway first. They were tying up in a line of other barges at 6pm in the evening, in a space overlooked by Holy Trinity church which sat high on the hill and dominated the skyline above them.

Charles puffed on his pipe and with his other hand, took his cap off and scratched the top of his head, absent mindedly. He didn't bother to dye his hair anymore as although he was starting to thin on top, it had turned a natural grey colour, partly as a result of the normal aging process and partly due to exposure to the sun over the last few years, while working long hours in the open air.

Eliza set to preparing a meal in the tiny, cramped cabin and the men needed no excuse or asking twice when she told them to get off to the pub for a beer. She was secretly hoping that Joseph would come back to the boat slightly merry as she had aspirations of starting a family. Her secret opinion of George Smith's Canal Act was that getting pregnant would be a good thing, particularly if she was to produce a little girl, as the new regulations prohibited any girl over twelve years of age from occupying a cabin as a sleeping place at the same time as any male person. There would then be little option when their daughter reached her twelfth birthday but for them to take a small house near the canal and for them to live on dry land once more, which she craved because she was fed up with the nomadic life. She accepted that Joseph would continue to work on the boat with his father but saw no male feet getting in her way as a good thing.

She shook herself out of her daydreaming and got back to the job in hand of completing the meal.

Meanwhile, the two men had clambered ashore from the boat and were walking along the towpath in the direction of the pub.

A voice called out and Charles froze on the spot, recognising the voice instantly. 'Well, well, well and if it aint me old mucker, Joe Clarke.'

Charles stayed still but Joseph turned in the general direction of the person thinking he was the one being spoken to.

'No, not you sonny, I'm talking to the engineer not the oil rag. Aint that right, Joe?'

Charles turned round and decided to try to blag his way out of the situation that he now found himself in. 'Sorry, my good man. Were you addressing me? I fear that you are mistaken as my name is not Joe whatever name you mentioned. I am Charles Tusker, owner of the canalboat *Bessie* moored just up the path, Sir. Now if you'll excuse us, we will continue with our evening.'

'Nice try, Joe but you should know you can't fool old Curly. Last time I saw you a few years back now, you may not have had your famous yellow hair and were pretending not to be Joe Clarke and I couldn't quite work out why. I knew you then and I know you now. You may have grey hair now but with the summer evening light reflecting down, I recognised you straight away. I've been quietly watching you.

'Oh, Curly, I didn't recognise you for a minute or two,' replied Charles. 'You are of course right but I owed some chaps a few quid after a card game went wrong and so became Charles Tusker, hardworking boatman.'

'Now then, Charlie, Charles or Joe. Call yourself what the 'ell you want to, but please don't call old Curly a fool. That just tends to make me cross….and you don't want to make Curly cross, do you?' came the response from the older bargee.

Charles remembered the story of Albert Bennett, a boatman from Small Heath who mysteriously disappeared one day after having had a dispute with Curly over a betting slip. His naked body was found floating in the lock basin the following day with a betting slip roughly sewn and attached to one of his testicles. Curly had many witnesses to confirm he was in Wolverhampton that day and so escaped the wrath of the law.

'Er, no Curly, I definitely don't want to make you cross, Curly,' stammered Charles.

'Now that's better. Wasn't too difficult, was it? You see, I made a few enquiries of my own at the time. Seems you disappeared for a few weeks when your Agnes got knifed and your boy, 'ere told that copper, Dawes, that you weren't in the house at the time it 'appened. His story was that when he called round, he found your poor late wife lying on the floor of the scullery as dead as a doornail with a kitchen knife stuck in her ribs and claimed it was a self-inflicted accident. Then the strangest of things, a few weeks later, my boys, keeping an eye on young Joseph 'ere, happen to be in the vicinity of the churchyard when that nosy Dawes got sorted and they saw you and your boy 'ere running away leaving that copper to give evidence to St. Peter at the pearly gates. Fortunately, or maybe unfortunately for you, *Charles,*' Curly added with a touch of irony, 'we also found his notebook at the scene and recovered it. Guess what? Dawes reckoned he was after you for killing poor Agnes. I reckon some would say it's my civic duty to hand over the notebook as lost property!'

Charles blanched and trying to stay calm, said 'Look I'm sure we can sort out this er, misunderstanding Curly, can't we?'

'Don't worry, Charles…….it'd be a good idea to stick to that name to avoid confusion, I think. You're right, we can sort this out, all right. You and your boy 'ere will do me a favour or two and I'm sure that I can rely on my memory slipping a bit. How does that sound….Charles?'

'No problem, Curly,' Charles responded assuredly, 'what do you want us to do?'

'Nothing for the time being, me old mucker, but you can be sure I'll let you know if I need a hand with anything. Now were you two on yer way to the pub? I've got a bit of a thirst on meself and so I might join you for a quick beer, if yer buying, that is?' and with that, he eased himself off his stool and after jumping down onto the towpath, followed Charles and Joseph through the door of the 'Anchor'.

CHAPTER 17 - IS CHARLES DEAD?...

Tom and Annie woke quite early the next morning with the usual disturbance that are taken for granted with hotel stays in a busy city, ranging from other guests banging doors, to the sound of early morning vehicles on the road outside.

After showering and dressing, they went downstairs to the hotel restaurant for breakfast but they were back in their room just before 8.30am.

'So, what's the plan today, Boss?' asked Annie 'are we off to the library again?'

'Well, we don't have to as we could just continue with the follow up research online with our laptops but a change of scenery rather than being cooped up in the hotel room all day would be preferable. Mind you,' he added slapping her backside gently, 'I could think of worse situations than being in a room with you all day! But I think yes, we will go back to the library and spend some time in the research room.

The environment there is much more conducive to concentrating on the task in hand.'

'Mmmm, I think you mean the Tusker in hand but yes, I agree with you and besides, perhaps there will be another chance for you to see Isabelle again,' she teased as Tom shook his head as his way of saying he couldn't believe she hadn't yet dropped that particular subject.

So, within half an hour and after a brisk walk along Broad Street, they were back at a table in the library research room with their laptops logged in and notebooks to hand, although there was no sign of the female archivist from the previous day, her place having been taken by a thirtyish something male colleague.

Their agreed plan of action was to start with the 1861 census with the hits identified from the day before and then to work forward with subsequent census returns up to 1901 with the idea that anyone still in Birmingham in 1901, was not going to be connected with Theodore or Lilian Tusker who by then would have been resident in the USA for several years. Tom had suggested that if they then combined this list with the baptism and marriage data to enable them to see how different families had expanded and developed.

He had also agreed with Annie's suggestion that the burial registers could then be cross referenced and would then be used to remove a number of possible candidates from their calculations for good.

They worked quietly together for an hour or so and had soon moved from the 1860's to the start of the next decade with no obvious candidates presenting themselves.

'I've just got to nip to the loo,' said Tom, 'I won't be a tick.' and he disappeared out through the double doors to the refreshment area. When he returned, he noted that Annie's chair was also vacant but a quick glance around the room and he saw that she was leaning on the counter, chatting to the archivist.

On seeing him sit down at the table, she walked back and said 'I was just talking to Geoff. He's a senior archivist here and I explained what we were trying to establish. He did explain to me that he had been setting up a database on canalboat records and a month or two ago, he remembered seeing the surname Tusker then,' she reported excitedly.

Oh really, that's interesting, 'replied Tom, 'did he say in what connection? A boat owner or a lock keeper perhaps?'

'No, that's just it. He can't remember the first name of the person concerned but he thought it might be something to do with a robbery or something. Unfortunately, the whole database has been sent off to be digitised and so, they won't be able to get it up online for a couple of months.'

'That's not a problem, surely?' retorted Tom, 'they must have kept a copy for safekeeping?'

'Indeed, they did, Geoff told me but unfortunately, it wasn't indexed at all and contains well over 300,000 entries relating to boat inspections, canal families as well as the companies that owned and ran the larger transport businesses and quite a few independent boat operators too. '

'Wow, that's a lot of entries,' Tom replied, 'and even though he thinks the man he remembers had something to do with a robbery, from what I recall from previous research I have carried out on canal families, honesty was not a genetic trait that many of them had!'

'That sounds a bit biased, Tom, if you don't mind me saying so. Tarring them all with the same brush seems to carry more than a smack of prejudice. Surely, there's good and bad in every industry and profession? In the States, yes, we have some low lives but we also have corruption amongst policemen, lawyers and politicians as well as crimes involving some from the poorer families. Rich, poor, white, black, gay and straight, I get really pissed when people are categorised as good or bad just because of their origins. You as a genealogist should be more than aware!'

Tom held his hands up in mock surrender, 'Whoa, steady on. I accept that I was generalising but I do agree with you, as it happens. There is a lot of evidence though through the years that there was a lot of social problems especially in the last part of the 1800's when the canal industry was under severe threat as a result of competition from the expanding rail network. Goods that were traditionally carried by boat such as coal, lime and metal could now be moved up and down the country much faster by goods train and in much larger quantities than a canal boat ever could. However, I agree with you 100% though that there's good and bad throughout humanity. '

'Ok, I'll let you off this time, 'responded Annie adding 'and in any event, Geoff only said that the incident he was trying to remember, *may* have had something to do with a robbery. It might also have been that a canalboatman called Tusker was the victim of a crime or even a detective. Geoff also said that he would access the unindexed database and do a Ctrl/F search for any mention of Theodore for us. Apparently, he quite likes the American accent,' emphasising the last sentence with an exaggerated drawl.

'You seemed to be getting on very well with Geoff?' commented Tom.

'Well, yes, but I was just taking your advice from yesterday. Now what was it? Something to do with keeping the archivists onside, wasn't it?' she added laughing, 'and something else of interest. Geoff mentioned that Isabelle is on annual leave for 3 weeks.

'I told you that my interest in Isabelle was purely professional,' Tom protested.

Apparently, Isabelle has gone to Florida on vacation. Now how ironic is that?' Annie said with just the slightest trace of a smirk.

'Right then, let's get back to it while we are waiting for Geoff to advise on the result of his search for Theodore in his database. Where were we?'

'So,' said Annie, we had just finished 1870 and were about to start at the beginning of 1871. I can see there's one to cross off the list straight away as there was that Charles Tusker killed while working on the railways that we found reference to before. I found his burial entry at Halesowen which was where he lived. I looked on a map and that's about halfway between Birmingham and Cradley Heath where the accident happened. '

'Yes, I agree,' confirmed Tom, 'you can cross Charles Tusker off the list as we can safely say that he is eliminated. We're on the right lines even if he wasn't!'

Annie winced at the somewhat bad taste joke on Tom's part but nevertheless, drew a solid line through the name of Charles Tusker.

A while later, the archivist came over and coughing quietly said 'Sorry to disturb you both but I did as I promised and searched the canal database for the name of Tusker. I'm afraid that there were no entries for either Theodore Tusker either alone or with a wife called Lilian. I did find an entry for a Charles and also a Joseph Tusker though, who seemed to be in trouble with the law on a few occasions.'

Tom looked up and asked, 'Do you have the details, at all?'

'Unfortunately, not, as I was explaining to Miss Kane earlier, it is just a very basic list of names that we have as the details are going through the digitisation process as we speak. I'm sorry but I can't even give you a date of the events in question at this stage of the project,' he added with an apologetic expression across his sallow features. 'I can tell you from our reference numbering system however that you would need to look at the 1870's and 1890's.

'No need to apologise, Geoff,' replied Annie, 'It was really good of you to try and help. Thank you very much.'

'If we need to check on the gentleman in question later, are the original records still here?' Tom enquired.

'Oh, most definitely, we wouldn't release those out of the library confines. If you can come up with a year of interest, then you can order the registers up from the archive for perusal. Just let me know if I can be of further assistance,' said Geoff smiling but seemingly just looking in Annie's direction.

'Thank you, we will indeed give you a shout if needed,' confirmed Tom giving just a slight hint of talking through gritted teeth, 'but we must continue from where we had reached,' he added as the library man returned to his place behind the counter.

'That's a co-incidence,' said Annie 'the name of Charles Tusker being mentioned again. We've just crossed one of those off the list and so it will be interesting when we come across this latest version to see if there is any connection between the two of them.'

'Indeed,' said Tom returning to his laptop, 'could be father and son or some other family relationship maybe.'

They finished early in the afternoon, their tired eyes telling them that they had done enough for the day. Unfortunately, their tired eyes had not passed on a vital piece of information to their brains that they had just missed a very important entry in the 1871 census.

'What would you like to do?' asked Tom, 'Let's leave research to one side for the day and start afresh tomorrow.'

'Well,' said Annie, 'I was thinking of some retail therapy. I did see some interesting underwear in one of the shop windows by the big mall, you showed me.'

'Mall?' questioned Tom, 'we're in the UK now remember! I suspect you are referring to the Bull Ring …….or the Bull Ring and Grand Central to give it the proper title. Come on then, your new underwear sounds interesting although I believe you will have to model it for me later,' he added laughing and avoiding a playful punch at the same time, 'here's New Street, we'll head down there.' And the couple headed off, all thoughts of Tuskers temporarily banished from their mind.

CHAPTER 18 – THE 1883 DIAMOND HEIST

The crew of the *Bessie* received the message that they had been anticipating, albeit not relishing. They had just exited the lock at Lapworth with a cargo of coal bound for Wolverhampton, when the lock keeper said to Joseph, 'I've just had a message to say that Curly wants you back in Camp Hill tomorrow.'

Over the few years since reconnecting with the crew of the *Bessie,* Curly had given them a steady stream of jobs starting with basic distribution of stolen goods using the canal boat as ideal cover. They had been recompensed by Curly who as well as paying them, had made it clear that continuing to co-operate with him was the real price of silence as to the real identity of Charles. Lately though,

Curly's errands had become more demanding and as well as direct involvement in petty thieving, had also included roughing up some of the local rivals, particularly the younger and self-styled members of the slogging gangs that were populating Birmingham's streets, trying and usually succeeding to terrorise both the local residents and businesses.

Joseph glanced at his father who had a bemused expression on his face.

'It's OK. It'll be something and nothing. We'll moor up for the night at Solihull Wharf near Elmdon Heath because then come tomorrow morning, it'll only take a couple of hours at most to get our *Bessie* over to Camp Hill.'

'Mmmm, what you forgot to mention is that while Eliza is clearing up after dinner, you two are planning to get bladdered at the Anchor!' exclaimed his daughter in law, naming the local pub near Wharf Lane.

'Never crossed me mind,' replied Charles 'but what a good suggestion. It would be rude not to sample the local ale while we are in the district!'

The next morning, just after first light saw the intrepid trio untie the barge from its mooring and slip away along the Grand Union Canal in the direction of Birmingham, passing through Olton and under the red brick Woodcock Lane bridge. The canal took a sharp left bend which was almost a 90-degree turn, before the vessel was navigating under the Yardley Road bridge which was just a headstone's throw from the site of the new Yardley Cemetery which was to have a great significance later in Charles' life even if he did not know it yet.

With only the occasional moorhen skittering away from the canal bank, all was quiet until they reached Tyseley where the din from the steam hammers at the nearby railway workshops spoiled the morning peace.

From that point onwards, Birmingham was a hive of activity as the *Bessie* was navigated through a number of locks before hitting the home straight alongside the railway at Small Heath from where Charles could see the first of the Camp Hill Locks.

'Ok, Joseph,' he called to his son, 'let's tie up here. Curly will find us when he's ready,' he added as he expertly brought the *Bessie* alongside the mooring pins on the towpath.

'Here you go, boys,' said Eliza, carefully placing two steaming mugs of tea, the contents having a darker hue than the canal itself, on the top of the cabin.

'Got another of those, Mrs Clarke?' and turning, Charles and Joseph saw Curly striding alongside the boat having crossed over the canal at the lower lock gate, unnoticed.

Curly climbed aboard and said 'Right, Charles. It is Charles, you're still calling yourself, is it? I've got a proper job for you. At 5 o'clock tonight, you will wait opposite Elkington's the Jewellers workshop in Great Hampton Street. All you then have to do is wait for old Elkington to come out. When he locks up, take a good look at him so that you'll recognise him next time. Shouldn't be difficult as he's a short fellow with a beard and walks with a limp. Got that?'

'Yes, Curly. Understood. Is that it?' replied Charles.

'No, Gawd blimey!' Curly exclaimed with a guffaw. 'No, every Wednesday morning, Elkington goes to London to sell his new stock to the diamond merchants in Hatton Garden. Tomorrow is Wednesday and so you two are going to follow him and help him to dispose of the said stock a bit quicker and for less profit than he anticipates.' and added 'now listen up, here's exactly how you are going to do it.'

Having run through the plan, Curly handed Charles a small leather satchel together with some money and two first class return train tickets from Birmingham New Street to Coventry for the next day.

Having identified their target the previous night as instructed, Charles and Joseph were waiting by the ticket barrier the next morning and before much time had elapsed, the jeweller's carriage arrived and as expected, he was carrying a leather satchel over his shoulder. As he passed the barrier, with Charles standing several yards away and with a medium sized brown suitcase at his feet, Joseph stepped in front of him and making it look like an accident, barged into the jeweller, nearly knocking him to the platform. 'Oh, I am so sorry sir, I didn't see you there. Here let me help you. Are you getting the Euston train too?' he enquired. He picked up the man's cane and newspaper which had been dropped in the confusion and at the same time opened the carriage door, stepping back to allow their victim to climb aboard, before following him into an empty compartment. Elkington put his satchel and cane on the rack above his seat and then sat down next to Joseph. Charles by then had entered the compartment, sitting at the other end of the opposite bench and placed his suitcase on the seat next to him. He listened almost in disbelief as Joseph struck up a conversation but introduced himself to the jeweller as Joseph Tusker, commercial traveller and informing him that he was travelling to Lambeth for a meeting with a prospective customer.

Roughly ten minutes before Coventry, Joseph started coughing and said he felt quite unwell. He told Elkington that he had consumed some sausage for his breakfast which didn't taste as fresh as it could have. 'I don't think I am going to continue with my journey today. I'll get off at Coventry, find myself some lodgings near the station and resume my trip to London tomorrow.' As the train drew to a halt, he stood up and promptly half collapsed back into his seat. 'I do feel markedly weak, could you kindly accompany me to the platform, just in case I fall?'

The old man agreed and taking Joseph's arm, helped him out of the compartment and then summoned the guard to assist Joseph further. As soon as the pair had left the carriage, Charles jumped up and swiftly opened his suitcase, taking out his leather satchel which was very similar to the one that the jeweller owned and exchanged it for his own, placing the jeweller's bag into the suitcase before walking out and passing Elkington in the corridor.

'Is your companion ok?' asked Charles, 'he did seem to come over rather queer.'

'Oh, he's not my companion, but just a fellow passenger I literally bumped into when we were embarking at Birmingham. He became indisposed but I believe he's feeling a little better for getting some air and the guard also found him a seat and a cup of water,' came the reply.

'Well, that's good,' responded Charles, 'Coventry is my destination and so I will bid you good day, sir and wish you a pleasant remainder of your journey.' He tipped the peak of his cap and stepped down from the carriage as Elkington resumed his seat, completely unaware that he had been duped.

Charles watched as the train left the station bound for London and turning smartly on his heel, he asked the porter from which platform and at what time was the next train to Birmingham due to depart.

'Platform 2, sir in 20 minutes time,' came the reply, 'can I carry your luggage at all?' he added, hopeful of a tip.

'No, thank you my man,' answered Charles, 'it is not heavy and I can manage myself,' walking off in the direction of the platform that had been indicated by the railway employee.

Part of the original plan prepared by Curly was that Charles and Joseph should return to Birmingham separately and meet up back at the *Bessie.* However, Charles was worried that Elkington would discover the theft earlier than anticipated and so he had visions of Sergeant Siviter jumping aboard the train to arrest him and so he had suggested an alternative rendezvous, which Curly had agreed to. He was quite relieved to see the train slow down as it approached Coleshill Station and with the solitary figure of Curly sitting on the platform bench as agreed. He picked the suitcase up off the floor where he had carefully placed it and as the train halted, he alighted and quickly put the suitcase down on the platform next to Curly.

'Well done, Charles,' said his employer, 'now, better jump back on that there train as there aint another one for another week. Otherwise, it's a long walk to Brummagem!' he added with a laugh, as the younger man hastily clambered aboard the otherwise deserted train. Before the train pulled away across the Maxstoke Lane level crossing, Charles watched as Curly climbed into a cart and flicking the whip at the old horse that was harnessed to it, he proceeded to head in the direction of the nearby town, although Charles didn't envy the horse having to pull its load up the steep hill leading to Coleshill.

Charles was tired. It had been an exhausting but exhilarating day and he was more than pleased to see the Bromford Bridge station where he could jump onto the down train to Bordesley, leaving just a short walk back to where the *'Bessie'* was moored. As he approached the boat, he saw Joseph poke his head out of the cabin hatch.

'How did you get here so quickly?' he enquired of his son in a puzzled voice.

'Easy,' came the reply, the porter at Coventry alerted the Station Master as to my "ill-health" and promptly arranged for me to sit in the guard's van on the Birmingham Express from London, rather than wait for the scheduled train. I've been back around an hour.'

'Yes, we were starting to worry about you,' chimed in Eliza, joining the two men near the tiller.

'What on earth made you tell Elkington that your name was Tusker? Are you stupid or what?' Charles asked angrily. 'Might as well walk along the length of Broad Street wearing a badge or waving a flag, telling the world it was us that stole the jewels!'

'It was the first name that came to mind. I panicked when Elkington introduced himself and asked me who I was. It's not as if I told him I was Joseph Clarke, is it?' he protested.

'Come on Charles, leave my Joe alone. It's not his fault he was last in the queue when they were dishing out common sense.' countered Eliza and turning to her husband said 'Be a love and go up to Iles the butcher on Garrison Street. Curly has told him to put a rabbit to one side for us. I foraged some vegetables at those allotments at Fenny Compton and so I'll be dishing up a nice stew for us tonight.'

'Ah, whoever said crime doesn't pay hasn't tasted your rabbit stew!' responded Joseph happily and he quickly disembarked and walked away along the towpath, heading for Kingston Road from where he could take a short cut to Watery Lane and then on to Garrison Street. If he had looked back, he would have seen Eliza grab hold of Charles's trouser belt and pull him down into the cabin. Charles half-heartedly protested and questioned whether Joseph might find out about their amorous and clandestine arrangement. 'It doesn't seem quite right to be bedding my son's wife!'

'Not a chance of him finding out,' replied Eliza, 'as I said, he was last in the queue when they were dishing out common sense,' pulling her bodice over her head as the pair sank down on the cramped bed. Besides, my husband's father is Joseph Clarke and not Charles

Tusker, I recall. Now come here, I need a real man, even if he does have a fake name.......'

CHAPTER 19 – A TUSKER REPORT
'I was thinking, Tom....' said Annie.
The pair were walking arm in arm along Broad Street, the next morning on their way to the library.
'Uh-oh,' replied Tom, interrupting her, 'should I be worried?'

'Very funny,' came the response, 'as I was saying, I was thinking about what Geoff told us yesterday about the canal database and the fact that there were references to canalboat crime of some form or another involving at least two of the Tusker clan. So, I was thinking that if they were significant enough incidents to get onto the database, then presumably, they would have originally been on the library card index?'

'Yes, but Geoff also said that the card index had been temporarily taken out of circulation to enable the new database compilation and so it's likely to be a non-starter.'

'Not what I am referring to, Tom,' Annie countered excitedly, 'what I meant was that to get to the card index in the first place, there must have been an original source such as a newspaper report. Why don't we access the British Newspaper Archive when we get to the research room and check for ourselves?'

'You know, that's not a half bad idea. I should have thought of it myself!'

'That may be so,' said Annie 'but in fairness, it's easy to overlook the obvious with so many different avenues of research open to us. I think you told me to think outside the box at all times?'

Tom looked ruefully at her but at the same time, was admiring the bank of knowledge that she had built up in the relatively short period of time since they had worked together on Annie's own family history when there was a definite professional and client relationship ….or at least there was to start with to start with. Now there was simply a relationship and it made Tom an extremely happy genealogist.

By this time, they were sat down at a desk in the research room with Geoff, the archivist from the day before, having signed them both in.

'Anything you need, this morning?' he asked helpfully.

'No. not for now, thanks,' replied Tom, 'we're following up on the two Tusker names you gave us yesterday and we are planning to search local Birmingham newspapers.'

'In which case, can I suggest that you concentrate on the Birmingham Daily Post and the Birmingham Daily Gazette? They were more focused on local news including the police courts than perhaps the Birmingham Mail may have been in those days.'

'Thanks Geoff, that's really helpful.' added Annie in response as the archivist walked off to answer a query from another researcher who was standing by the counter.

'Right,' said Tom, 'let's just check yesterday's notes. The two names that Geoff mentioned were, let me see, er Charles and Joseph Tusker.'

'Shall we take one each and then compare notes?' suggested Annie.

They both booted up their laptops and quickly navigated to the BNA website with Annie using the library free login, while Tom accessed the database by inputting his own account details.

After searching the 1870 to 1890 period, they had both downloaded different articles from the various local papers and had made notes after reading them through.

Shall we compare results then, Tom? asked Annie

'Fine by me,' he confirmed, 'do you want to go first?'

'OK, so I had Charles Tusker. There were quite a few articles about the one we found before. If you remember, he was the one killed working on the railway in 1871 and before you start, no more of your *on the right lines* jokes!'

'I promise,' he said solemnly, 'Let's stay on track….any more on him?' he replied with a grin.

Annie chose to ignore Tom's perverse sense of humour and said that she had found several articles on the late Charles Tusker, including some family details from an obituary. It was mainly stuff about the accident itself though and the inquest on the poor man.

'No mention of Theodore, I suppose?' questioned Tom.

'None whatsoever,' came the reply, 'but I did find references to another Charles Tusker. Well, obviously a different one, anyway,' she added for good measure.

'Go on,' encouraged Tom.

'OK, this is from August 1875, I found reference to a court case in a place called Aston. Is that in Birmingham?'

'Ah that I can tell you,' advised Tom, 'Aston is a bit of a run-down area on what used to be the outskirts of Birmingham, but is now a very busy suburb. So, what have you got?'

'Well,' replied Annie, 'I transcribed from a few reports on the same incident but to summarise, this Charles Tusker was the owner of a canal boat called *The Bessie* and he lived aboard with another couple, Joseph and Eliza Clarke who were married. There was a twist in that Joseph Clarke was apparently the son of this Charles Tusker who had allegedly reverted from being a Clarke to using his mother's surname of Tusker after he discovered he was illegitimate. Anyway, the Charles Tusker in this report was up before the court charged with stealing two windlasses, whatever they are?'

'A windlass is a metal handle in the shape of the letter L which is used to wind and unwind the lock gates on a canal. It's quite heavy manual work,' answered Tom.

'Ah,' acknowledged Annie, 'thank you. So, the Charles Tusker in question was up before the court, charged with stealing two of these windlass things from another boat, parked further up the Birmingham and Fazeley canal at....let me check...yes, a place called Camp Hill. What?' she questioned, noting that Tom was trying to suppress more than a slight hint of laughter across his face.

'Moored is the word you are looking for. You moor a boat or park a car. A boat is not parked!'

'Oh ok, Mr Perfect! Moored then. So, while their boat was *moored*,' she said emphasising the word, 'it was alleged that Charles Tusker stole the windlasses as well as some horse feed from another boat. Unfortunately for him, it seems he was being watched by two policemen, let me see....oh yes, Sergeant Siviter and Constable Nevill. The police constable said that as he had walked up towards Charles Tusker, he had dropped the windlasses onto the towpath and then tried to run away.'

'Oh,' acknowledged Tom, 'so he could have been in a lot of trouble then. Stealing was regarded as a very serious offence at that time and even minor offences such as stealing a chicken could be met with hard labour or for repeat offences, transportation to Australia for several years. So, what did the court decide in the end?' he asked.

'Well, from what you just said about punishments for theft, it seems that our Mr Tusker was a very lucky man then,' she replied. 'When they called the police officer to read his statement, it seems that he didn't actually see Charles Tusker aboard the boat from where the goods were stolen. He just caught him red handed on the towpath, carrying the goods. Tusker's statement as to the charges against him was to the effect that he had found the equipment on the towpath, having seen another man carrying the goods but who had promptly dropped them and run off in the opposite direction. Tusker then gave evidence that rather than leave the windlasses where they were, he picked them up intending to leave them with the lock keeper while he could find out to whom they belonged.'

'So what happened at the court hearing?' asked Tom.

'Well,' Annie said in response, 'the newspaper report was suggesting that because there had been a history of thefts from boats in the area, then as all boatmen were a thoroughly bad lot and all as dishonest as each other, Charles Tusker had to be guilty because he operated a canal boat. It was no co-incidence that the police were there as one of the newspaper articles suggested that they were there to watch the boatmen as it was reasonably certain that there was a lot of criminal activity going on. Fancy that, Tom, a sting operation even in those days! I thought it was a relatively new concept found in modern movies. Anyway, the Chairman of the Court must have been in a good mood and was feeling lenient but also it seemed he was fair, given the lack of evidence against this Tusker fellow. Anyway, he let him off with a warning that he had better stay out of court in the future or otherwise, he would not be so easy going.'

'Mmmm,' said Tom thoughtfully, 'you're right, it seems he was very lucky. Anything else?' he asked.

'Isn't that enough?' Annie answered eagerly. 'What about you? You were looking for articles concerning Joseph Tusker, weren't you?'

'I was and I've got another newspaper report about six months after yours. Here is the headline,' he added and then pushed a printout of the article in Annie's direction, where he began to read for himself

BRICKS FOR JEWELS IN DARING BAG EXCHANGE.
TRAIN THIEVES ESCAPE WITH £2,000 HAUL
A diamond merchant has been robbed of a bagful of jewels valued at over £2,000 whilst travelling from Birmingham to London. A case, similar in appearance to that containing the jewels was at some point substituted by the thieves and was found to contain two bath bricks. The victim of the theft is Mr. Jeremiah Elkington, a local businessman of excellent repute who, during the course of an interview, told this newspaper that he had left Birmingham on Monday last on the London train and it was while climbing aboard, he fell into conversation with a fellow businessman by the name of Joseph Tusker who relayed to him that he was a commercial traveller, also heading for London. His new companion appeared to be an amiable chap and to the best of Mr Elkington's recollection, Tusker had fair hair with a light moustache. He was dressed very smartly in a brown striped suit and a straw hat. As he had said, Tusker seemed to be most affable, but as is the custom with commercial travellers, Mr Elkington did not inquire into the nature of his business. It was just as the locomotive was approaching Coventry Station, that Tusker confided that he was feeling unwell and then asked if the victim of this heinous crime could assist him to reach the platform so that he could locate some lodgings. Tusker had added that he had decided to rest overnight in Coventry before continuing his journey to London the following day. There was a second man in the carriage at the time who had a slightly scruffy appearance and Mr Elkington recalls that he could not help but observe the fellow's somewhat dirty fingernails and the fact that he seemed uncomfortable in formal clothing as he was observed fidgeting in his seat with some frequency. When Mr Elkington returned to the carriage after assisting

the aforementioned fellow traveller to the platform, this other rough looking man was standing up in the carriage, carrying a small suitcase and advised Mr Elkington that he was also leaving the train, which seemed a little odd at the time.

After the train had completed its journey and Mr Elkington had arrived in London, he retrieved his cane and bag from the luggage rack, but he realised immediately that the bag was without a doubt far heavier in weight than when he had placed it there at the commencement of his journey at Birmingham Terminus. He immediately opened the bag and found to his shock and considerable consternation that his consignment of very valuable jewels had been stolen and that they had been replaced with two bricks. The gems were mostly diamonds in mounted rings although some were unmounted, one stone itself being worth at least £800.

The following is the official list of the stolen jewellery: two black leather cases, one containing diamond rings and the other, diamond and coloured stone rings, three boxes being in each case; three brown cases each containing six diamond and coloured stone rings, all stock-marked and initialled "JE."; several diamond and sapphire brooches, several single-stone diamond tie pins, an opal pendant, several miniature brooches, a wallet containing a quantity of uncut diamonds as well as two or three parcels of cut diamonds, two parcels of sapphires, two parcels of six pearls apiece, one dozen brooches as well as an assortment of nine-carat pearl pendants.

The property unfortunately was only partly insured.

The police officer in charge of the investigation has advised that the two men were almost certainly in cahoots and that the first one who said that he was called Joseph Tusker, was almost certainly using a false name and that along with the other person mentioned, had duped Mr Elkington, relying on his good nature to help a fellow passenger that he felt was in some distress. This is a shocking crime against an honest, reputable merchant, but it is good to learn that the proprietors of the Hand-to-Hand Insurance Company are offering a reward for information leading to the apprehension of these callous thieves.

The police have since discovered that as a result of taking a statement from a porter at Coventry that the younger man must have made a remarkably quick recovery from his discomfort as he had in fact returned to Birmingham in the guard's van of the fast train just a few minutes after disembarking the London train. The porter had provided additional information that another man, bearing a close resemblance to the second passenger that Mr Elkington had observed in the carriage, had stopped briefly to exchange a few words with the so-called Tusker, before being directed to the north bound platform to await the next stopping train to Birmingham.

'What an interesting story!' exclaimed Annie, 'It seems that these Tuskers have a few naughty streaks in their genes. I am wondering whether the Joseph Tusker in this last article may have actually been Joseph Clarke. It seems a bit of a co-incidence.'

'Absolutely, he could have been', replied Tom. 'Mind you, we've still got to link these Tuskers to the Chief's Tuskers but I have a feeling in these old genealogical bones of mine that there is a connection. Let's keep looking – I suspect the best way to do it is to try and pick up this Charles and Joseph to see if they are in the census, although given that Charles was a canalboat master, he may have managed to avoid the enumerator, especially if he wasn't moored over the night the census was taken.'

'Shall we call it a day, Tom? I'm starving. Let's go back to the hotel and if you are not hungry yet, we can always work up an appetite', she added with a wink.

CHAPTER 20 - THE PLAN

Charles and Joseph were sitting at a table in a smoke filled back room in the *Spread-Eagle* pub. At the head of the table sat Curly, pulling on his pipe and contributing to the general fug in the air.

Charles himself was smoking a cigarette but Joseph who didn't smoke was coughing, clearing his throat and hoping that the meeting would be ending soon.

Each of the men had a pint of beer in front of them and after taking a long swig from his glass, Curly said 'Well boys, it's time for the big one. This is where we really get rich. Are you in?' he asked.

Charles looked at the older man ' I'm guessing that you're not wanting a reply to the question, Curly?' he asked, 'I be thinking that provided we say yes, then you continue to have a bad memory about my real identity?'

'Charlie, Charlie, no you do me a great disservice. It must be what, nigh on 20 years since you and the boy 'ere,' nodding in Joseph's direction, 'topped that copper?'

'No,' he continued, 'that's old news innit? I don't think that the boys in blue would be much interested in you anymore for that little indiscretion!'

Joseph spluttered, partly aided by a smoke assisted cough. 'You mean we're under no obligation to you anymore?'

Curly gave him a hard stare and then laughed out loud 'Oh, Charles, where do you suppose he gets his silly ideas from, do you think? You wouldn't imagine he's a Clarke, sorry Tusker. There I go again!'

He turned towards Joseph and said 'No, son, I have plenty more on you since then, you useless cumberbound! Plenty of people will be able to make statements about windlasses and jewellery robberies to put you both serving time in Winson Green for a few years. Now get up to the bar, boy and bring us all another beer, he added, draining his glass, leaving a frothy moustache around his mouth. After Joseph had closed the door behind him, Curly looked Charles straight in the eye and said, 'I wonder what the boy would make of his old Dad shagging his wife when his back is turned, eh?'

This time it was Charles' turn to go pale as Curly added 'Indeed, there's not much goes on that old Curly doesn't get to hear about. My eyes and ears are everywhere seeking out information for me. I know that you and the lovely Eliza have been doing a blanket hornpipe on more than a few occasions! So, I think you will both be working for me for a while yet or at least until I get bored with the pair of you.'

At this point, Joseph returned carrying three glasses, although managing to spill a good quantity of beer as he made his way across to the table, drawing yet another scathing glare from the boss.

'Right,' said Curly, 'down to business. Pin yer' lugholes back, here is the plan.'

Both Charles and Joseph listened for the next hour or so in ever growing amazement as Curly outlined his audacious scheme. He was right about one thing and that if they succeeded, they would be very rich indeed, even allowing for the fact that their share would only be a fraction of the overall haul.

'So, let's get this straight,' said Charles, thoughtfully, 'We take the *Bessie* and moor her on the Grand Junction canal under the railway bridge approaching Curzon Street Station. Then some helpful Post Office employee opens the window of the mail carriage and throws parcels down to us in the boat below? It sounds crazy even by your standards!'

'Crazy maybe', came the considered response but obviously I have extra people on the payroll. Do you know what a TPO is or was?', he asked the two men sat across the table from him.

Charles and Joseph glanced at each other, shook their heads and turned back to face Curly.

'Right,' said Curly. 'Every day is a school day, it seems. A TPO is a Travelling Post Office. Now a TPO is, or at least was, a post office on board a train which was staffed by employees called Travelling Sorters. As the name suggests, they sorted the mail while travelling between the bigger cities in England. This was seen by the powers that be in the Post Office to be an efficient use of time and to speed up the whole mail delivery process. So, rather than sort the mail in a post office building, deliver it to a station and for it to sit in a mail coach, with a postal guard who more often than not was asleep on the journey anyway, they used a TPO.'

Charles asked, 'When you say it *was* a post office aboard the mail train, are you trying to say it doesn't exist anymore then?'

'Spot on the money, sunshine,' answered Curly, 'the post office reduced the use of separate Travelling Post Offices around 10 years ago and along with it went the very well-paid job of Travelling Sorter, which was usually carried out by a higher paid senior clerk. A lot of the sorters were pensioned off before their time as the role passed to the London Postal Service in a department called the Circulation Office.'

'I don't get it, 'interrupted Joseph, who had been listening intently to what the older man had to say.

Curly with an annoyed look on his face turned to Charles and said 'Didn't you ever teach your boy some manners, Charles? He should know better at his age than to interrupt grown-ups when they're talking!' he added.

'Now just listen a little longer and all will be revealed,' he said, 'so, what were well paid jobs with a few perks along the way, lost a lot of importance and the men who held the jobs before, found themselves on a much lower wage and longer hours as their own local sorting offices would loan the men to London on 5-year contracts. However, many of the men still lived in provincial towns and cities and this meant them travelling long distances without getting paid for the time travelling and being away from their families. Now one of the chaps here in Birmingham who is one of the very few travelling sorters left, goes by the name of Kenny Keeping has been told that he's going to be laid off at the end of the month and I've been helping him and his family, just by way of a gesture of generosity, mind.'

'Ah, I see,' said Joseph, 'so this Kenny fella is on the payroll, just like me and Dad, then?'

'Mmmm, sort of, although Kenny has got some brains. He was nearer the front of the queue than you two! He tells me that a lot of them are pretty unhappy with their lot and so between us, we've devised a little get rich quick scheme.'

Charles thought for a moment and replied 'I don't get it. If you've got it all worked out, where do me and Joseph come into the picture?'

'Quite simple, really,' said Curly, 'we've got a train, we've got the mail but you two have got a little lady that I need.'

Before he could continue, Joseph jumped up and grabbed Curly by the lapels and shouted 'You aint having my 'Liza, she's mine! You leave her out of this!'

Curly swung his right arm and his fist connected with the side of Joseph's face, catapulting the younger man backwards hitting the pub wall behind him.

'Don't you ever.......and I mean ever, put your dirty paws on me again. Otherwise, your Liza,' Curly added, mimicking Joseph's comment a few moments earlier, 'will be sorting out her widow's weeds and sobbing at your funeral. I meant *Bessie,* your bloody canal boat, not your bloody wife, you gibface. Charles, sort your lad out once and for all, before I sort him meself.'

Joseph with a fast-developing red bruise on his left jaw sat down again, sullenly looking in Curly's direction but wisely saying nothing.

Curly continued, 'Now where was I before I was so rudely interrupted? Oh yes, the *Bessie* and where she and of course you two, come into my plans. When the Liverpool to Birmingham mail train approaches Curzon Street Station, it runs very slowly at a snail pace, waiting for the signal to change. The post sorting vans are always the last two on the train behind the passenger carriages and Kenny is arranging that next Friday night, as the train passes over the canal bridge, one of his men who is also a travelling sorter will be throwing selected bags of mail out of the carriage door so that they land on the towpath. All you two have to do is collect them, load them onto the *Bessie* and sail away into the sunset, so to speak.'

'Well, that's brilliant, Boss,' said Charles 'but why only selected bags and won't they be missed?', he added, glancing over at the still sulking Joseph.

'Now there's a question.' responded Curly, 'Think about it for a moment. What does the Post Office have that's made of paper and very valuable?' he asked.

'Ah, I know that one, Boss' said Joseph enthusiastically trying to get back into the older man's good books. It's stamps, isn't it?'

'Oh, good grief,' replied Curly slapping his hand over his eyes in a gesture of disbelief. 'No, not stamps you idiot! Bank notes is what I mean. The Post Office is also a savings bank. As well as sending birthday cards from Aunty Maud to Cousin Madge, it also deals in huge amount of money that is deposited by all of its customers. The Central Post Office in Liverpool collects large numbers of twenty pound and fifty pound notes and once counted, they are parcelled up and then sent on the train to Birmingham, en route for St Martin's Le Grand Head Post Office in London. Any questions so far?' he asked.

'Only one thing I'm puzzled about,' said Joseph, 'is I haven't got an Aunty Maud or a cousin called Madge. Who are they?'

This time it was Charles' turn to show his exasperation, 'Shut up, Joe. For Christ's sake, just shut up. It's only a figure of speech!'

Joseph didn't take too kindly to a public talking down by his own father but realised that for now, it was best to keep quiet, but made a mental note to get even on another occasion. He had lived in his father's shadow for too long. He had covered for him following his mother's death and somehow had got dragged into the death of Inspector Dawes in Birmingham and now was completely integrated into a life of crime. He didn't like it as all he had ever wanted was a quiet life for him and his wife, Eliza. He had never been an overly ambitious man but now thanks to his father, he was continually looking over his shoulder.

For now, all he could think of was 'Yes Dad, sorry Dad and sorry, Curly,' in a pretend apologetic appearance, 'so what happens with these parcels of bank notes?'

'That's more like it,' acknowledged Curly, 'as I said, after Kenny's sorter has thrown the parcels down to you, you have to be pretty quick because I dare say, some will end up floating in the cut and you are going to grab them before they get too wet.'

'How many parcels do you reckon on there being, Boss?' asked Charles, 'will it take us long to pick them all up and get away from the scene before the alarm gets raised?'

'By our reckoning, there should be about twenty bundles in all with each being wrapped in brown paper about a foot square and deep.'

Joseph cleared his throat and asked nervously, 'I hope this isn't a stupid question but what happens to Kenny's sorter chap? Surely, he's going to be in a lot of trouble when the parcels are missed at the station?'

'No and it's not a stupid question, Joseph,' replied Curly, muttering 'for once' very quietly under his breath which neither of the other two men heard. 'No, we have arranged for it to look like our man has been attacked by some robbers on the train and although I don't know the details, it's quite likely he will have a bruise or two and be left tied up and gagged in the mail van. He is going to be well rewarded for the part he is playing in the robbery....as of course will you two,' he added with a grin.

'Really?' replied Joseph, his eyes lighting up, 'how much?'

Curly rolled his eyes but staying calm answered by saying 'well that depends on how much we get away with but if there's as much in those packages as I reckon, you should end up with a couple of hundred quid each.'

Charles and Joseph looked at each other and it was Charles who spoke next, ' Bloody 'ell, that's a fortune, Boss!' he exclaimed.

'It is,' responded the gang leader, 'and now for the next part. From the time the train stops on the bridge and the parcels get chucked out of the carriage, you should have around ten minutes to pack them inside the cabin and make your getaway. Once the train gets to Curzon Street, the Post Office Staff based there are usually waiting on the platform with a handcart. There are normally three men and a couple of security guards to watch over them while they transfer the mail to the London train which will be waiting on the opposite platform. So, at most, around another five minutes before they find a trussed-up sorter and realise that a robbery has occurred. They will be calling the coppers at that point but by that time, you and your *Bessie* should be well away, heading back to Camp Hill but just keep going. I'll get a message to you, never fear, but just don't moor up until you hear from me, clear?'

'Clear, Boss,' they chorused.

'Now get out of here, both of you,' ordered Curly 'and one last thing, you'll be pleased to know that your debt to me will be paid in full if this all goes to plan. I'll be retiring and won't need you again and after we sort out the proceeds of this little enterprise, I never want to see you again.'

CHAPTER 21 – WHERE ARE THOSE TUSKERS?

The following day, Tom and Annie had decided to work from the hotel. They had set up in a quiet area of the ground floor bar area which gave them more space compared to the confines of their own room, as well as easy access to snacks and drinks. They didn't see the need to go to the library that day, simply because they had decided to work through the census entries to follow up Charles Tusker and to look for any additional information on Joseph Tusker, the person who, according to the newspaper report, seemed to have been involved with the diamond robbery on the Birmingham to London train.

'So, the way forward here,' suggested Tom, 'is to set up a basic timeline using a simple spreadsheet. We have a tab for each decade and then put the year of each event in the first column of each sheet and then note events that happened in chronological order.'

'And then what?' quizzed Annie

'Very simply, look for anomalies or patterns, connections between people, events or that sort of thing and between census entries in different years using news articles, parish registers and things like that to see if we can establish a connection,' Tom replied.

'Ok, shall I prepare the spreadsheet on my laptop?' suggested Annie 'and then you can access the databases and our notes from the last couple of days.'

'Sounds like a plan, Annie,' agreed Tom, 'Let's get down to it!'

'Easy, Tiger,' purred Annie with an exaggerated wink, 'genealogy project research first and fun later,' not missing the innuendo from her companion. 'We've got the targets of Joseph Tusker and Joseph Clarke and possibly two Charles Tuskers to source,' she added.

'OK, Charles Tusker No.1 is the railway worker who was killed at the end of 1870 so let's try and pick him up on the previous census in 1861,' Tom answered, inputting the data into the Ancestry search, adding Halesowen and his approximate date of birth of 1830 which he had calculated from the newspaper articles. 'Here he is….living at Halesowen with his wife Mary. It doesn't tell us much more to be honest. No children with them and both him and his wife shown as being aged 31 and born Birmingham, although that could of course, mean born 1829 or 1830 for either or both of them as it would depend as to whether they had already reached the age of 31 in 1860.'

'That's right, so I will add Mr & Mrs Tusker down on each of the tabs for the 1820's, 1830's and the 1860's with a note in the comments box, identifying him as the deceased railway worker and then I'll add him to the 1870's as well, as that was the year that he was killed according to the newspaper story.' Annie added.

The pair worked diligently for the next hour and then broke off to take a coffee break, pleased with their morning's efforts. They had now added the notes to the spreadsheet, cross referencing the information on the windlass theft, the diamond robbery as well as having added the names of Charles Tusker aka Charles Clarke as well as Joseph Clarke and Joseph Tusker.

Tom disappeared into the bathroom and when he came back, Annie was facing away from him, bending down to retrieve something from her laptop bag which was on the floor. She had on a pair of tight pale blue capris' which showed the outlines of her backside off very well indeed. Tom moved swiftly forward and as there was no-one else in the vicinity, he stroked the left buttock as Annie straightened up in surprise.

'Good job we stayed in the hotel today, that's not the sort of thing that would be welcomed in the library!' Annie said with a smile.

Tom just raised his eyebrows and they both returned to the table to continue the research.

'So, where were we before our, err, coffee break?' asked Tom.

Annie refreshed the spreadsheet on her screen and said, I think we need to get some flesh on these two Tuskers in particular ….'

Tom considered the problem and responded, 'It might be best to look them up in reverse order as it were, starting with the 1891 census and then working backwards, followed by the 1881, based on the fact that the diamond robbery was in 1883 which was in between those two dates. Then although we have looked it up already, we can re-check the 1871 as the windlass court case was in the mid 1870's. It might be we will get diverted in other directions as we go, maybe to check some parish registers or the GRO birth, marriage or death index.'

'OK,' said Annie, 'you take the spreadsheet this session and I'll do the look ups,' logging into ancestry.co.uk as she spoke, 'Charles Tusker from the *Bessie* first, although we don't know his age with any real confidence. That might be a problem?'

'Well, we can take an educated guess for now. We know from the court case that in 1875 that he was on board his canal boat with his son and daughter in law. There were no children mentioned in the article and so it is probably fairly safe to assume that they are relatively young, maybe in their 20's. Therefore, if we were to assume that Charles would have married, say 20 to 30 years before the court hearing, we can take an educated guess at a birth year of around 1825 to 1835. I would suggest we input 1830 and wild card for 5 or 10 years either side and we'll see what we get returned,' Tom suggested.

'Gee,' Annie answered, 'great to get the benefit of your experience.'

'Seems only fair, after all I had the benefit of yours, a while back,' he countered, the memory of a spontaneous bout of lovemaking, still very fresh in his mind.

'Yes, c'mon, back to the job in hand and get that mind of yours out of the gutter and back on track!' Annie exclaimed, with just the slightest hint of a blush evident on her cheeks, before turning back to face her screen.

'Umph,' she grunted, 'no trace of Charles Tusker at all. She tried again but this time without the birth date range but still the laptop refused to introduce her to the elusive quarry.

'I know,' Tom interjected, try for Charles' son and daughter in law, Joseph and Eliza Clarke, probably aged 40 to 45 now?'

'I've got them,' Annie exclaimed excitedly, 'They are on a canal boat but it's not *Bessie*, it's called *Lottie,* this time. Joseph is 42 and his wife is a year younger, but I wonder where Charles Tusker is? '

'Well,' said Tom, thoughtfully, 'he would have been around 60 years old by then and so I guess he could have retired from the canal life or perhaps he may even have died. Can I see the census entry for Joseph Clarke please?'

Annie pushed the laptop nearer to Tom so that he had a better view of the screen. 'Ah, that's interesting,' he said, 'Joseph is shown as Head of the family and Eliza, quite naturally is his wife. I wonder what happened to dear old *Bessie* though?'

'Well,' Annie replied, 'with or without *Bessie*, I'm more interested in what happened to Charles and so we had better continue on the trail.'

Annie changed the search parameters and called up Joseph and Eliza in the 1881 census, using the same years of birth based on their ages in the 1891.

'I'm going to put Charles in under the father category because we know he was in the boat in 1875 and so hopefully, he will still be aboard in 1881.'

'Good thinking,' Tom agreed 'Yes, that must be them' and Annie read out the details to be transcribed onto the spreadsheet:

1881 census RG11/3311 Folio 54, Page 23, Civil Parish: Fenny Compton, RSD Southam, Parish of St. Clare, Fenny Compton

Canalboat, Bessie

Charles Tusker   Head   Wid'r 49   Boatman   Warwicks, B'ham

Joseph Clarke   Son   Mar   32   Labourer   Warwicks. B'ham

Eliza L Clarke   Dr in Law   Mar   31   Cook   Toxteth, Liverpool

'So, that possibly confirms Charles' story to the court about changing his name back to Tusker after his wife died. He's certainly a widower now.' observed Tom.

'It's interesting that Joseph's wife was born in Liverpool, quite a distance from Birmingham?' quizzed Annie.

'Quite normal though, especially as there is a canal connection between the two cities,' replied Tom 'OK, what's next, 1871?'

Annie confirmed that he was right and soon they had the entry for that year too, with the address of Joseph and Eliza's old house at Court 4 back of 15, Frederick St, Birmingham.

'Hey, that's weird!' said Annie and continued. 'Joseph is shown as the Head of the household and Eliza as his wife which is expected. Their ages are a couple of years out, but I know that's not major. However, Charles is also there living with them, shown as a widower and already taking the name *Tusker*. However, he is shown as a lodger and not as Joseph's father. The other thing that is odd and I didn't twig it in the 1881 census just now, is that he's 39 years old and a fireman on the railway. Doing the math, as Joseph is showing as being 22, Charles would only be 16 or 17 when Joseph was born, based on the age of 39 shown here. It's also a bit of a coincidence that he is shown as a railway employee, just like our other Charles Tusker that was killed in that terrible accident.'

'Mmmm, ok, but having a child at that age might be unusual but not impossible. We can try to find marriage records for Joseph and Eliza and possibly a baptism entry for Joseph, either online or at the library as they have a large collection of parish registers there. What about looking for them in the 1861? It should help with the age query and might shed some light on the occupation. Charles should be shown as Charles Clarke then, of course.' replied Tom.

Annie was soon searching for Charles Clarke born Birmingham with an approximate age of 29 and with a son called Joseph but drew a blank.

Tom suggested that she tried looking for the son, Joseph, next who should be approximately 12 years old and living with both parents.

'Now I am confused,' she added, 'I think that this looks like them,' and she read out the details for Tom to transcribe:

1861 census RG9/1009 Folio 23, Page 79

Civil Parish: Birmingham, Parish of St. Paul, Birmingham

Court 3, bk of 24 Vittoria St

Joseph Clarke   Head   Mar   35   Furnace operator Birmingham

Agnes Clarke   Wife   Mar   33 Birmingham

Joseph T Clarke   Son   Unmar   12   Scholar Birmingham

'That's more confusion, stated Annie, 'this time he is not shown as Charles but down as another Joseph. He's also showing as being older than in the later years, which is more like it from an age perspective but whilst he told the court, he'd changed his surname, he didn't mention a different first name. What's going on, Tom?'

'I don't know,' came the swift answer, 'but I think we're on to something. We'll check the remaining census entries for good measure to help confirm his age. Then we can look for the death of Agnes and maybe check the newspaper archive too. She would only have been between 33 and 43 when she died and there might be a story there, although of course she may have not been in the best of health, especially in the poor sanitation that they would be experiencing. It's also possible that she could have died in childbirth which was a frequent cause of death in those days!'

The 1851 census wasn't a source of much additional information as the family were living in the same house, albeit all three of them were 10 years younger.

'Ok, parish register time,' suggested Tom 'let's see if you can find the marriages of Joseph and Agnes, also of their son Joseph to Eliza, as well as the birth or baptism of Joseph the younger.'

'Challenge accepted,' replied Annie eagerly and already logged into the *Ancestry* database, she was soon entering the details onto the spreadsheet of the elder couple's marriage which had taken place at St Martins in 1848. Annie left the name as Joseph Clarke but then keyed in a year range from 1865 to 1871 so that the search parameters would now relate to the son.

She explained her logic 'We know that Joseph junior and Eliza were married by the time the 1871 census was completed and so were likely born about 1850. Is that ok, Tom?' she checked.

He nodded his agreement and the programme returned four possible entries which they studied in turn. 'That will be the one,' said Tom, pointing out one of the entries which read:

4 July 1870, Holy Trinity Church, Bordesley, Joseph T Clarke, 21, bachelor, tin plate worker of Court 3, bk of 24 Vittoria St, married Eliza L Parkes, 19, spinster, with the consent of parents, housemaid, 219 Watery Lane, Fathers - Joseph Clarke, Furnace Operator and Harry Parkes, Labourer, Albert Dock.

'Even if there was the slightest doubt after the address and Joseph's occupation, the Albert Dock in its heyday was one of the biggest dock areas in Liverpool. If you recall, Eliza was on one of the census entries as having been born in Toxteth in Liverpool, so there are a lot of matching facts,' he added enthusiastically.

'I can't find the son's baptism,' she said in a resigned tone of voice, some 30 minutes later. 'I've tried a number of combos of the name, as well as the father's name being either Charles or Joseph but nothing.

'It's possible he wasn't baptised at all,' Tom suggested, 'some families tried to avoid the church routine if they could. I did find the birth on the GRO index while you were trying to locate the baptism. This is him, showing as Joseph T Clarke, Birmingham 6d 405, March quarter 1849. I also found Eliza L Parkes, Liverpool 8b 119 June quarter 1850

We can order the birth certificate, but it will be a few days before we receive the details even if we choose the online pdf route.'

He quickly jotted the details down, before completing the online order form and paying the certificate fees for the two, using his saved debit card details.

'Ok,' agreed Annie, 'let me check on the death or burial of Agnes Clarke and then you can take me out for a very nice lunch,' she added, navigating to the Birmingham burials on Ancestry.

'While you're doing that,' responded Tom, 'I'll log in to the British Library Newspaper Archive and see if there's a story on her death.'

'Well, if it helps, I have the burial already,' said Annie, 'it doesn't say much, other than Agnes Clarke of Court 3, bk of 24 Vittoria Street was buried 28 February 1871 at St Paul, Birmingham with her age shown as 42. It doesn't really confirm much or add anything to what we already know, does it?'

Tom was busy concentrating on scrolling through the search results returned by the newspaper database. 'What…. Oh wow! Listen to this from the *Birmingham Post* 15 February 1871. Now this could be very relevant.'

He quickly downloaded the article and started to read it out loud to Annie:

'POLICE SEEK FUGITIVE AFTER STABBING!

Inspector Dawes of Birmingham Police has informed our reporter that the force is actively seeking a man by the name of Joseph Clarke who has disappeared following the death of his wife, Agnes, who died after being stabbed at the family home in Vittoria Street. The incident was witnessed by their distraught son Joseph, who has made a statement to the police to the effect that his mother's death was accidental. He had reported that on entering the house, he had found his mother in the kitchen. She told him that she had slipped, whilst cutting a loaf of bread, stabbing herself in the ribs, causing her to bleed profusely. Mrs Clarke sadly expired at the scene.

Inspector Dawes has urged any member of the public that may be sheltering Clarke to give him up so that he may be interviewed, adding that at this stage, the circumstances of the death of Mrs Clarke have to be regarded as suspicious, made more so by the fact that Mr Clarke had disappeared immediately afterwards.

The coroner has released the body and the funeral will be at St Pauls church on 28th inst.

'Gee, that is an amazing find,' answered Annie, 'do you think that this could be the real reason that Joseph Clarke changed his name to Charles Tusker? It's a load of lies, straight out of the trash can, about taking his mother's maiden name.'

'It looks likely, I agree,' said Tom, 'while he was on the run, he must have read the story of the death of the real Charles Tusker on the railway and assumed his identity, whilst at the same time probably, he changed his appearance to avoid being apprehended by the police. It looks like he was in hiding at his son and daughter in law's house.'

'Mmmm, that does seem a little odd. Surely, the police would have been watching his house or the home of his son to see if he re-appeared. He was obviously there in the 1871 census under his newly acquired false name?'

'Ok,' replied Tom,' let's knock it on the head for now and go get that lunch you promised that I was going to buy you!'

CHAPTER 22 – THE GREAT TRAIN ROBBERY

Charles and Joseph had arranged for Eliza to stay overnight with her best friend, who lived with her family in the Nechells district of Birmingham. To start with, Eliza was miffed at being excluded from the planned robbery but in the end, had agreed to staying off the *Bessie* that night. She knew that it was a dangerous plan but that if it came off, she would be able to afford a better life with Joseph and if the robbery failed, she would be miles away from the scene.

A few years before and prior to meeting Joseph, she had experienced one temporary stay for a night in the cells at Bradford Street, after a mistake over a stolen handkerchief and she was in no hurry to repeat the experience.

It was just after 7pm and the *Bessie* was moored once again at Camp Hill Locks. Charles and Joseph heard Curly's tuneless whistling, long before he appeared from the other side of the railway bridge.

'Good evenin' chaps,' he greeted them, jumping aboard the boat, causing it to rock slightly. 'All ready, then? You know the plan, just get up to Curzon Street bridge and tie up underneath out of sight. A few minutes before 10 o'clock, you'll hear the sound of the mail train approaching. Our postman on board has been briefed on the special delivery, so to speak,' sniggering at his own joke, 'and so get the boat moving at that point. At least you have a steam engine now and don't have to rely any longer on that old nag of an 'orse pulling you along. Right, I'll be off now and 'ere, take this, you may need it if it gets rough.' At this, he placed an oilskin pouch tied up with string, onto the cabin top, before jumping down onto the towpath, whistling again as he disappeared into the swirling early evening mist.

Joseph untied the string on the pouch and pulled back the corners of the package to reveal its contents to the two boatmen.

Charles gasped as he saw an easily identifiable howdah pistol which he recognised immediately, as he had seen one very similar the previous year, when a soldier returning from India had been trying to sell one in Charles' local pub. The soldier had explained to his audience that this was a high calibre pistol designed to enable huntsmen to kill wild animals from the safety of a howdah, while perched in relative safety on top of an elephant.

'Jeez!' he exclaimed recoiling in horror, 'that is a powerful shooter if ever I saw one. I don't want anything to do with it,' he added, pushing the pistol away from him along the cabin top.

Joseph picked up the revolver and examined it closer. 'What did he mean when he said in case it gets rough?' he questioned. 'Perhaps we ought to keep it handy in case of trouble?'

'I don't know,' replied Charles, 'as I said, I'm not getting involved with guns. You can get away with killing someone in a fair fight….and sometimes an unfair one but kill someone with a gun and it's premeditated if you were carrying the weapon. It's a sure way to be having an appointment with Tommy Scott at Stafford,' he added, referring to one of the current Home Office hangmen.

'I don't get you, sometimes,' replied his son, 'you stabbed and killed Mom which we accepted was an accident, then you beat the life out of that copper Dawes and yet you're reluctant to use a gun? I know that if push comes to shove, I'd rather shoot it out than be shot. It'll be safe in here,' he argued, picking the pistol up and placing it inside the upside-down bucket which stood in the stern of the *Bessie* and was decorated in the traditional waterway roses and castles pattern.

'As you wish, Joseph, just don't involve me. You're on your own if you use the gun. Just don't forget what I'm telling you.' replied the older man. 'Come on, let's get underway. Best to get to Curzon Street early rather than late. That's one train I don't want to miss,' he added with a nervous laugh as he jumped back on board, having untied the boat from its mooring point on the canal side.

Around 40 minutes later, the intrepid pair were out of sight in the shelter of the railway bridge, following Curly's instructions to the letter. Joseph who was steering the vessel, cut the engine to an idle before turning it off altogether. Charles jumped onto the towpath and wrapped the mooring rope loosely around a nearby steel stanchion to prevent the boat from drifting.

Neither man spoke as the minutes ticked by until Charles pulled the half albert from his pocket and told Joseph to look sharp.

'There's still around 10 minutes before the train is due to arrive and stop directly above us as the driver waits for the signal on the railway line', he confirmed.

A few more minutes passed by with the nerves of both men taut with anticipation of the robbery that lay ahead. Technically, they were not robbers themselves but mere accomplices.

They heard the train before they could see it, as the metal lines above them started to whistle at first and then hum as the noise of the train wheels contacting against the lines started to vibrate within earshot. Then came a gentle screeching at first, followed by a louder harsher noise as the engine driver applied the brakes to bring the engine and its entourage of carriages to a halt.

Charles had unwrapped the temporary mooring rope and from his position on the towpath, was gently pulling the *Bessie* to a point underneath the edge of the parapet of the bridge above them.

The arranged code was the postal worker above their heads tunelessly but loudly whistling *'The Blaydon Races',* a song published by its author only a couple of years before even though he had penned the lyrics some 30 years earlier in the early 1860's. Joseph got a stern look from Charles when he started to sing the words to the ditty, 'Bloody 'ell man, we're here to do a job, not to take part in a music hall concert!' he snapped as the pressure and stress of the evening finally exploded within him.

Disgruntled at once again being the subject of a put down from his father, Joseph had no time to respond as a loud splash interrupted the night air caused by a bundle of some description landing in the canal just in front of the boat, followed by another four or five similar splashes all within six feet of the bows. A dull thud from the towpath as a couple more of the packages narrowly missed Charles where he was standing and trying to extract the packages floating in the canal by pulling them towards him using a boat hook.

With his back towards Joseph, he didn't see the younger man pick up one of the smaller packages and when his father wasn't looking, conceal it under the bucket that was also the hiding place for the pistol that had been provided earlier by Curly.

Soon, all of the packages with the exception of the one hidden by Joseph were stowed safely out of sight inside the cabin. As Charles started the engine and the canal boat started to chug away from the towpath, there was an almighty splash, as something much larger hit the water, sending huge sprays of water in every direction, scattering the moorhens that up until then had been swimming peacefully nearby.

Charles and Joseph both looked over the side to see what had caused the commotion and were horrified to see the grinning face of a man still in his post office uniform staring back at them. Then their horror increased as they realised in the semi darkness that the man was not grinning at them at all but what had appeared to be his mouth, was actually a huge slit under his chin where a knife had been used to cut his throat. Quite clearly, he was already no longer in this world and had no doubt already started on the long journey to meet his already deceased ancestors.

Joseph grabbed the boathook and pushed the corpse away from the *Bessie* and the last they saw of it was a column of bubbles as the man's lungs filled with the murky Grand Junction water and he sank to the bottom of the cut, no doubt aided by the weight of his boots and the two bricks that had been pushed down the waistband of his trousers by his unknown assailants.

'Quick, let's get out of here!' yelled Charles, 'Curly has really set us up this time,' he added, setting the engine to the maximum power possible to get away from the crime scene as quickly as possible, leaving a wake of white water behind them. After around half a mile, he cut the revs and slowed the engine right down.

'What are you doing?' questioned Joseph, 'We need to get as much water under the bows as possible, then pick up my 'Liza and get off to the safe house at Knowle that Curly told us to go to.'

Charles replied 'Firstly, if we maintain that speed for much longer, we'll probably blow the engine up as it won't take that steam pressure for long and secondly, you well know that there's a maximum speed that all of us boatmen have to comply with. If the canal company get wind of us going too fast, they'll likely call the constabulary and that might just be a tiny problem for us, carrying the packets stolen from the post office train.'

Neither man could get the image of the dead postal worker out of their mind as they could not rid themselves of the memory of the grin from the slit in the man's throat.

'Curly said he would just be roughed up a bit so as to make the robbery look realistic,' protested Joseph, 'if anyone has seen the *Bessie* in the vicinity of the Curzon Street bridge, we could be in trouble!'

'You be right, there,' replied Charles grimly, his jaw set square, 'let's look sharp, there's Eliza on the wharf. Get her aboard quick and let's get some water between us and Curzon Street.'

After a brief stop to allow Eliza to board, they were soon retracing their route from a few days before, passing through Elmdon Heath and Catherine De Barnes before they navigated the long 90-degree right hand bend on the way to their safe haven at Knowle. Just short of reaching Knowle Locks, they tied up at Kixley Lane bridge, so that they would avoid having to navigate through the steep descent of the five locks which dropped the canal down more than 40 feet over a short distance.

'OK,' ordered Charles, 'let's collect our extra cargo and take it to our rooms at the *Greswolde Arms Inn.* Curly has booked us two rooms there, one for me and the other for you and Eliza and then we wait for Curly to make contact.'

'The *Greswolde Arms?*' questioned Eliza, 'That's a bit posh, aint it. Wasn't that the place where Lady Byron stayed whenever she was in the area?'

'Yes,' replied Joseph, 'a chap I know worked on the lime wharf at Knowle Hall and he told me that his father used to recount stories of famous people staying in the village.'

Charles interrupted them, 'Well, don't get carried away as actually, it won't be that posh because the rooms that Curly has arranged with the Landlord for us to take shelter in are actually in the stable block! So, when you two have quite finished giving me a history lesson, grab some of these packages and let's get to the bloody place. I'm thirsty, I'm tired and I need to rest.'

Charles didn't see Joseph and Eliza exchange knowing glances. Eliza distracted Charles' attention for a moment as his son picked up the items hidden within the bucket at the back of the boat and slid them into the small space underneath the bed before he closed the cabin door, locking it behind him.

It was almost total darkness with the moon just poking out from behind the thick cloud, as the trio then made their way along Kixley Lane to the outbuildings at the Inn.

After being greeted by the landlord, who had introduced himself as William, they were shown to their overnight accommodation, which consisted of just two animal stalls. On top of an upturned box in each was a glass and a jug of water, along with half a loaf of bread and a lump of cheese.

'Curly said to spare you no expense,' laughed the landlord, 'help yourself to fresh hay, so that your stay is more comfortable!'

Charles, Joseph and Eliza looked at each other in disbelief. 'Are you serious?' he asked, his question directed towards William.

'Just following instructions,' came the reply. 'Oh, and Curly did say he would be along tomorrow morning bright and early to collect his stuff. As I have been passed a message about the murderous robbery in Birmingham earlier and also see the Post Office emblem on those packages you brought with you, I reckon you be in no position to argue, eh?'

CHAPTER 23 – THE TOURISTS

The next day saw Tom and Annie walking in the Birmingham city centre. Tom had told Annie that the day was reserved for sight-seeing to give them a day off and a break from their intensive research.

As they turned from Hill Street into Hurst Street, Annie said 'You've been very secretive this morning, Tom. Where are we going?'

'Have patience and all will be revealed. It's not just any tourism tour you see, but a genealogy related tourism tour,' he replied, as they continued walking.

The streets were quieter once they had left the main New Street thoroughfare, where for a change, they had enjoyed a breakfast outside of the hotel environment.

'Ok, here we are, Inge Street. You might remember in our research some of the homes were described as back-to-back houses? Well, I have booked a couple of tickets for a tour of the back-to-back museum, said to be the last surviving houses of their type, certainly in Birmingham.'

'Yes, of course,' responded Annie, 'I recall that you said they were tiny houses, with lots of families all crammed together, with shared rest rooms?'

'Mmmph, I can't see that the residents would have seen them as much of a place for resting! Often, they were just buckets under a bench type of seat. It wasn't until the 1930's that the flushing water closets that you will see on today's tour would have been installed. In fact, in the late 1800's, the facilities wouldn't even have been that far advanced. To start with, there would have been a single water pump, which eventually would have been replaced by a tap to be shared by up to 40 people who would do their business in buckets. These in turn would then have to be emptied onto strategically placed dung heaps in a corner of the yard. Then it would be the job of men employed by the local corporation to cart the waste away at night and take it down to the wharf where they would load it onto a special canal boat called a scud. This would then be used to transport their cargo out of the town boundaries, where it could be dumped out of harm's way in a field or bit of waste ground.'

After a few moments thought, Annie said 'I think you said that the Clarke and Tusker family would have been living in a back-to-back. So, what we are going to see today would be very similar to what our friends would have been experiencing in, where was it, Vittoria Street?'

They had arrived at the front of the museum now and Annie read aloud from a tourist leaflet on a stand outside. *'Take the family for a tour around the only surviving back-to-backs in Birmingham where originally, there would have been thousands of similar houses, with all of the residents putting up with incredibly insanitary conditions. Authentic sights, sounds and smells make this an unforgettable day out.'*

'Phew,' she exclaimed, ' I hope that the smells are not too authentic!'

The pair were introduced to their tour guide and with the rest of the small party, had an intriguing and exciting introduction to the three storey houses.

Jane, their guide, explained that the conditions were so bad that a new law under an Act of Parliament in 1875 meant that no more back to backs would be built, after that date. Even so, it wasn't for nearly another 100 years, that the housing would be phased out with the tenants being moved to other areas, often into new high-rise housing estates, which some observers would question whether these represented an improvement in conditions or not.

Tom had been on the tour before, but Annie was visibly shaking as they left the museum building. 'Are you OK, Annie?' he asked.

'Yes, I think so but whilst it is a fantastic exhibition and the guide was so informative, I couldn't get it out of my head what the conditions must have been like for the poor families that lived there in the late 1800's. I got so immersed in it all and I sort of pictured the Tusker family living there. All of the rooms were so tiny and they must have been so cramped. It makes you appreciate what we take for granted but still moan about …but thank you for taking me. I appreciate it,' she added and pulled him towards her and kissed him on the cheek. 'So, where's next?' she asked.

'Well,' came the response, 'we're carrying on with the theme of cramped conditions and we are going on a cruise!'

Annie looked puzzled 'A cruise? In Birmingham? Are you kidding me?' she fired at Tom.

'Nope,' came the response, 'I remembered that one of Aunt Jemima's friends has a narrow boat and so, we are going to walk back to Broad Street and then down to Gas Street Basin where we will find Jim, his wife, Peggy and of course, Aunt Jemima. We're going out for the afternoon, stopping at a pub for lunch and then returning in the late afternoon. How does that sound?' he asked.

They were soon aboard *'Polly Anna'* which turned out to be a 72 ft narrowboat which Jim and Peggy had lovingly restored several years earlier. After Aunt Jemima had made the introductions, they all clambered aboard and were soon chugging their way along the canal. They paused at a set of locks and Tom pointed out that they were at Camp Hill, in the imposing shadows of Holy Trinity Church.

'Hey', yelled Annie, 'that's where the Tusker boat was par….*moored*….', she quickly corrected herself remembering her faux-pas and Tom's put down from the previous day.

They both watched, fascinated, as Jim and Peggy expertly manoeuvred the boat through the locks and they were soon making good headway in what had turned out to be a lovely sunny, late morning. Peggy took Annie on a guided tour of the *Polly Anna* with Annie being forced to stoop down as she was shown round the cabin interior. It was explained that at 72ft, this was generally the longest boat available on the canal network as otherwise, it would not fit the length of the locks.

'Jemima has explained that you and Tom are over here doing some gynaecological research. Is that right?' she asked.

Annie collapsed in a fit of giggles 'No, it's genealogical research, you know, family history!'

Peggy joined in the laughter at her apparent slip of the tongue, 'Eh well love, they both deal with births, I suppose!'

Back on deck, after Jim had taken Tom on a similar tour of the living accommodation, he said 'So Jemmy here,' referring to his pet name for Jemima, 'has been telling us about this canal family you've been checking up on and so I have been doing my own checking with a pal of mine at the National Waterways Museum in Gloucester. There they have a database compiled from the canal boat inspection records and this boat *The Bessie* that you were interested in, was registered in the name of Charles Tusker from 1871. It was licenced for 2 adults and 4 children or alternatively, 3 adults and no children.

If you consider that according to the records, she was only 52ft long and her cabin would only have had headroom of just over 5ft, then it would have been pretty cramped in there,' he explained.

'From what I remember though, Charles Tusker lived aboard with his son and daughter in law so that would be the three adults permitted,' replied Annie, 'not just cramped but also not much privacy either! I particularly feel sorry for the daughter in law. Effectively sleeping with her husband when her father-in-law was essentially in the same room as they were,' she continued, 'especially if they both snored as most men seem to,' glancing a firm look in Tom's direction.

'From what I read,' mused Tom, 'there would probably only have been a curtain separating them, which possibly explains why we found no record of any children for Joseph and Eliza. Not much space for a quick cuddle, let alone any baby making!' he laughed.

Jim turned to the rest of the party and then pointing to a spot on their left-hand side, told them 'That's Yardley Cemetery, over there. If you ask me nicely, I might stop on the way back and tie up for a while to show you something.'

Tom's ears pricked up and he responded, 'What are you going to show us at Yardley, Jim? I know it's a large cemetery, as I've done my share of grave hunting there in the past.'

'All will be revealed,' said Jim, exchanging an unseen wink with Jemima, 'but first, it's lunchtime!'

The five of them enjoyed a lovely lunch at the Blue Ball, which Tom remembered from his youth as being a canal side pub specialising in cider. He laughed as he recounted some of his experiences to Annie, who having confessed that she had never tried that particular alcoholic beverage, was now eagerly losing her cider virginity.

'They always used to say that the cider was made with water pumped straight up the bank from the canal,' he said and added 'we used to drink pints of cider, laced with blackcurrant because it was so strong, but boy, did it taste good!'

'Ok,' said Jemima, 'enough of these tales of your mis-spent youth! I always thought you were a good boy! Now, I think it's time for Jim's secret to be revealed. Shall we set sail back to Yardley, Cap'n?'

After a short journey, they were soon mooring along the towpath, having just passed under the Yardley Road canal bridge.

'Right then.' Jim said, after he had got their attention, 'You will be wanting to hear mine and Jemmy's little secret? What she hasn't told you is that I'm also a keen genealogist and like Jemmy, Peggy and I are both members of the BMSGH which is the Midland Ancestors Family History Society.'

'It's where we met,' explained Jemima, 'and when we found out that we had a mutual interest in canal boat ancestry, we became firm friends and I have been on a few floating holidays with Jim and Peggy, over the years.'

Annie interrupted, 'Hey, hang on just a mo,' she said, 'so why did you call family history, gynaecology earlier, Peggy?'

'Sorry, I was just pulling your leg luv, as we didn't want to give the game away to you and Tom!'

Jim continued with the story, 'so when Jemmy told us about your research into this Tusker family and what you'd found in relation to your Clarke and Tusker conundrum, I did some research using the member only, BMSGH databases and found a burial plot right here at Yardley, that I thought might be of interest to you.'

The group climbed the embankment up the very rough-hewn steps in the grass and soil before they then walked a short distance along

Yardley Road, until they came to one of the cemetery entrances, opposite Mansfield Road.

Once inside, Jim led the way, occasionally referring to a plan that he had downloaded from the internet the previous day. He stopped suddenly and then said 'Right, it's just along here' and walked past several graves, counting the rows as he went.

'Here we are, this is the one that I wanted to show you,' he said, pointing to a small white headstone.

Annie stepped forward and knelt down on the grass to get a better view of the inscription on the memorial, which she read out aloud to the others who were listening intently,

Sacred to the memory of Joseph Clarke and Charles Tusker,

One man but two people

who died 2 April 1891.

'Mmm,' she added, 'there are more words at the bottom of the headstone, but I can't make them out very well, as they are a bit obscured by the moss.'

Tom got down on his knees beside her and stared closely at the remaining letters in front of them, 'It seems very odd, but I think it reads *'I'm sorry.'* I must admit to saying that I've never seen an apology on a headstone before!'

Jemima chipped in 'Well, we have the answer for you or at least part of it, anyway. When we found the grave, a few days ago, we also looked on the British Library Newspaper site and found a couple of interesting articles.'

'We checked them out,' added Peggy 'and basically, it turns out our Mr Tusker or Mr Clarke, whichever name you prefer, had been shot with his body having been found floating in the canal which runs to the north of Acocks Green. At the time it would have been little more than a village, as opposed to the busy, slightly run-down typical Birmingham area, it is today. The doctor who examined the body, thought his death was very recent, given the lack of decomposition of the corpse and so they decided to record his death as occurring on the same date as when his body was found, as it was unlikely that he had been in the water for long.'

'Did they find out what happened to him?' questioned Annie, 'was there an autopsy?'

'So, it would have been an inquest over here in the UK, as opposed to an American autopsy and whilst there was one, they didn't completely reach a conclusive verdict on the cause of death,' replied Jim, 'as according to a later article in the Birmingham Mail, the Coroner's ruling was a case of death by misadventure. So, at the end of the day, while it looked like murder, it seems he could not definitively rule out suicide or confirm an accident. At the same time however, his son and daughter in law had also gone missing. Their canal boat, or rather Charles' canal boat, *The Bessie,* was later found burned out, empty and abandoned at Wolverhampton.'

'If you remember, Tom,' interjected Annie, 'we didn't find Charles Tusker on the 1891 census, but we did find Joseph and Eliza on board another boat. Can you remember what she was called?'

'Hold on, I'll look at the notes on my tablet,' he said, pulling the digital device out of his inside pocket and after scrolling through a few pages, said, 'yes, here we are, it's '*The Lottie.*'

'It's getting interesting,' said Jim, I guess we need to look up this *Lottie* on the museum database, although unfortunately, my friend isn't back as he's taking a few days off. I'll let you know when I can get hold of him.'

'Have you tried the 1901 census?' asked Peggy.

'No,' replied Tom, 'If they are the Tuskers we want, they emigrated to America in 1893. We have still to prove the link to Theodore and Lillian, but I think we've made real progress today, thanks to you guys.'

'OK,' said Jim, 'let's make our way back to the canal. I'd like to be back in Gas Street before dark.'

CHAPTER 24 – GUNSHOT NEAR THE GRESWOLDE

Charles was the first to wake up the next morning.

His head hurt and his back ached. The former was without doubt due to the tankards of ale that he and Joseph had shared the previous night and the latter down to the stable stall where he had slept. There was no floor and only the scattered straw separated him from the damp soil that formed the base of his temporary bedroom.

He stretched and yelped as his nerve ends also came to life as he gingerly stood up. It was still not fully light, but his eyes adjusted quickly at the same time as his bladder reminded him of the folly of the previous night's drinking. He walked past the adjoining stall, occupied by Joseph and Eliza and who were still fast asleep, as evidenced by Joseph's light snoring.

The couple were entwined on the floor and Charles could see a flash of Eliza's right breast through a gap in the opening to her blouse. Sensing his presence, she opened her eyes and realising what he was looking at, shifted her position thus affording him an even better view.

Embarrassed at being caught but mindful of his needs at the same time, he walked round the back of the stable block and quickly urinated in the bushes behind, out of sight of the eyes of anyone inside the main pub building.

Startled on hearing a rustling noise, he hastily started to fasten his trousers and looking round, saw Eliza standing watching with a sly grin on her face, 'Aww Charlie, don't put him away, he's a sight for sore eyes, to be sure, especially when your husband has one that hardly ever wakes up!'

'For goodness' sake, Eliza, keep your voice down. Joseph's only the other side of that brick wall,'

'Oh, the ale will probably ensure he stays that way too, unless I go give him a kick,' came the reply, 'but you're right, best to play it safe.'

At that moment, they heard Joseph's voice, as the man staggered round the corner of the building. He glanced suspiciously at Charles and Eliza and asked, 'What's going on here, then? Looks a bit shifty, a bit awkward like, seeing you two standing there.'

'What are you talking about Joseph?' retorted Eliza, 'I was just stretching my legs, looking for the ladies' room, when your father came back from a walk and I was asking him to disappear a while to give me some privacy. Now if you both, don't mind, a lady has to do what a lady has to do!'

The two men shuffled back to the stables with Joseph giving Charles an angry look, as if by way of a warning but then the tension of the moment was interrupted by a deep voice booming out, as the landlord William, appeared in their vision.

'Oh, there you are, chaps, I brought you some bread and dripping which I had left over from last night and there's also a mug of tea each,' and he placed a wooden tray for them on top of one of the animal troughs.

Eliza had by this time reappeared and as they were all starving as a result of only having eaten some of the nearly stale cheese from the previous evening, they tucked into the makeshift breakfast with the bread accompanied by some wilted watercress on the side of the plate.

'That's very kind of you, William,' said Eliza, 'I'm really hungry!'

'Very kind? Very kind?' came the response from the burly man, 'that'll be one shilling and sixpence each, when you're ready. I'm sure you will be able to afford it once Curly meets up with you,' he guffawed, giving them a big theatrical wink, before he turned away to return to the bar.

As he did so, Charles called him back, 'Did Curly give you any message as to what time he's coming by this morning or where we're supposed to meet him?' he asked.

'Oh, Curly's already here,' came the reply, 'in fact, he's been here all night, staying in one of our best guest rooms. He was tucking into his breakfast about ten minutes ago and so I imagine he'll be out to see you soon. Oh, talk of the devil, here he is now,' he said, nodding at Curly as he came out of the pub door and headed in their direction.

'Morning all, did you sleep well,' he asked, 'I had a very comfortable room and a jolly good breakfast too, courtesy of mine host, William,' he added.

'Have you been out here, all night?' he asked with an innocent expression, 'such a shame that there was no room at the inn, eh?'

'Look Curly, can we get this sorted quickly,' growled Charles, 'you left us in possession of a revolver and you clearly told us that the post office man would just be roughed up a bit to make it look like a genuine robbery. Yet, the last time we saw him, he had a slit in his throat and was fast becoming fish food in the canal!'

'Oh him, don't dwell on that, it turned out he was a little disloyal, that's all. He tried to keep some of the haul for himself and as you know by now, nobody gets the best of Curly. I've been too many times round the block to fall for an employee trying to put one over on me!'

Joseph and Eliza exchanged glances, blanching a little, but still trying to concentrate on what Curly was saying.

'So, where are my little packages, still in your care, custody and control, I hope?' he asked, waiting for an answer from the crew of *The Bessie.*

'Yes, Boss, no worries there, 'answered Charles, 'All present and correct. Your parcels are all in the end stall there, under the bales of straw. I counted them out myself,' he added, 'all nineteen are there and after I checked on them, I slept next to them all night, in the same stall so as to keep them safe.'

Curly replied, 'Oh, I love your little joke, Charles, what a wonderful sense of humour you have,' and turning in the general direction of where Joseph was standing next to Eliza, he added, 'Isn't he a little tease, Eliza? I bet you find that as well, don't you?', nodding at her with a serious expression but winking at the same time.

Eliza now had a worried expression as she realised that somehow Curly knew about her affair with her father-in-law and was frightened that he was about to reveal all to Joseph.

Charles looked puzzled at this little exchange, 'Sorry Boss, I'm not with you. What joke? I'm telling you that all nineteen of them are here, all safe and sound. Come on and I'll show you.'

'Charlie,' came the response, 'as you might have realised by now, I'm not laughing because a total of twenty packages were thrown out of the window of the carriage by my little helper. That means that there's one missing. What about you, Joseph? Any thoughts? You've been quiet up to now, anyroad.'

The younger man paused before answering, 'Er well, the only thing I can think of is that perhaps it caught on the embankment on the way down…..or hit the edge of the railway bridge and fell back onto the side of the track,' Joseph stammered, trying to avoid looking Curly in the eye.

'Of course, now why didn't I think of that? Unless of course it fell on the boat somewhere unnoticed,' he questioned, 'it could have fallen onto the prow of *'The Bessie'* and not observed by you two in your haste to secure the rest of my packages that were floating in the cut. Do you know what? I think we should all go down to the wharf and check her out, just in case.'

Joseph and Eliza again looked uneasy at the suggestion as they realised that their attempt to cheat Curly might be about to be discovered. For Joseph, in particular, the memory of the postal worker and his second smile bubbling on the way to the bottom of the canal as a reward for his disloyalty came back fresh in his memory. He had to think and think fast if he wasn't going to become fish bait himself.

He stepped forward 'Tell you what, Boss. No point in us all going back to the boat. Me and Dad will go back and have a quick shufty. It's not as if she's a big boat after all, tha' knows? It'll only take us a few minutes to check her over,' and added 'we can check the cabin too as the hatch would have been open at the time and I suppose it's possible that a package could have rolled into the accommodation? Just a thought really.'

'That's a great idea, Joseph,' replied Curly, 'I'm sure that your Eliza will be able to look after Old Curly, won't you? he added, looking directly at the young woman. 'I'm sure we can have a nice chat while you're away, eh love?'

Eliza looked quite uncomfortable at the implied suggestion. 'Well, it'll only take them ten minutes to get down to the wharf at a quick pace and ten minutes back again and so as it won't take long to carry out the search, so they'll be back quite quickly. I'll go and see the landlord and ask him to make a mug of tea for us all, as the men will be likely shrammed when they get back from the waterside.'

'Now that, Eliza, is a sound plan and just to put your mind at rest, you had no need to get yourself all flustered. It's not like you would be attracted to an older man now, is it?' This time, his exaggerated wink was aimed to where Charles was standing, but he was still maintaining an innocent look across his weatherworn features.

It was as if Joseph had suddenly woken up out of a deep sleep as his brain caught up what it was that the gang leader was implying. He struggled to process the thoughts that were forming in his head but realised that now was not the time or the place to take any action. No, he would keep his powder dry for now and wait for the opportunity for revenge that he realised might present itself in the not-too-distant future.

He turned and started to walk out of the pub yard, waving his hand to Charles, signalling for him to join him and the pair were soon out of sight as they headed back in the direction of the towpath. Eliza had also been quick to move towards the main building but found her way blocked by the older man.

'Lo…look Curly, are you trying to stir up trouble between me and my 'usband?' she demanded, 'Joseph is a possessive man and gets very worked up if he thinks another man is paying too much attention to me,' she offered by way of an explanation.

The older man grabbed the woman by the shoulder and pulled her closer, 'Now then, I know and you know, that my old mucker Charles and you, have been 'aving it away whenever Joseph's back is turned. Don't forget, my spies are everywhere. Information is knowledge and knowledge is power.'

Eliza's blouse had popped open at the neck as Curly had grabbed her and taking his opportunity, he thrust his hand inside and fondled one of her breasts, causing her to gasp. She pulled back, with Curly removing his hand at that point.

'That was a nice little feel, Eliza, no doubt about that and as long as we understand each other, then everything will be just fine, know what I'm saying?' he questioned, 'I also know that it was either your loving husband or Charles that stole one of my little parcels too. Not sure which one yet but the truth will out, as sure as eggs is eggs,' he said laughing, 'now where's that tea? Don't want young Joseph to think we were up to some malarkey behind his back, do we?' he added laughing again, before patting her on the backside and pushing her in the direction of the door to the bar.

Meanwhile, Charles and Joseph had reached the canal with Charles slightly breathless with trying to keep up with his son who had set a quick pace and had not said a single word since leaving the confines of *The Greswolde Arms.'*

'Hey, slow down, Son,' protested the older of the two, this is a bit of a wild goose chase, anyways. I think we would have seen any spare packages as we left Curzon Street. We had to cast off fore and aft and so would surely have seen anything on the foredeck or in the stern before we set off?'

Joseph had been getting angrier every step of the way back to *The Bessie'* as the realisation that his wife and father had been making a fool of him. In his mind though, Eliza was the innocent party here and he slowly became convinced that either she had been seduced or worse still, coerced into having a relationship with his father. He began to wonder on how many occasions it had happened and he could feel the rage building up inside him, fuelled by the jealous streak that was part of his DNA.

The fragments of his plan were coming together and he knew that now was his time. Time to get even for the put downs, the minimal paternal love shown during his childhood and although several months had elapsed since the incident, he also recalled the violent death of his mother, Agnes, following the so-called accidental knifing at his parents' home and then being persuaded to cover it up afterwards.

Although his father had always claimed it was an accident, Joseph had been a witness to the truth and there was no doubt that Charles' actions that night had been the result of him being beered up prior to the incident and now more doubts crept into Joseph's mind as little voices told him that it was time and that he now needed to exert his authority on the situation.

A couple of minutes later and they had reached the spot where '*The Bessie'* was moored and both men boarded quickly with Charles producing his bunch of keys, unlocking the main hatch, fumbling a little in the chill of the morning air and a bout of coughing that had been exacerbated by the recent fast walk.

'Give me the keys!' insisted Joseph, 'you check the foredeck and the ropes. I'll go inside and check out the cabin. The sooner we're back at the pub, the better. I don't trust that Curly with my Eliza.'

Charles nodded and stepped down onto the towpath, cursorily checking the side of the vessel, before mounting again at the front.

Meanwhile, Joseph had disappeared inside and quickly unwrapped one of the packages that he had secreted under the bed the evening before. He checked it out and then made his way back up the few steps to the tiller and pretended to look on the starboard side.

'Nothing here,' he called out to his father who had his back to him at this point.

'No, I can't see anything either,' replied the older man and turned to make his way back towards where his son was standing, stopping suddenly when he realised that he was staring into the barrel of the revolver.

'What the hell are you doing?' he asked, 'Why did you keep that gun that Curly gave us. I thought you had chucked it over the side. I told you that I wanted nothing to do with it. For Christ's sake, that's a bloody dangerous joke. It might even be loaded; you just don't know!' he exclaimed in a frightened tone.

'Well dear Father, that's where you're wrong. You see, I do know that it's loaded because I just put the bullets in the chamber myself.' replied Joseph, intensely.

'What? Why? Put that thing down now, it's not like the toy pistol that you used to play peaky blinders with as a kid back in the courtyard. Even then you wouldn't have hit a brewhouse door at twenty paces, mind,' he retorted.

Joseph snarled back 'You see? There you go again, can't resist knocking me back, can you? But this time, I've got the upper hand,' he added, waving the gun in the air. You think you are so clever, don't you? But I knows that you've been bedding my 'Liza when I aint be looking. Taking advantage of her pure soul, if not quite her pure body!'

Charles stiffened as the seriousness of the situation finally dawned on him. 'Now then son, let's not be silly. She came onto me and it was just the once, after all. What's a man supposed to do faced with the temptations of the flesh?' he said, glancing quickly over the water to his left.

The momentary distraction was enough as Joseph followed his eyeline and Charles took the opportunity to launch himself at his son, reaching out to grab the hand that held the revolver. The force of the impact was all that was needed to knock Joseph off balance and the two men fell into the stern, with Charles just managing to avoid smashing his head against the tiller, as they rolled together.

There was a loud bang as the gun went off and blood splattered against the hatch that led to the cabin. One of the men got up off the floor, his clothing already soaked by the other's blood and looked down at the motionless form below him.

He looked in horror at the smoking gun and then quickly hurled it over the side with a splash and waited for someone to respond, wondering if anyone had heard the commotion.

But no-one came. It was still relatively early, but the other working boats had already departed from the wharf and the lime workers were not yet due to start their daily shift.

Minutes seemed like hours as he worked out his next moves. Although what had happened was an accident, a jury wouldn't believe him. He went down into the cabin and saw Curly's missing package where it had been dropped on the floor and knew instantly what his best course of action was. He picked up a tarpaulin folded neatly in the hold and covered the body up to avoid it being seen by someone walking past on the towpath. He grabbed some fresh clothing that was close to hand and then put on the coat that was thrown over the bed so that the existing blood-stained attire was concealed before he started to make his way back towards *The Greswolde*.

Curly shrugged his shoulders in a silent response to Eliza's question 'Where are they? They've been gone for ages!'

'Oh, stop mitherin' woman. Here they come now,' and he pointed in the direction of the lane that led to the wharf.

'Yes, I see Charles, easily recognizable by his blue overcoat and he's carrying one of your packages, but why is he on his own? Where's my Joseph?' she added, staring into the distance as the approaching figure drew nearer.

CHAPTER 25 – ANYTHING IN THE PAPER?

After they had disembarked back at Gas Street Basin, Tom and Annie had said their goodbyes to Jim, Peggy and Jemima, thanking them profusely for both their hospitality and the help with the research.

They went straight back to their hotel where they took turns to shower and dress in time for their evening meal.

Over food, they discussed their next moves with both being puzzled as to the strange epitaph on the Yardley grave of Charles Tusker.

'One man and two people……clearly refers to the fact that the two names referred to one person, confirming that Joseph Clarke became Charles Tusker!' said Annie excitedly, 'but I am puzzled about the reference to someone being sorry. Who was sorry and what for?'

'My guess,' replied Tom, 'is that whoever arranged the burial and purchased the headstone was doing the apologising, but we will probably never know for sure. Come on, back to the room. I know it's late, but I want to check the laptop to see if the birth certificate for Joseph the younger and Eliza are back…….because there's something else that has been niggling me but I may now have the answer as to the identity of the mysterious Theodore and Lilian that emigrated to the USA and who they actually were.'

'Oh Tom, stop teasing! Who are you referring to?' demanded Annie.

'I'm not sure yet,' came the considered reply, 'it's just a hunch for now and so rather than lead you up the garden path at this stage, all I'll say is that I'm hoping that the birth certificates that we're waiting for from the GRO will confirm things, one way or another!'

'The garden path?' she spluttered, ' I guess that's just one of your quaint English sayings? I'm not even going to ask!'

The couple made their way back to their room at a quickened pace, eager to check Tom's email to see if the pdf certificates ordered from the GRO were waiting for them in Tom's inbox. Firing up the laptop, he opened *'Outlook',* scanning the inbox as several emails appeared, each with the familiar ping.

Disappointed, he turned to Annie and told her that the missing certificates were still awaited and that she would have to be patient if he was to prove his hunch one way or the other.

Annie yawned, 'Sorry, Tom but I'm pooped. It's been a long day what with walking halfway round Birmingham this morning and the effect of the fresh air. I'm off to bed……to sleep, before you get any ideas either,' she added, climbing into bed in her underwear.

They had both ordered a light continental breakfast for the next morning and this had been delivered to their room at 7.00am, as requested, so that they could make an early start.

Tom hopefully checked his email again but still the wanted certificates remained wanted and were quite clearly still in the GRO pipeline. He quickly checked the website of the Birmingham Register Office in Holliday Street to see if there was an alternative to waiting for the electronic certificate service. However, he was again knocked back when he saw a banner notice advising that the walk-in service had been suspended and that the certificate service was solely by appointment. Not only that, but the advice that certificate production was currently taking two to three weeks before issue, only added to his rising disappointment and sense of frustration.

'Look, I don't think we can move further on parish registers or certificates that we have found or ordered to date until we have the relevant documents,' said Tom.

'So, it's a vacation day then,' replied Annie hopefully, 'perhaps another visit to the mall?'

'Not so fast, pard'ner,' responded Tom in an exaggerated southern drawl. What I was going to suggest is some intensive newspaper searching around Joseph Clarke aka Charles Tusker, looking for anything on his death, to add to the information that Jim and Peggy found.'

'Okay,' said Annie with a long sigh, feigning disappointment, 'I guess that we could also check up on anything additional on the Agnes Clarke death to see if the intrepid Inspector Dawes managed to advance his investigations into her demise? Right from the get-go, there's been something funny going on here.'

'It'll be best if we go and work at the library,' Tom suggested, 'if we do find something in the newspaper archive, we will be handily placed to follow it up in the parish registers perhaps?'

They made their way over to the Central Library building and were soon sitting down at what was becoming their usual table. The archivist who had signed them in winked at Annie, a fact that did not go unnoticed by Tom.

'Better get your laptop fired up, Annie,' he said gruffly, 'we haven't got all day.'

Sheepishly, Annie nodded and sat down quickly sitting opposite Tom.

'Ok, British Newspaper Archive it is then,' she said, and with the slightest hint of a grin across her features, she tapped a few keys on the keyboard to enter her username and password.

The familiar BNA website flashed up in front of them, 'What should we search for first?' Annie asked.

Tom suggested that as they now knew the basic facts about the untimely demise of Agnes Clarke, they could perhaps look for further articles on the investigation into her death, 'Put Inspector Dawes and Birmingham Police into the search box, then see we might just learn as to why he didn't apprehend Joseph aka Charles Tusker.'

Annie quickly typed in the suggested search and promptly received several pages of hits. She scanned the side bar menu and told Tom that she would add filters to narrow the results to all of the Birmingham newspapers for a 10-year period, commencing 1870. The revised results flashed up on the screen and so Tom carried his chair round to where Annie was sitting on the opposite side of the table and sat down next to her. He could feel the warmth of her arm through the thin fabric of her blouse, as their arms touched fleetingly as he moved closer to get a better view of the laptop screen. She added a further filter to change from the default *'Relevance'* to *'Date (Earliest)'* so that they could work up the timeline.

They could see that there were only six results for 1870, several for 1871 but strangely there was nothing returned for the years 1872 to 1879 from the years that they had selected.

'OK,' said Tom, 'let's just take them in turn,' and so Annie clicked on the first headline from March 1870 in which the detective was being praised for his part in the detection and arrest of the leaders of a stone throwing slogging gang who had been terrorising residents in Milk Street, Watery Lane and Heath Mill Road and several others in the Digbeth and Aston areas.

Two of the other articles were from the same month, referring to the trial of the young men concerned, recording the satisfaction of his senior officers at the Kenyon Street Police Station where Inspector Dawes had been based.

Annie navigated to the next article from July 1870 where Dawes was reported as receiving yet another commendation, this time for bravery after rescuing a young child who apparently had fallen into the canal. The newspaper stated that Dawes could not swim and had an aversion to the canal since being thrown into the water several years earlier, after trying to break up a bare-knuckle fight which was taking place on the towpath.

The next search result received the attention of the cursor, but when the article opened, it turned out to be a false return from the website algorithm as there were two adjacent stories, one involving a Henry Dawes and the other referring to a Board of Trade Inspector and so had nothing to do with the intrepid policeman who was the target of their research.

Annie raised her eyebrows and sighed before clicking on the final article for 1870 but again, it did not give them much insight into their quest for information.

This time, although the report was in connection with *their* Inspector Dawes, the information was to do with a small ceremony at the police station to celebrate the fact that the Birmingham City Police Force now consisted of 400 constables and that Dawes was to be in charge of a small group of detectives to be based at the new police headquarters in Moor Street.

'It's an interesting insight into our man,' said Tom, thoughtfully, 'he was obviously well thought of in the force. Let's get onto 1871, there's a cluster of articles that start in the middle of February.'

'Well, that makes sense,' commented Annie, 'we found the first article on the death of Agnes which, according to our notes was on 15 February, followed by her burial on the 28th of the same month.'

There was indeed a number of articles reporting on the death of Agnes, in addition to the one that they had found previously but all churned out much the same facts, to the effect that the police were searching for the husband of the deceased, namely one Joseph Clarke who had disappeared from the family home shortly after the stabbing.

Annie thought for a moment and added 'Strange there's nothing about her funeral. It seems the newspapers are very eager to report on the nasty stories, the violence and that sort of thing but nothing from the family point of view. After all, Agnes was a human, someone's mother.'

'Unfortunately, sentiment doesn't sell newsprint,' replied Tom, 'whereas murder, manslaughter and mayhem does. I'm not playing down Agnes' death but they were an ordinary family, living in poverty in a slum area of the city.'

'So, what you are saying, Tom Harding, is that her life doesn't matter?' responded Annie angrily.

'Hey, Annie, no not at all,' said Tom, 'I was just saying how it is with newspapers, not saying it's right or that I agree with them. Surely, it's no different in the States?'

'Sorry Tom, I don't mean to be kinda grouchy,' Annie said apologetically, 'shall we get back to the articles?'

Their search had moved into early March 1871 but it seemed that the search for Joseph Clarke had disappeared from journalistic attention.

Annie clicked on the next article in the list before them, in a state of near automation without taking too much notice of the headline. Clicking through and starting to read, they gasped and just stared at each other as the story from the *Birmingham Daily Post* opened in front of them,

POLICEMAN MURDERED – HEINOUS ATTROCITY

This newspaper is saddened to report the murder most foul, of one of the most respected police officers in the Birmingham City Police Department. Readers will be familiar with the name of Inspector Percy Dawes who only last year it will be recalled, received a commendation from the Mayor, the Rt Hon Mr Braithwaite Lloyd, following a display of bravery in rescuing a drowning child from the canal near Deritend. However, now we despair to report that Inspector Dawes has been the victim of a particularly violent and fatal assault on his person.

His lifeless body was found outside St Pauls Church by a person walking on his way home and was taking a short cut through the

churchyard before he stumbled upon the lifeless body of the unfortunate officer.

It is thought that the good Inspector was attacked whilst going about his lawful business by opportunist thugs, possibly with revenge as a motive.

An inquest will be held shortly.

'OMG!' exclaimed Annie, 'Tom, this sure gets worse!'

'Well, it definitely explains why there are no articles in later years and also, why Joseph Clarke alias Charles Tusker wasn't apprehended following the death of his wife,' Tom replied. 'Click on the next article and see what can be added,'

Annie did as instructed and soon they were reading the newspaper report of the inquest on the policeman that the then newly named Charles Tusker had read nearly 150 years earlier and from the very same newspaper that had originally given him the idea of starting a new life on the canal.

There were two further articles essentially informing the readership that enquiries into the murder of the murdered policeman were not progressing well, with the second one quoting Chief Inspector Lomax, the officer in charge of the enquiry, to the effect that the investigation was being closed given the lack of evidence that had been obtained to date.

'So that's it, then,' said Annie and was about to continue when she was interrupted by a ping from Tom's laptop on the opposite table, signalling the arrival of an email. He got up and casually looked at his inbox with his face lighting up.

'It's the birth certificates for the younger of the Joseph Clarkes and Eliza Parkes, who became his wife!' he exclaimed and eagerly opened the first pdf from the GRO as Annie scurried round to his side of the table and peered over his shoulder.

The familiar General Register Office birth certificate format came into view confirming that Joseph Clarke had indeed been born in the Birmingham registration district .

After they had both read the usual introductory script on the certificate, confirming the document was a certified copy of an entry of birth in the registration district of Birmingham and the sub district of All Saints, Tom scrolled down to the important data which informed them of the details:-

NO.441 13 March 1849 at Court 3, bk of 24 Vittoria St, Joseph Theodore, Boy,

The next two columns confirmed the parents as being Joseph Clarke and Agnes Clarke formerly Atkins and that the occupation of the father was furnace operator, pen manufactory. The certificate went onto state that the informant was Agnes Clarke, Mother, once again confirming the address.

'Oh, wow!' exclaimed Annie, turning to Tom as the mutual penny dropped.

'Oh, wow indeed,' said Tom excitedly, 'it's Theodore, his middle name is Theodore!'

'This must be the proof of the connection between the Clarkes, Charles Tusker and the Tuskers that came over to the USA!' said Annie, loudly.

'Mmmm, not so fast, we still don't know who the Lilian was that accompanied him to Amer…..oh, but we do now,' he added, stopping in mid-sentence, contradicting himself, as he had clicked on the pdf that contained Eliza's birth details, just as they were discussing the first of the birth certificates that they had opened.

'What do you mean?' asked Annie, turning towards his laptop screen to read the later set of birth details,

'Well, I'll be darned,' she added, and after again skipping the formal parts of the document, she read out aloud 'Eliza Lilian Parkes, 29 May 1850 at Treborth Street, Toxteth, Liverpool RD, Girl, mother's name, Mary and the father's name, Harry Parkes. That matches the details on their marriage certificate and is probably sufficient to confirm that this can only be the birth details of the Eliza that married Joseph Clarke in 1870.

'So,' said Tom enthusiastically, 'we have Theodore and Lillian by the look of it. All we have to do now is figure out how and why they left England!'

CHAPTER 26 – COVER UP

'Where's my Joseph?' Eliza repeated her question, staring into the distance as the approaching blue coated figure drew nearer to where they were standing in the back yard of the *'Greswolde Arms.'*

'Who bloody cares?' growled Curly, 'as long as he's found my package!'

'Hey, hold on a minute!' exclaimed Eliza, 'that's not Charles. It *is* Joseph after all, but why is he wearing his father's grubby overcoat? It's about two sizes too big for him.'

Eliza launched herself forward and broke into a quick walk towards the oncoming figure and soon confirmed that it was indeed her husband.

'Joseph? What are you doing and why are you wearing that awful coat?' she demanded.

'Erm, we have got a problem,' he replied and turning to Curly who by this time had joined the couple, added 'and here's the missing package. I managed to recover it for you.'

What's happened to Charles?' persisted Eliza.

Joseph was ready to give his version of what happened on the *Bessie* and had practised it over and over in his head on the way back.

'Well Boss,' he said handing the paper wrapped package over to Curly, 'Charles was acting strangely and when we reached the canal, he told me to search the outside while he would look inside the cabin,' the lies tripping off his tongue, coming quite naturally to him by now.

'So, I quickly made sure there was nothing on the cabin roof and then crept back to the open hatch to see what my dad was doing. I looked in the cabin and saw him on the floor reaching under the bed to retrieve something and then, he pulled out your parcel. I asked him what he was up to and he told me he had hidden it back at

Curzon Street. He said that you'd never miss one little parcel and it was then that I realised he was holding that gun you left with him *and* it was pointed at me! He ushered me back into the stern and then followed me out, still pointing the gun at me.'

'Hold on a bit, Joseph,' Eliza interrupted, noticing that the coat had become unbuttoned, 'why have you got blood on your sleeve?'

'Well, that's the problem I mentioned earlier,' he replied. 'I told Charles that we had to return the package or otherwise, we'd both end up feeding the fish. He refused to listen and said that there was enough money for us to get away and live a decent life, away from the canal.'

'And then?' interrupted Eliza.

'Well, there was a splash next to the boat as a duck or something landed in the canal and as he looked away, distracted like, I went to grab the gun off him but he stumbled against the tiller and the gun went off. I saw blood spurting and thought he'd shot me at first, but I can only think that he must have accidentally shot himself as he lost his balance. He just went straight down in a heap on the deck of the boat. That was the moment when I realised that he had a big wound and he was bleeding from his chest. I knelt down on the floor and tried to lift him, but he expired on the spot, right there and then in front of me. I half expected to see or hear someone come running along the towpath to see what the commotion was about but thankfully, I guess that most of the other boats had already left for the day.'

Curly launched into self-preservation mode 'So you just left him in the back of the boat in the open, grabbed the package and came back here, did you? You bloody idiot!' he screamed.

'No, no Boss,' protested the younger man, 'I dragged the body so it was a bit more out of sight and covered it up with a tarpaulin. I then grabbed his coat off the bed to cover up the blood on my clothes in case I met anyone on the way back, locked the boat up, picked up the package where he'd dropped it and came back to return it to you. I didn't know what to do next but thought you'd have a plan and that I should wait until I'd reported back.'

'Well young Joseph, you thought right, you done good,' he said, calming down and patting the younger man on the shoulder, 'now let's get this straight. You have just shot your father and now he's dead and we do know that people who kill other people, end up on Hangman's Hill, yeh?'

Joseph paled visibly, 'but Boss, it was an accident and you can't turn me in, I was working for you, remember?'

'Ah, don't worry Son, if you're worried about your Eliza, I'll look after her after your body has finished dangling from the gallows,' and then let out a huge burst of laughter, 'Ha-ha, ha -ha, sorry, couldn't resist that! Don't worry, I'm not about to hand you over to the coppers, I'm as involved as much as you are in this mess and I don't want to be swinging any more than you do. I have an idea to sort this out and then we can all start afresh without ever having to worry about money again. I'll get the landlord to pass a message back to some of my associates but in the meantime, let's get ourselves back to the *Bessie.*'

The trio gathered up the packages from the mail train and stuffed them equally into two brown hessian flour sacks that their host, William, had produced. With each man carrying a sack each, they silently trudged in single file back to the boat, which was still tied up at its wharf side mooring.

The first task was to move the body of the now deceased boatman inside the cabin, completely out of sight.

'Get the kettle on then love,' Curly said to Eliza.

'Gawd, you must be joking, I'm not going in there,' she answered, nodding in the general direction of the cabin. Not wiv a dead body to step over, anyways,' she added, 'Nah, I'm going to sit down on the deck at the prow. I can keep my eyes peeled for trouble as we go.'

Curly and Joseph set to, cleaning up the blood that Charles had spilled into the stern area earlier, made worse when Joseph and Curly had dragged the corpse to conceal it earlier, spreading the dark stain over a wider area. They filled a bucket with water from the canal and sloshed it into the footwell and then Joseph was on his knees, kneeling on the blue overcoat, using the scrubbing brush and detergent that Eliza normally used for general cleaning. Between them, they made a passable job of hiding the stains just in case any by-standers wandered near and got too close to the scene of the earlier fight and its fatal conclusion.

'Joseph,' ordered Curly, 'turn the *Bessie* round down by the locks and let's head back to Brummagem. We'll moor up near Yardley, wait until it gets dark and then we can get rid of Charlie's body.'

The temperature had dropped as by now it was early afternoon and it was cold as they travelled back along the canal. A light persistent drizzle did nothing to improve their situation or the sombre mood, but no-one had any desire to go inside the warmer confines of the cabin to keep Charles company. It was a subdued and somewhat dampened crew that eventually reached the canal bridge at Yardley.

Curly ordered Joseph to cut the steam engine and they moored up by tying the ropes to a tree stump on the embankment on the opposite side to the towpath, just as daylight was starting to fade.

'Less likelihood of us getting disturbed here,' said Curly, 'right Joseph, as you were the one that put him in the cabin, so you can be the one to get him out. Wrap a blanket round him and he will be easier to drag….and yes, I have done it before and it is the reason I know, before you ask,' he added.

Joseph did as he had been instructed and soon, his father's crumpled corpse lay curled up and covered with the blanket on the floor of the well deck at the stern.

'Right Eliza, time for you to stop being a wimp, 'demanded Curly, we'll keep watch and what we need you to do is go inside the cabin and collect anything that's important to you that you want to take with you. The *Bessie* is about to embark on her last journey.'

Eliza cautiously stepped through the hatchway, screwing her nose up at the odour of death starting to permeate through the cabin. She quickly grabbed at a pillow covering and picked up bits and pieces including a brooch that had belonged to her mother, some lace handkerchiefs and some clean clothes for both herself and Joseph as well as some soap and Joseph's razor.

She was about to leave when in one of the soap hole storage slots in the bulkhead, she caught sight of a small daguerreotype picture of Charles and Agnes that must have been taken in happier times. Joseph had brought the picture with him when he cleared their house of personal belongings in a similar exercise, prior to starting their life on the canal in what almost seemed like a lifetime ago. She took a last look around the cramped accommodation space of the saloon, realising wistfully that hers and Joseph's whole life could be summed up by just a few contents that could be crammed inside a pillow covering.

A shiver rippled down her spine and without further hesitation, she joined Curly and Joseph in the much fresher air, but she had no sooner done so than she realised that she could hear the chugging from the engine of another canal boat approaching but was as yet, still out of sight around a bend in the canal on the other side of the bridge.

'Ah, here are my boys,' said Curly, 'just in time to take care of things,' and as he spoke, the prow of the second boat appeared and after manoeuvring, it drew alongside, breasting up to the *Bessie* with the other crew securing the second boat, skilfully using the anser pins on both vessels to prevent either moving.

'OK, you two, your time is up….on the *Bessie* anyroad,' said Curly, addressing both Joseph and Eliza.

Seeing that Curly had a small black revolver in his hand, Joseph stuttered, 'c-c-c'mon Curly, there's no need for that, is there? I-I-I did recover the missing package for you, after all.'

'Eh?' and realising that Joseph was looking at the gun in his hand, replied, 'No, no son, don't worry. I have been keeping this on the *Lottie*. This is my main boat when I'm lying low. With all that's gone on, I feel more comfortable with a little fire power in my pocket. Don't worry m'boy, one corpse to dispose of is an inconvenience but three would be a downright bloody chore!'

Joseph and Eliza visibly relaxed at Curly's words as the older man continued 'Now we have to dispose of Charlie here. Let's roll him up in the blanket, lift and dump him over the side and onto the bank.'

The problem was that Charles had been a big man when he was alive but now, he seemed even heavier in his deceased state with rigor mortis having started to set in over the last few hours. Eliza watched as Joseph, Curly and the two crewmen from the *Lottie* struggled as they tried to lift the body over the side of the boat.

'Come on, Joseph,' grunted Curly, 'don't forget this was the man that was shagging your missus when your back was turned!'

With a roar of anger and finding a reserve of strength from an unknown source, Joseph heaved his father's remains over the side of the boat. It hit the muddy bank with a soft thud before rolling down and was only prevented from entering the canal by the hull of the *Bessie* which was butted up to the bank.

'Well done, Joseph,' said Curly, patting him on the shoulder congratulating him.

Joseph stayed where he was sitting on the floor of the boat, hunched up and sobbing to himself. Eliza knelt down next to him and put her arm around his shoulders. 'C'mon Joe,' she said, 'it's all finished with now. You did what you had to do.'

'I know,' came the semi snuffled reply, b-b-but he was still my dad. I know he did some terrible things to Mom and then taking advantage of you, but while I felt like punching his lights out, I didn't want to see him dead!'

The conversation was interrupted by Curly, 'Right, let's get cracking and get away from here. You two have done right by me and so here's what we are going to do. You said you had thrown the revolver into the canal this morning but the London detectives that will be deployed from Scotland Yard will probably assume it's there and comb the bottom of the cut and then using this latest ballistic knowledge they talk about, they might be able to trace the gun back to the *Bessie* and therefore back to you two. So, we're going to swap boats, my canal days are over as your help has guaranteed my retirement fund! You can take *Lottie* and do what you like with her as long as you just disappear and be sharp about it!'

It was time for the quietly spoken Eliza to pipe up angrily, 'That's ok for you Curly, but we need some money if we are going to really disappear as we won't be able to work the canals in *Lottie*. I think we need some money to help us on our way *and* to help us forget the events of the last 24 hours.'

Joseph looked worried and was clearly of the opinion that Curly might change his mind about disposing of three corpses being a chore because he intervened with 'Calm down 'Liza, we are getting our very own boat, after all.'

'No young Joseph,' responded Curly, 'your good lady wife is quite right and don't worry, I always intended to slip you a few quid so as to see you alright.'

At which point, he picked up one of the paper packages next to him that had been stolen from the train and which were still in the hessian sacks. With a grubby thumb nail, he split it open, flicking through the bundle of notes with the fingers of his other hand. He split them roughly into two equal parts and lobbed one part to the two-man crew that had brought the *Lottie* alongside and the other half he passed to Eliza, 'Here you are, darling. I reckon there's about three hundred quid there and that should bide you over until it goes quiet, or you work out what to do. Gawd 'elp us, you might even go on a cruise,' he added guffawing at his own joke as he helped Eliza climb into the stern of the *Lottie.*

Joseph followed her, carrying the pillow slip containing all of their worldly possessions and asked, 'and what will you do with the *Bessie?*'

'Less you know, the better it will be,' came the reply, 'but James and Harry here will take me back to Birmingham where I have made some travel arrangements of my own and then they'll go up the cut a bit and get rid of the dear old *Bessie,* blood stains, gunpowder residue and all.'

At this point, he unhitched the two boats and pushed the Lottie away while Joseph fired up the steam boiler in their new vessel. The last sound as the party separated was from Charles, his body now unrestricted by the hull of the *Bessie,* rolling down the last bit of embankment and landing in the water with a gentle splosh, but not loud enough to alert any curious passers-by.

CHAPTER 27 – PUTTING TWO AND TWO TOGETHER

Tom and Annie were heading for something to eat and a beer in a pub, but the establishment that Tom had selected turned out to be no ordinary pub.

Tom had promised Annie that they would have a night away from hotel restaurant food and so they walked the short distance from their Broad Street hotel and were soon in Brindley Place and entering the *Malt House* a pub that backed onto the side of the canal, giving fantastic views of the water-based nightlife.

"So, Annie, do you realise that this place is quite famous in your country because it also has having a connection to the United States?' he asked.

Annie thought that this was probably one of his jokey moments and so, with a touch of sarcasm replied, 'Oh yes, why's that then? Let me guess, it's because they serve a reuben sandwich or hot dogs, I suppose?'

'Nope, nothing to do with the food. We're talking politics now. This Pub once had a very famous visitor,' he answered, with a semi serious expression.

Annie glanced up from studying the menu and gave him a puzzled look, one eyebrow half-cocked and the expression on her face telling him to continue.

'Well, back in 1998, I was living in Birmingham. In fact, I was staying at Aunt Jemima's house as at the time, I had a full-time job in the city centre. Anyway, there was an international political conference which took place at the International Convention Centre in Birmingham which is just over there on the opposite side of the Canal and involved most of the major world leaders.'

Tom continued 'Mr Blair represented the UK, Boris Yeltsin was there for the Russians, Jacques Chirac in attendance as he was the French President at the time and then from the USA, came the one and only Bill Clinton.'

'And?' asked Annie impatiently, her stomach telling her that this was the time to be ordering their food and not engaging in small talk.

'And' continued Tom calmly, 'Bill Clinton came into this very pub and enjoyed a couple of pints of best bitter. It made the *Birmingham Mail* at the time and there were photos of him on this very balcony, knocking his beer back. Now isn't that impressive?'

'I'm not that impressed, to be honest,' Annie replied nonchalantly. 'He's a Democrat and I'm a Republican so I never did see eye to eye with his policies.'

Seeing the slightly deflated look on Tom's face, she leaned across the table and kissed him on the cheek, 'but thank you for the history lesson as always and also for bringing me here. It certainly is in a lovely position.'

After selecting from the menu, they ordered their food and changing the subject quickly, Tom asked Annie what she thought their next research move should be.

She thought for a moment, 'Well, we have connected Joseph and Eliza Clarke as also being Theodore and Lilian Tusker. I guess we need to try and locate some evidence to prove that they are the same couple that emigrated to America in 1893 but by then they had taken the Tusker surname. It doesn't seem unreasonable that if they assumed a fake name, it would be the same fake name as Joseph senior took when he changed from Clarke to Tusker?'

'Good thinking,' replied Tom 'I thought of another angle as well. You remember when we were on the boat with Jim and Peggy?'

'Yes, of course,' she answered, 'It was a brilliant day!'

'Exactly, now do you remember that Jim said he had a friend at the museum who had access to the canal boat database?' Seeing Annie nod, he continued, 'I phoned Aunt Jemima while you were getting changed back at the hotel and she is going to ask Jim to check with his friend to see if there is any record of what became of the Tusker boat *The Bessie* which was the name we found on the census with our family aboard.

She's seeing him and Peggy tonight at a family history meeting and she'll ask them. It might shed a bit more light on what happened to our intrepid crew and if there is some additional information, it might move us a little nearer to establishing the connection between the Clarkes' canal cruises and the Tusker transatlantic trip.' he added grinning at his attempted joke but this only drew an exaggerated imitation slap by Annie to her own forehead.

Annie turned to him and said, 'The other thing that's bugging me is that weird inscription on Charles Tusker's headstone at Yardley. I mean to say, what sort of grieving relative inscribes a memorial with an apology?'

'Well, the headstone itself was quite ornate and would therefore have been fairly expensive to erect. As it was reported that he was a victim of either manslaughter or murder, it seems odd that there was any headstone at all. Have you got your tablet with you, by any chance?' he asked.

'Yep, sure thing, it's right here in my tote,' she responded, picking up her shoulder bag on which Tom could see the distinctive Michael Kor's logo.

'What do you want me to check on?' she asked

'If you can navigate to the British Newspaper Archive, Jim mentioned there was a report on the discovery of Charles Tusker's body. I wondered whether there were any further articles on the funeral. I imagine that the authorities would have buried him, probably in a paupers' grave which is why it makes even less sense that an expensive memorial was erected. We can check the date of the funeral on the Birmingham burial records website and then see if there was anything in any of the local newspapers.'

Annie quickly found the burial entry and then made a note of the date of the interment before she proceeded to logon to the Newspaper Archive website but Tom stopped her and said 'Before you do that, please can you download the full burial entry. It'll cost £5 but it might be worth it.'

Annie did as she had been instructed and they were soon opening the pdf which was almost instantly returned by the Bereavement Dept database site.

Tom studied it and after a little thought, told her that he was puzzled because the entry confirmed that the burial had actually been a private family ceremony as opposed to the anticipated pauper service and had been conducted by *Furber Bastock*, one of the oldest established family firms of funeral directors in the Birmingham area. 'That's really useful to know,' he said out loud. 'I happen to know that they have one of the largest archives of funeral records with details of every single ceremony that they have arranged since 1868 which was when the firm started trading. Now we have the date that Charles was laid to rest, it should be straight forward for them to check their ledgers and give us some detailed information.'

Annie googled the funeral director's website and found an enquiry form which she completed, giving their contact details before she then entered the burial date and the fact that it had taken place at Yardley Cemetery.

At that moment, their food arrived and so Annie quickly hit the submit button to send the request. The waitress placed their plates on the table in front of them, but just as Tom was about to pick up his knife and fork, his mobile rang. He mouthed to Annie that it was Jim on the phone as he answered the call.

Annie could only hear one side of the conversation and Tom was listening intently, interrupting Jim only with an occasional 'Really?', 'Oh OK' followed by a 'that's interesting,' and finally 'wow!'

He added 'Thanks for the information, Jim, we appreciate it.' ending the call and after putting the phone back down on the table, he innocently speared a chip with his fork, chewing it very slowly.

'Tom! Don't be a pig, tell me what Jim just told you', she demanded impatiently. 'It must have been something very interesting, judging from the fact that your eyebrows were raising and lowering thirteen to the dozen while he was speaking! It's a dead giveaway whenever you're talking to someone!'

Tom speared another chip and was about to pop it into his mouth but seeing the expression on Annie's face, decided it may not be the most prudent thing to do.

'Ok, ok, busted,' he replied with his hands up in an imitation of fake surrender, 'In brief, Jim told me that his friend has found the *Bessie* in the logbooks and canalboat registration documents. It seems that about a week after Charles was killed, she was found ablaze on the Wyrley and Essington canal section, near Wolverhampton …… or

'Ampton, which Jim reliably informed me was the boaters' name for the town for many years. Nobody was on board at the time of the fire it seems, but the police found evidence of this being a deliberate blaze as there were traces of an accelerant, likely paraffin. The *Bessie* was all but destroyed in the fire and the remnants deposited into the nearby scrapyard. Jim also checked the newspapers but there was no report of anyone being apprehended for setting fire to the boat.'

Annie was listening intently to what Tom was saying and interrupted him by saying 'Now, I distinctly heard you say *wow*. What you have just said is very interesting but nothing that I would call as deserving a Tom Harding wow!'

'Ok, ok,' Tom replied with a grin, 'you're obviously becoming quite the detective. What Jim went on to tell me, was that his friend also did a search for Joseph and Eliza Clarke on the boat owners register and he found them aboard another canal boat which carried the name *Lottie*. His friend is going to do some additional checking on the history of the *Lottie* for us and said he'd get back to Jim if he found any more information.'

'Oh ok, I'll let you have your wow. That's quite exciting by way of a turn of events. C'mon, back to the hotel,' she said, 'time for bed!'

'What?' Tom replied, 'it's only early!'

'Who said anything about sleeping?' Annie answered with a wink, 'It's time for my wow moment now, I think!'

CHAPTER 28 – BOATING WITH LOTTIE

Joseph was getting used to navigating with *Lottie* as she was a little bit shorter in length and slightly narrower in beam. He found their new boat quite easy to manoeuvre.

Eliza had asked him whether narrowness in beam and ease of manoeuvre was the way he preferred his women and maybe one of the reasons that he had married her.

Whilst the size of the vessel may have been a factor in his overall sense of relief, he also felt that a heavy burden had been lifted from his shoulders now that his father was gone, he still felt more than a little bit guilty at the part that he had played in Charles' demise.

It had only been a few days since the boat exchange at Yardley and he and Eliza had resumed their usual runs up and down the Grand Junction canal, carrying their cargoes, which consisted mainly of coal and lime.

Interspersed with the carriage of conventional goods, it was general knowledge that the pair were not averse to carrying unconventional goods from time to time too.

With the money that Curly had given them from the robbery proceeds, Joseph and Eliza had opened a bank account at the Bilston branch of the Metropolitan and Birmingham Bank, just a short carriage ride from the Walsall Canal.

Joseph and Eliza had spent some of their money on new clothing and the pair looked rather dapper as they alighted outside the bank, before going inside to conclude their business of setting up an account by depositing £250.

It was a sunny day and so they walked in the general direction of the canal and then walked along the towpath, hand in hand until they reached *The Lottie* moored alongside Darlaston Brook.

Once aboard the vessel, they both changed into their day clothes, more befitting of canal boat folk. They were planning to stay moored up for the rest of the day before moving up the cut to Wombourne, a village a few miles southwest of Wolverhampton to meet up with a local man by the name of Robert Henry who liked to refer to himself as a 'businessman' but in reality, he was a well-known fence for the easy disposal of stolen goods for those in need of such services. Having moored up, Eliza stayed on board whilst Joseph made his way to the nearby *Boat* public house, which was around 200 yards away from their mooring. Although it was a reasonably respectable establishment now and a popular beer house for the heavy drinking canal boatmen and women, Joseph recalled the stories that back in the day of the canal being built, it had become a brothel of some notoriety, servicing the needs of the hard-working navvies who put in long hours completing the construction of the waterway.

Joseph pushed open the door of the bar and hesitated briefly as the bright lights, the noisy babble of the conversation and the smell of stale beer assailed all of his senses simultaneously.

He glanced round and spotted Robert Henry sitting on his own at a corner table with a half full tankard of beer on the table in front of him. As he approached the table, the other man nodded for him to sit down and signalled to one of the serving wenches who after returning to the bar, promptly placed another beer in front of Joseph.

The two men had met before although it had been when Charles was still around and so Joseph was cautious, 'Evening, Mr 'Enry,' he began, 'I understand that you be needing our transport services again?'

His companion for the evening nodded back in reply, 'Indeed I do Joseph, but first can I express my condolences on the sad news of your father's demise? He was a fine man. Let us hope they do catch the scoundrel that shot him and soon. Sometimes it seems it is not safe for those of us that just want to make an honest living.' he added with a wink.

'Thank you,' responded Joseph and changing the subject hurriedly, added 'but we must look to the future now. How is it we can be of assistance?'

Robert took a swig of the ale and after wiping the froth away from his mouth with the cuff of his jacket, as it seemed most menfolk did when on the beer. He leaned forward and speaking in a quieter voice said, 'Some associates of mine came into possession of a large quantity of silver plate, candlesticks, trays and the like.

They are currently concealed in one of the outbuildings of this public house but seeing that your boat is moored just a short distance away, we will bring the goods to you at midnight. There is good cloud cover and so no bright moonlight. Once safely stowed, you should convey them to a spot four miles down the canal where the arrangements have been made for you to be met and the goods offloaded. At that point, you will receive the usual fee of 10 guineas for your help, 'he said firmly, closing off any hope of negotiation that Joseph may have harboured.

Instead, he replied 'That's fine, Mr 'Enry. My father always said what a pleasure it was to do business with you. I take it the er, cargo has come from the recent burglary at Wightwick Manor?'

'The less you know, the better it will be,' came the answer, 'just be ready at midnight!'

Joseph trudged back to the *Lottie,* feeling tired after quaffing two tankards of ale at *The Boat* and after climbing back on board, he recounted to Eliza what their instructions were. He was hungry and helped himself to some crusty bread and a lump of cheese that Eliza had put out on the table area in preparation for his return.

At fifteen minutes to midnight, he got up and left the cabin to await the delivery of their consignment. Right on time, two men appeared out of the darkness and after placing two wooden crates next to the tiller, instructions were passed on for the next stage of the transaction and just as quickly, they disappeared from view.

Joseph quickly transferred the boxes into the hold and covered them over with a tarpaulin.

Suddenly, he heard whistles blowing, the sound of which pierced the night air, coupled with the sound of heavy boots echoing off the cobbled paving. The noise came from the back of the warehouse in which direction the two men who had delivered the crates just minutes before had hurried towards. Realising that the police were approaching, Joseph quickly and skilfully cast off from the wharf with the vessel's steam engine just making a quiet puttering noise as the *Lottie* also vanished into the swirling mist.

The instructions that they had been given were clear and under the light of the full moon with the mist clearing, Joseph made for the agreed meeting point, just south of Wolverhampton. He was being quite cautious as he approached the rendezvous. How had the police found out about the goods being disposed of that night?

Eliza came up and stood next to him in the stern. 'What's the delay, Joe?' she asked.

'I'm not sure,' he replied 'the agreed signal was that a lantern would be left alight in the upstairs window of the abandoned lock keeper's cottage and this would mean that it was safe for us to moor and unload, but there's no lantern and it's ten minutes overdue already.

We'll wait here out of sight for another little while and then if there is still no signal, we will sail right on past the designated unloading place, carrying on down the canal for a couple of miles and then try to find a quiet place to tie up and work out what we should do next.'

It was all quiet apart from the hooting from the beak of a distant owl. Eliza made a mug of tea and they quietly sipped from the enamel mugs but the silence seemed to get even quieter, which is at least how it seemed to the hapless pair of boaters.

'Okay, times up,' said Joseph in a hoarse whisper and handed Eliza his mug, 'let's crack on. They're obviously not coming for their stuff!' and at that, he restarted the engine and once again, they were on the move, visibility limited by the darkness of the night. They continued until they reached the Aldersley Junction where Joseph tied up fore and aft on mooring pins, about half a mile from the point where the Wolverhampton Canal joined the Birmingham Canal Navigation.

'Right 'Liza, pass me that jemmy. Let's see what we have in these crates that were of so much interest to the coppers back there. Sort of makes me nervous carrying stolen goods …. or at least stolen goods that I haven't stolen or been told what they are,' he added with a nervous laugh.

He took the metal lever from his wife and under the light of an oil lamp tried to get a grip under the lid of one of the crates. Uttering a grunt of force, the wood gave way and with a large splintering sound, the lid of the first crate gave up its resistance, broken into three pieces.

The contents inside the crate were covered by sheets of old newspaper and Joseph gingerly lifted the top sheets back.

He recoiled as he realised that he was not staring at some items of silverware as he had been expecting following his discussion with the fence in the pub, just a few hours ago.

Instead, his eyes alighted on bundles of five-pound notes, each secured with a length of brown twine.

Joseph and Eliza immediately turned to the second crate and followed the same process but with increased vigour. This time, the lid gave way a bit easier and they were soon looking at the identical twin of the first crate with the interior also lined with the tied-up bundles of bank notes.

'Strewth!' exclaimed Eliza, 'that's a small fortune, aint it?', she asked of her husband.

'Aint it indeed,' came the instant response.

Joseph picked up a strip of paper which lay underneath the money, but with the last inch or so still protruding from one of the wads of notes.

'I recognise this', he said, 'it's the same wrapper that was around each of the money bundles from the Post Office raid.'

'This must be Curly's money!' he added.

Eliza's eyes widened, 'We've got to get rid of it, we'll be for it when Curly finds out. We'll be helping yer dad to see who can make the best fish food!' she cried.

'Are you bloody stupid, Liza?' demanded Joseph, 'there's an absolute fortune here. It'll set us up for life, just think, no more hauling limestone, coal and manure up and down the cut, in all weathers.'

'Aye and if Curly finds out we've got 'is money, then it'll be a short life that we'll be set up for and all,' Eliza continued in a frightened tone, her voice quietening to little more than a whimper.

'We'll 'ave to lie low for a while, that's plain to see,' replied Joseph and adding 'we'll get off the Union and take the Dudley No.1 down in the direction of Stourbridge and Worcester. We can moor up at a quiet wharf near Brierley Hill until the fuss dies down.'

'Mmm, ok,' said Eliza 'but only because I don't have a better plan. I'm just really worried that Curly is going to catch up with us though.'

'We'll get underway while it's still dark, tie up at dawn on the opposite side of the towpath and then take it in turns to sleep. We'll be down by the Factory Locks, north of Tipton by the morning and then tomorrow night, we can continue on our way to Stourbridge. Don't worry, my love, we'll take the Netherton Tunnel rather than having to leg it through the Dudley,' he added as an afterthought, referring to the long limestone tunnel where engines were banned for fear of tunnel collapse. This would leave the boating community to lie on their backs on the deck and use their legs on the tunnel walls and roof to propel the vessel forward.

They executed the plan perfectly and spent the following day moored in a quiet location, away from any other boats, keeping a watch out for possible trouble.

As darkness fell, they were just about to set off when another boat came upstream and Joseph recognised Daniel Turner, a veteran boatman, originally from Liverpool with whom he had shared many a pint with, in the past.

Daniel pulled alongside and shouted 'Oi Joseph, how are you both doing. Haven't seen you for months, I was sorry to hear about your dad by the way. Charlie was a good bloke,'

He added. 'Oh, I've just come up from Birmingham and have you heard the news? Old Curly's been nicked by the rozzers. He's in a cell at Steelhouse Lane. Seems like someone grassed him up as being behind that Post Office train robbery at Curzon Street when that sorter was killed! They reckon it's Hangman's Hill for him.'

'Thanks for letting us know, Daniel,' shouted back Eliza, 'we're on our way to Worcester. Heard there's a fair bit of new work around,' at the same time waving goodbye to their fellow boatman as he continued on his own journey.

'Right, Joseph, I said last night I didn't have a better plan but now I have! Hearing Daniel's scouse accent has made me a little homesick. I reckon we should turn round and head north to Liverpool!' she exclaimed, excitedly.

'But we were going down the Dudley, we decided last night and we just told Daniel that as well, didn't we?', he protested.

'Aye and Daniel's got a loose mouth on him, too. If someone grassed Curly up, then chance is they know you and Charles were involved too and they'll be after us soon. We can rely on Daniel telling everyone we're down Worcester way, while we head up north instead.'

'Eliza, that's brilliant. Now I knows why I married you, beautiful and brainy at the same time. Fast ahead, Captain!'

CHAPTER 29 – CURLY'S SUSPENDED SENTENCE

The next morning, after having eaten breakfast in their room, Tom had just walked out of the shower when he heard the familiar ring tone on his phone as the device jumped around on the top of the table, because he had left the vibrate function on as well.

He could see the caller id and called out to Annie 'It's Jim, he must have some more information for us.'

Annie put her laptop down on the sofa beside her and listened as Tom answered the phone.

'Hi Jim, how are you today and has your friend managed to find anything else out about the *Lottie* for us?' he asked.

He listened for a while and Annie watched as he grabbed one of the hotel pencils and scribbled away on the notepad provided.

'Ok,' she heard him say, followed by another 'ok'.

His face gave nothing away as he concentrated on what Jim was telling him but eventually, he passed on his thanks and ended the call.

'That is incredible,' he said, referring to his notes, 'the amount of detail they have on that database is amazing. It turns out that the *Lottie* was transferred to Joseph and Eliza Clarke in 1893 and then about a month later, was re-registered, but this time, to Theodore and Lilian Tusker!'

'So, it looks like our theory was right about Joseph and Eliza changing their name, picking up the Tusker surname that Charles had "borrowed" and then each of them using their middle names, dropping their original birth forenames of Joseph and Eliza!' Annie exclaimed and almost without pausing for breath, added 'but why, Tom? Why? It seems a little extreme to be honest.'

'It may have something to do with the previous owner,' Tom responded, glancing down at the pad again, 'apparently it was a man by the name of Curly Harris who had been running the *Lottie* up and down the canal for many a year. Jim said that there were some notes to the effect that he had been in trouble with the canal boat inspector for either having too many people on board or carrying unauthorised cargoes but to be honest, he doesn't sound any different from a large percentage of the canal population.'

'So, I guess he retired and sold the boat, then?' enquired Annie.

'No, well that's the strange thing,' replied Tom, 'there was nothing in the logbooks about the sale and no bill of transfer either which was usually a legal requirement on such occasions. It would seem that the ownership of the boat just changed to Joseph and Eliza, aka Theodore and Lilian, shortly after the remains of the burned-out *Bessie* was found up near Wolverhampton.'

'It doesn't really make sense though,' interjected Annie, ' I don't imagine that they were insured and so where on earth would they get the money from to buy another boat and so quickly too?'

'There's nothing much else in the museum files but maybe we could try the British Library Newspaper Archive? I know Jim said there was nothing on the *Bessie* but there might be some additional information on this Curly Harris character,' Tom suggested.

Annie moved back across to the sofa and retrieved her laptop. 'I was already on the BNA website, just going back over some of the older records to make sure we hadn't missed anything or that the site hadn't been updated with some extra page scans,' she said.

She quickly woke the laptop up from its temporary slumber and Tom watched as the familiar page appeared on the screen. Annie typed in the advanced search box "Curly+Harris"+canal+Birmingham and then added a date filter for the years 1875 to 1899. After a few seconds, the results were returned and as expected, there were a couple of articles from the magistrate's court reporting some instances of petty crime but then, they both saw the same headline from late September 1893, from the *Birmingham Post,*

BOATMAN TO HANG FOR POST OFFICE MURDER

At the Birmingham Quarter Sessions today, canal boatman Stanley Harris, known in the boating community as "Curly" received the death sentence after His Worship, Judge Harcourt donned the black cap and passed the ultimate penalty on this weasel of a man.

The jury had heard that the police had been convinced of his involvement in many serious crimes in the past but had been unable to procure sufficient evidence on any of the previous occasions.

The facts of this case proved just how vile a man Harris was as the police now had clear evidence to prove that he was the mastermind behind the Curzon Street Postal Train robbery when a young 23-year-old Post Office Sorting Clerk was murdered trying to protect his employers' property. The Court had heard that the victim, a man who had been married for just a few months, had been set upon by a gang of robbers, masquerading as passengers on the train. Despite his brave attempts to prevent the heinous crime occurring, his throat was cut and his body unceremoniously thrown from the railway carriage into the stagnant canal waters below.

The Police were given evidence by an informant that it was Harris who had organised the robbery and although some of the stolen money has been recovered, a substantial amount of the robbers' haul is still missing. Some paper notes and a map were found at the Harris accommodation and the fact that the man was linked to the robbery is beyond doubt.

The train had been robbed whilst stopped at the signal and afterwards, a number of passengers on the train made statements to the effect that a canalboat was seen heading away from the railway bridge immediately afterwards.

The Police have also been investigating a possible link between the robbery and the discovery of the body of a canal boatman by the name of Charles Tusker, with the cause of death being a bullet wound to the heart which was now without doubt the result of foul play.

The body was discovered in the canal near Acocks Green, two days after the robbery and a search is underway for the remaining two members of the crew of his canalboat who are a married couple by the names of Joseph and Eliza Clarke. The Police believe that based on some additional information gleaned from their informant that Tusker and the Clarkes' played an instrumental part in the train robbery and by association, in the murder of the post office employee.

What has added to the mystery of this situation is that the vessel that Charles Tusker operated under the name of the 'Bessie', has since been found burned out, north of Birmingham.

Harris has already been refused leave to appeal and it is expected that the sentence will be carried out at Winson Green prison within the next few weeks.

Annie and Tom looked at each other in disbelief at the report that they had just read.

It was Annie that broke the silence, 'This looks like this could be the answer, Tom? This man Curly is responsible for a murder that Charles Tusker and the two Clarkes were also involved with and then the body of Charles Tusker is found shortly after the robbery.'

'I agree, it is a bit too much of a coincidence,' replied Tom, 'especially as the *Bessie* is burned out and then almost immediately after, Joseph and Eliza are aboard Curly's boat the *Lottie* and at about the same time, they also change their name.'

'It suggests that they have something to hide, without a doubt,' answered Annie, thoughtfully, 'look, there is another article here. It looks like our friend Curly did hang after all,'

CURLY HARRIS HANGS ~ BIRMINGHAM IS A SAFER PLACE

At 8am this morning, the ultimate sentence was carried out at the new execution shed adjacent to C Wing at Winson Green Prison on the convicted murderer Stanley Harris who was also known by the name of Curly.

James Berry Esq. was the hangman and it was reported that despite him being a practiced executioner at the Winson Green gallows, having been employed there on three previous occasions, the despatch of Harris did not go smoothly as the drop was inadequate and he struggled for nearly four minutes after the trap opened.

A crowd of over 500 bystanders had gathered outside the prison walls to witness the raising of the black flag to signify the eventual death of Harris. It is understood that there were several postal workers present in the crowd and applause broke out at the raising of the flag at 8.05am.

The condemned man had reportedly consumed a hearty breakfast and afterwards, he walked unaided to the gallows. Harris made a statement confessing to his crime and acknowledged the justice of his sentence.

Tom and Annie finished reading the article from the screen in front of them and sat quietly for a moment or two, digesting the information from the newspaper.

It was Tom who spoke first, trying to lighten the mood of the moment 'There's an old genealogist's joke which is a euphemism about ancestors who were hung, as getting a suspended sentence. It seems that this Curly fellow definitely received his suspended sentence, even if it looks like he may have been suspended a while longer than normal!'

Annie visibly shivered as she took in what she had just read, 'The article describes him as a vile man and so whilst in general, I disagree with the death sentence, I find it hard to argue against crimes such as this one. What I don't understand yet is the connection between this Curly character and our Clarkes or Tuskers. The newspaper seems to be making a definite connection between them by referring to the discovery of the body of Charles Tusker in the canal with gunshot wounds, shortly after the robbery?'

Before Tom could reply, his laptop pinged to signify the arrival of an email and opening up his Outlook account, he said 'Perhaps this might tell us something. It's the reply from the Furbers, the funeral directors.'

The email was brief and merely thanked Tom for his enquiry and referred him to the pdf that was attached, stating that it was a digital scan of the appropriate page from their ledger, relating to the funeral of Charles Tusker at Yardley Cemetery.

Tom quickly clicked on the pdf icon and they watched as the document opened almost immediately.

The writing was in perfect copperplate script, no doubt from a very practiced 19th century clerical hand and so proved very easy to read. At the top of the page was the name of Charles Tusker but alongside was a note in brackets *'Also known as Joseph Clarke the Elder'* stating he was of unknown age.

In the box for the address of deceased, the words *'abode unknown'* but in brackets, the word *'boatman'* had been added, as if that was sufficient as an explanation for the lack of an address.

But it was the details lower down the page where Tom and Annie's gaze was drawn, where they read that the invoice would be remitted to Joseph Clarke the Younger and in brackets, the words *'Son of the Deceased'* had been added, followed by *'(Also known as Theodore Tusker)'*

In the special instructions box at the foot of the page was a note confirming the inscription required for the headstone and the additional words which just a few days earlier, they had read for themselves at the cemetery, simply *"I'm sorry, I didn't mean it."*

'That's a little odd, 'said Annie, 'why pay for the headstone and then disappear for good and what does he mean when he says he was sorry? It sounds like a confession to me.'

'Well, I must admit that is exactly what it does look like,' replied Tom, 'but what it does prove is that Charles Tusker was actually Joseph Clarke. It also goes to prove that Theodore Tusker who emigrated to the USA was his son, under a false identity. Don't forget also that Theodore and Lilian's son born just after their arrival in the United States was called Joseph Charles, surely a nod to his father and grandfather?'

'By default, then his wife Eliza must have been Lilian, which is what we concluded from her birth certificate!' responded Annie , her voice trembling with more than a trace of excitement.

'It most certainly proves the connection and is the link between them and Bob Tusker. Of course, that means that the Chief is descended from a murderer or even murderers!' she added.

'I think our job over here in Birmingham is nearly done,' replied Tom, 'we can finish writing up the report and return to Florida, if you are ready to go back, that is? Obviously, we have to say our goodbyes to Aunt Jemima first but if you want to look for some flights, let's get back to some sunshine!'

CHAPTER 30 – GOODBYE TO LIVERPOOL

The *Lottie* was moored up with the thick rope knotted round a large branch of an oak tree growing out of the top of a small embankment on the opposite side of the canal to the towpath.

'Should be safer here,' commented Joseph, 'but I think we should still take turns to keep watch while the other gets some shut eye. We've not only likely got the coppers but also some of Curly's cronies keeping their beady eyes open for us. There are only his two henchmen who helped with the body at Acocks Green that would know that it was us that took over the *Lottie* but I don't imagine for a minute that they will be shopping us to the cops for fear of incriminating themselves.'

'Yes, but they might earn a little reward money for pointing Curly's men in the direction of the *Lottie.* Anyway, where did you disappear to this afternoon, Joe?' asked Eliza, 'I was quite worried aboard the boat all by myself. Every time I heard another boat engine, I had to dive inside the cabin so I wouldn't be seen!'

'Stop blatherin', woman,' he replied, 'I 'ad some business to attend to, I went off to the telegraph office and sent money and instructions to Furbers, the funeral people in Birmingham and arranged a decent burial and a headstone for me dad, over at Yardley.'

'That's a bit risky, Joe, sending money by a messenger. It could get lost or stolen, couldn't it?' Eliza replied.

'Not as risky as sending it by train,' sniggered her husband, 'what with all these robbers around!'

They both spent a restless night, neither sleeping when it was their turn to do so and it seemed like an eternity until the first shafts of daylight dispersed the darkness as dawn broke. Joseph and Eliza grabbed some bread and jam for their breakfast and washed the food down with a mug of hot tea each, sufficient to fend off the cold early morning temperature.

'Come on, let's get moving. It'll take two or three days to get to Liverpool unless we get delayed.' Joseph instructed as Eliza finished tidying the tiny kitchen.

'I can't wait to see my dad,' exclaimed Eliza, 'it shames me to say so but it is over twenty years since I last saw him when he and me mam came down to see us when we moved into our house after we was wed.'

'Seems like a lifetime ago,' agreed Joseph, wistfully, 'c'mon woman, we got to go to Liverpool because Liverpool certainly won't come to us!'

The pair were soon on the move again. Joseph, or Theodore as he had to keep reminding himself was the name that he would now be known by, had studied the charts by the flickering light of the candle in the cabin the previous night when it had been his wife's turn to catch a couple of hours sleep.

He had learned from the chart that the route would take them from the end of the Birmingham canal out onto the Staffordshire and Worcester line followed by a forty-mile length of canal which would see them linking up with the Ellesmere and Chester canal near Nantwich.

The canal would then carry the crew of the *Lottie* to the junction with the River Mersey and the lights of the metropolis of Liverpool, where they would eventually moor up.

Having completed their journey without incident, they made their way to see Eliza's father and the rest of her family, who still lived in the terraced dockers' cottage which they had occupied as a family for over 50 years.

Alighting down from the cab, Joseph turned and helped Eliza step down onto the street, her boots scuffing up a small cloud of dust as she did so.

She counted the houses down in her head although she didn't really need to do so as she knew where her family home was and she marched on ahead, eager to see her father again.

The brown paint on the door was peeling and the net curtains looked as grimy as she seemed to remember them the day she had left home in what seemed to her to be half a lifetime ago.

Before she could knock however, the door was yanked open and a hand grabbed her arm and pulled her roughly into the hallway and her father's gruff voice yelled at Joseph to also get inside quickly and the insistent nature of the command made her husband also scurry inside the house without delay.

'Wh...what's going on, Dad?' she cried out with surprise as she was not expecting such an aggressive nature for their reception.

Her father led them into the small sitting room at the back of the house, crammed with furniture collected over the years all now with faded fabrics and well-worn arms, before he replied to his daughter's question. 'I'll tell you what's wrong my girl. If only I knew what you and your feller 'ere 'ave bin up to,' his nasal scouse accent serving only to elevate the concern in his voice. 'We had a visit from three heavies from the High Rip Gang telling us that they had been asked by some of their mates in Birmingham to call on us to say that if you was to show up 'ere, we 'ad to turn you in to them as otherwise, they would give a proper thumping to one of us. Apparently, there's a bounty on your 'eads for grassing up and robbing Curly Harris, that boatman who was hung at Winson Green.'

'We didn't grass up anyone and we definitely didn't rob Curly,' protested Joseph, 'we're not that stupid! We were asked to collect some crates for him but he got arrested before we could deliver them,' and then added 'that's when we found out the crates contained the money from that train robbery.'

'Well, we're made up to see you, of course, but if you think you're staying here, you've another think coming,' interrupted Eliza's mother who, as if by magic, appeared from the scullery, her pinafore covered in flour and traces of what appeared to be some sort of jam, although it was difficult to be sure as the spillages were obviously several days old.

Eliza's mother continued 'I.....err.....that is we, are fed up with the gang life and the daily threats of violence just by walking on the same pavement as some of these thugs. Started with the Cornermen, the Logwoods and now this High Rip mob, makes your Brummy Peaky Blinders so called hard knocks look like wet nursed babbies!'

Eliza's father took charge of the conversation, 'Ok, here's what we'll do. The neighbours may have seen you but none of them will grass us up to the High Rip, but we can't risk them coming back tomorrow and finding you 'ere. It won't just be us in for a thumping but it will be you two as well!'

Harry Parkes continued, 'So, the light is starting to fade and so we wait a while longer until it gets properly dark and then we'll sneak you out the back. We'll organise a carriage to take you back to your boat. After that, you have to disappear and it's not up for discussion.'

Joseph turned to his father-in-law, 'We have already changed our names, Harry. Theodore and Lilian are how we are known now. '

Harry Parkes grabbed his daughter and gave her a huge hug and with tears streaming down his face, said 'I guess this is the last time we see you then. Take care of yourself and that big lummox of an 'usband.'

Peering into the darkness of the back yard, Harry ushered his daughter and son in law to a carriage waiting nearby and watched as they climbed aboard. With a crack of his whip and a curse, the driver moved the horse forward.

A little over 10 minutes later, they climbed down and started walking swiftly along the towpath to where the *Lottie* was moored, the third of four boats tied up abreast of each other.

Roughly 20 yards from the vessel, Theodore pushed his arm out in front of his wife and stopped her from advancing further, at the same time putting his finger to his lips, indicating that she should keep her voice down.

'What is it?' she whispered.

'We have had, or we might still have some visitors,' he replied, 'I placed the bucket in the middle, directly above the lock to the cabin hatch and it's been moved to one side. '

They crept silently forward and stepped aboard the first of the boats which was tied up to the mooring pins on the towpath and quickly walked across the decks until they were standing next to the *Lottie*. There was movement inside the cabin as the sound of footsteps as well as things being picked up and put down again and it was apparent that a search was in progress in the cabin of their boat. Joseph aka Theodore crept silently along the deck until he was level with the prow of the *Lottie* and kneeling down, put his right hand inside and felt around the deck box which previously had held horse feed until the advent of the steam engine had made their old nag redundant before he had ended his days in the knacker's yard.

The box was now filled with sand designed as a DIY fire extinguisher in the event that the worst disaster that could strike a boat family was ever to occur. Whilst unlikely to save a vessel, it was hoped that there would be sufficient time to evacuate the crew to a place of safety.

He felt around in the sand and then pulled out an oilskin wrapped package and carefully discarded the outer wrapper, revealing the gun that had originally been given to them by Curly, which he had kept hidden and had not thrown overboard as he had told their ex-employer.

Ignoring the fact that he was holding the revolver with which he had shot his own father, he turned to his wife and remarked very quietly 'Well, Curly gave it to us for protection and blimey, that's what we need right now,' indicating that she should climb into the stern of the boat on which they were standing. Remaining on the deck of the boat moored alongside their own vessel, he quickly moved towards the hatch of their own boat and signalled that she should crouch down, out of sight and possible danger from the altercation that was surely about to occur.

Joseph removed his boots and very gently lowered himself, noiselessly into the stern of their own boat, concealing himself to one side of the hatch, peering out from behind a tarpaulin that had been very roughly folded.

As he did so, there was a curse from inside and as the hatch was slid backwards, a bald head appeared followed by a man's trunk, as the intruder hoisted himself out of the cabin. He was joined almost immediately by a companion who stood next to him on top of the cabin.

'The money must be 'ere somewhere,' said the first man with the twang of the Liverpudlian accent, 'they had it in Birmingham and must have brought it with the….' and stopped in mid flow as from his vantage point, he had spied Eliza curled up and cowering in the ineffective shelter of the boat next to them.

'Well, George, look down there,' he said, nudging his companion in the ribs and pointing downwards, 'if I'm not mistaken, I recognise her as the wench from the good ship *Lottie.* I think that we could be in for a bit of sport tonight. Wonder where that no-good lunkhead of her husband is? You keep watch and I'll go first,' he commanded. As he spoke, he jumped down into the stern of the boat and started to undo the belt on his brown corduroy breeches.

'The no-good lunkhead is right 'ere,' yelled Joseph, shrugging the tarpaulin to one side, and as he stood up, took aim with the pistol quickly and fired in the general direction of Eliza's would-be assailant.

The bullet hit his foe in the left shoulder and with a yell of pain, he fell backwards and stumbled against the low interior perimeter of the stern. As the gangster lost his balance, Eliza got to her feet and hit him hard, swinging the windlass at his head, which caused him to tumble over the side and into the murky water of the Mersey.

The other man, George, had watched with horror and realising he was the next target, jumped from the boat onto the next vessel moored abreast and started running across the decks towards the bank. As he leaped onto the boat nearest the bank, he was oblivious to the fact that he wasn't being pursued, as Joseph was still checking that Eliza was ok.

However, there had been some light drizzly rain earlier and in his attempt to escape, he stepped onto the damp, perilously slippy deck top and as his feet shot up in the air, he fell, hitting his head against the tiller with force, sending blood spurting into the river, as the rest of his body followed suit with a loud splash and instantly sank out of sight.

The silence of the night was disturbed by laughing and singing nearby and Joseph's puzzlement turned to realisation that it was chucking out time at the many nearby pubs. The chances were that they would have company soon as inebriated boat people returned to their nearby vessels, thus increasing the chance of discovery.

Joseph took control of the situation and told his wife to haul in the short anchor chain which disappeared into the river at the bows of the *Lottie.*

'Anchor, Joe? When since have we used an anchor?' she questioned, adding 'We be tied up to the next boat!'.

'Just do as I say, wench,' came the reply 'and all will be revealed.'

The chain links clanked as they coiled on to the floor of the boat helm and then a yelp of surprise as Eliza realised that there was no anchor attached to the chain but instead, a waterproof sack was revealed which Joseph helped manhandle so that it too swung onto the floor of the vessel.

Joseph grinned at his wife ' I think that this is what those High Rip boys were after. I wasn't going to leave all of the money to fall into the hands of some thieving scousers.'

Seeing his wife's happy face change to her best insulted look, he added quickly 'not that all scousers are thieves, of course….'

'What next then, Joe?' asked Eliza, in a more forgiving tone.

'Firstly, we stop all this Joe and Eliza nonsense,' came the reply. 'From now on, we have to be consistent and remember that we are Theodore and Lillian now as we agreed. I recall seeing a poster when our carriage went down past the docks earlier, advertising that a ship is due to leave tomorrow bound for New York. I say we bundle this cash into a holdall, check into lodgings near the docks and tomorrow, we'll get ourselves tickets and we'll set sail for America aboard the *RMS Scythia!'*

'We need to pack another bag with some bits of clothes to tide us over. Da' used to say from his days in the dock that it takes about 8 days to sail to America and unless you get a change, you'll stink more than you usually do,' she added with a grin. 'Let's get ourselves down to the Dockside and we can check into the Mercantile as it's awful posh there!' she exclaimed. 'We can't stay here any longer that's for sure.'

CHAPTER 31 - BACK HOME?

With a screech of rubber and a couple of bumps on the tarmac, the plane carrying Tom and Annie touched down at Tampa Airport. They had been lucky enough to get a short notice direct British Airways flight from Heathrow.

After completing the formalities of passport control and collecting their luggage off the carousel, it was shortly after 6pm US time that they were in a hire car south bound on the I-75 heading from the glow of the lights from the Tampa skyscrapers towards the much quieter and less commercial area of Anna Maria Island.

Their report was written up with the conclusions regarding the Chief's ancestry, all evidenced by the essential source material that had been obtained and analysed during their stay in the UK.

Annie had emailed Bob Tusker to alert him to the fact that his project was complete and they had agreed to meet him the following day to guide him through their detailed research.

'What do you think he is going to make of it, Tom?' asked Annie, 'It's gonna be a bit of a shock for him when he finds out he's descended from thieves and murderers!'

'Maybe, maybe not,' mused Tom, 'over the years, I have had a few unhappy clients who don't want to believe that they are descended from wrong-uns, but on the whole, most are happy with a bit of notoriety.'

'It might be different with the Chief though,' replied Annie, ' after all he is a police officer and it might be embarrassing for him, perhaps? I know he was hoping for a promotion and so if this all came out, that might be the end of his career.'

'Well, the one thing you can't change is your family history, as much as someone might like to. Ancestry shouldn't be embarrassing, as a descendant can't be held accountable for an ancestor's misdeeds.' came the considered response.

Annie continued, ' So what you are saying really is that unless said descendant repeated the crimes or wrongdoings of an ancestor, then they are OK?'

Tom was distracted for a moment as he looked out of the window and his jaw opened as he took in the view from the Sunshine Skyway. 'Wow, that is awesome,' he said mimicking his American partner's accent and getting a mock glare in return.

Returning to their previous discussion, he responded with '...and yes, I strongly believe that everyone should celebrate their ancestors, good and bad. Often there were perfectly valid , or at least understandable, reasons for so called wrong doings. Inevitably poverty, hunger, or both were factors as families had to do anything they could to feed the many mouths around the table.' and added, 'Often the only alternative to crime was the workhouse and everyone lived in fear of having to go in the "house" because there was more embarrassment with that than there was with being up in front of the magistrate, not to mention the harsh conditions suffered by the inmates.'

The journey continued and Tom told Annie more about the workhouses and the masters' cruelty that was often evident as husbands were separated from wives and in a similar vein, children were kept apart from their parents.

Although the poorest of families had a roof over their heads, very basic food to eat, this was often in return for extreme hard labour for both men and women inmates.

By this time, they were nearing the end of their journey as they had arrived in Palmetto and were soon in the Bradenton City Limits.

Tom noted that Annie ignored the first turning to Anna Maria as this would have taken them along the SR64 and over the bridge which had been the scene of the car accident where her parents had been killed after her deranged brother, in the hope of getting rid of Annie, had tampered with the brakes on her car, just a few weeks earlier. Instead, she drove straight past the junction and continued ahead before turning onto the Cortez Road. Tom didn't say anything as he knew that she had avoided that location ever since the accident. 'I'm sorry Tom,' she said 'but I will get over it. I realise that I need to celebrate their lives, not grieve their deaths. Tomorrow, I will get some flowers and perhaps we can drive down to the bridge, park up and I can spend a few minutes in reflection? I know Mom and Dad would have loved you, despite your annoying habits,' she added, grinning.'

After the transatlantic flight followed by the hustle and bustle of Tampa Airport, they were exhausted as they walked through the front door of Annie's Key Royale home. Soon they were showered and asleep, unsure of what the next day was going to bring them. After a fitful night's sleep, Tom woke the next morning to find Annie missing from the bed but with a wonderful aroma of bacon and coffee.

He wandered into the kitchen, rubbing his eyes, not quite taking in what he saw with Annie by the hob, naked apart from a full length apron.

'Wow, that's a sight for sore eyes!' he said.

'Aha. So, you like what you see?' she questioned, smiling.

'Definitely, what isn't there to like about crispy bacon and fresh coffee?' he replied jokingly, receiving a flick of the tea towel across his butt as a reward.

They had agreed to meet the Chief at Grassy Pointe Preserve off East Bay Drive, at 7.30 that evening which gave them plenty of time to fulfil Annie's pledge to drive to the scene of her step-parents' death crash. She had been to the florist located on Gulf Drive North and bought a posy of red roses which, she explained to Tom, had been one of Bill and Amy's favourite flowers.

The traffic was busy and it was almost 15 minutes later that they pulled off the SR64 into the parking lot on the Island side of the drawbridge, spanning intra-coastal waterway. Annie walked to the water's edge where the gentle wash from a tall sailboat lapped her toes. She stood quietly for a few minutes staring into the distance as if willing Bill and Amy Kane to turn back time and surface from the water.

The glare from the late morning sun gave a halo like reflection to the scene and the florist had attached a large piece of foam plastic to the flowers. Bending down, Annie placed her posy onto the water and gently pushed it away, watching as the tidal water and current pulled it further out into the waterway until the wash from a powerful launch caused it to rock and finally succumb to the waves, sinking slowly beneath the surface, disappearing from sight.

Annie wiped away a tear that was making its way down her cheek and pressed herself against Tom, drawing comfort from him. 'C'mon Tom, let's get out of here. We can get some R & R on the beach and maybe get a little bit of colour on your pale English body!'

However, the scorching relentless afternoon sun meant that the beach was crowded with tourists and so the couple made their way back to the house to review their report in readiness for their meeting with the Chief later that evening.

"So where is this Grassy Pointe Preserve that the Chief wants to meet us at and why can't he just come to the house?' questioned Tom.

'Well, as to the where, it's a community wetlands area used for tourism, designed to protect the ecology of the region .' Annie responded, adding, 'There's a boardwalk which connects to the wetlands and all sorts of mangroves, trees and shrubs. It's a bit swampy in places, but very pretty.'

'And as to the why?' asked Tom.

'He simply said he would be on duty,' replied Annie, adding that the chief had told her that there had been reports of anti-social behaviour in the area but he that he was too excited after reading Tom's very brief emailed summary of his ancestral research and couldn't wait until he was off duty to learn the full details of their research outcomes.

'There is something that I feel is a little odd though. If you can give me a minute please? I need to call Patrick Stringer back at the office and ask for his advice before we set out?'

CHAPTER 32 - GREAT EXPECTATIONS

Having checked into the Mercantile Hotel, Joseph using his new Theodore persona had walked down to the Cunard Ticket Office and although most of the 3rd class tickets had been sold, there were still a number of cabins left for the more well to do or more discerning passengers as the shipping company posters referred to their wealthier clientele.

He wasn't aware of it but at the very same time, his wife was meeting someone whom she had arranged to meet in secret back in their hotel room. The man confirmed her suspicions and left shortly afterwards giving the newly named Lilian plenty to think about.

Back at the ticket office on the dockside, no questions were asked as the clerk took details for the Board of Trade manifest, aided by a generous tip.

Thanks to Curly's unintended generosity, money was now no object and as Joseph and Eliza were now officially Theodore and Lilian Tusker, both aged 39, they were soon to be heading for a new life in the United States of America.

The RMS Scythia was due to sail at high water at 11am the next morning with Theodore and Lilian on board the 4,556-tonne vessel early enough to enjoy a good breakfast in their well appointed cabin.

Their steward who had introduced himself to the couple as Michael had brought them scrambled eggs with bacon and hot toast to their dining area. Theodore noticed that his wife was just picking at her food and asked her if she was going to finish the meal.

When she replied in the negative, a huge grin came over his face and he picked up her plate and scraped the remainder of her food, adding to the heap of food already in front of him on his own plate.

'I am sorry Th…Th….Theodore,' she said, 'I don't feel too well and will take a little air if you don't mind?'

'Allow me, Madam,' interrupted Michael, holding the door open for her. I will show you to a deck chair on your balcony if I may?'

'Yes, do that, Michael,' called out Theodore, belching out loud but then returning his attention to the slowly reducing mountain of food in front of him. 'Oh, do come back quickly afterwards man, as I will need some more coffee to wash this lot down with!'

Some thirty minutes later, his stomach somewhat distended with the first meal of many during the imminent transatlantic crossing. He found Lilian sitting on a red and yellow striped deckchair, staring across at the Liverpool Town Hall and the George Dock, a tear in her eye.

'What be up with thee, my love?' he questioned gently, 'what is it that is upsetting you?'

Lilian looked up at him and replied quietly ' Liverpool, that's what's up. It's probably the last time I shall see my hometown and more importantly, my family. I know that I had not seen them for many a year when we were on the boats in the midlands but I could have seen them anytime if I had just made a little more effort and got on a stagecoach or travelled by the railway. Now we will be more than 3000 miles apart and it won't ever be safe to return to England again anyway, as we will likely still be wanted by both sides of the law!'

Theodore sat down on another chair next to her and took her hand. 'I think it's time to think of new beginnings and our new life in America. We have more money than we have ever had before so we can settle down and perhaps buy a small farm or another business of some kind. We could even start a family...'

At this remark, his wife turned bright red and started crying for real 'Do you mean that, Jos---- Theodore, I mean?' she said hastily correcting herself, forgetting their new identities for a moment. 'I've been frightened to tell you because I didn't know how you would react but, errrm, well, we have already!'

'You've lost me there, my sweet Lilian,' came the reply, 'what have we done already?'

She looked him straight in the eye and responded ' Start a family, that's what we've done already! I was two months late but then you wouldn't notice whether I was on the rag or not! So, while you were down on the dock getting the tickets yesterday evening, I arranged with the concierge at the Mercantile to send a doctor to the room and well, he confirmed my suspicions. I'm pregnant! We're going to have a baby after all these years married and there was me thinking yours didn't work either,' she added, holding back on the full truth, as she knew her husband would not take kindly to knowing all of the facts about her interesting condition.
'Whaaat?' was the response from the shocked Theodore, 'how did that happen?'

She chuckled 'well if you don't know by now, my love, then there's little hope for you,' she replied, embracing him tightly, her mind flashing back to the several instances on board the *Bessie* with her father-in-law Charles, when caution and care had been overtaken by passion and pleasure on more than one occasion. Even a makeshift bed of reeds at the side of the canal towpath had been the scene of one of their amorous couplings.

She knew without a doubt that the rare occasions between the sheets with her husband had been unproductive given the unsatisfactory cramped accommodations that their canalboat had provided.

She still believed that the shooting of Charles had been an accident and would have been shocked to learn the truth that her husband had killed his father in an act of revenge and that he already knew the full truth of the clandestine affair with his wife.

Not as shocked as Theodore would have been if he had realised that it had been his wife that had instigated the relationship, of course!

The couple continued chatting about the future and Lilian realised that she had possibly got away with hers and Charles' subterfuge, when she realised that her husband had reverted to the subject of the impending birth.

'Shall we call him Charles after my father?' he was asking, 'it might be that he will look like him after all.' he added.

'What? Why? It might be a girl…..she stammered, ' why would we name the child after your father?' she added, searching his face for any clue that he might know the truth about the paternity.

'Just the practice in our family,' he replied,' the first born is named after his….or her….grandfather, so I thought Charles, even though that wasn't his real name….or maybe Agnes, if it turns out to be a girl?'

Lilian considered his idea for a moment or two. 'I have a better idea,' she said, 'in my family, we tend to name the first child after the parents and have a middle name honouring the grandparents. So, I think, ' it should be Joseph Charles if it's a boy and a girl should be Eliza Mary,' she said excitedly, trying hard to get her husband away from the topic of her dalliances outside of the marital bed.

'My love, that sounds like a plan. It's quite funny really because if it IS a boy then the Joseph represents mine and father's real names as in the ones that we were baptised with and then Charles after my dad's alias! I like it.' he said loudly and with enthusiasm.

Lilian sighed with more than a little relief and signalling to a passing steward, she ordered a pot of tea for them both and perhaps as a gesture towards their now relatively wealthy situation, requested a plate of biscuits too, which seemed a real extravagance to her, based on childhood memories of poverty and the years of struggle, make do and mend.

The earnest conversation had distracted her and she realised that the Liverpool skyline had disappeared into the mists as the British coast passed out of sight.

'Did you say it would be eight or nine days to reach America ? Where will we land anyway? In our hurry to get away and all of the excitement, I forgot to ask.' she giggled.

'If the weather is kind, then yes it will be around that time to get across the ocean to where we will make land in the port of Boston. All I know of it is that it is a big city, on the east coast of America. I believe that the prices of property will be higher there and so I think we should head further south to the country but we can take some advice when we make land. We don't want to draw attention to ourselves unnecessarily and so I suggest that we check into a small comfortable hotel under our new identities. Lilian responded enthusiastically 'No-one will be any the wiser that we are anyone other than Mr Theodore Tusker and his good lady wife, Mrs Lilian Tusker, immigrating from England to a new life in the United States!'

The crossing was excellent in many respects, marred only by Lilian suffering regular bouts of sickness, but whether this was pregnancy related or the motion of the vessel, she was never too sure. She was certain however, that the sooner that they arrived in the eastern seaboard port, the better that she would feel.

Theodore did not seem to notice his wife's discomfort at all. He knew that the price of their passage provided all of their food and drink, including more than the occasional alcoholic beverage and he made sure that he took full advantage of the facilities on offer so that he could get his money's worth.

After a week had elapsed, their attendant Michael had advised them just before dinner, that the captain had announced that the next day would see them arrive at their destination. Michael was a font of all knowledge and readily answered questions as to what the process was for disembarking and what they could expect once they were on dry land.

He also explained to them that the Immigration Act passed in America two years earlier, meant that they would have to undertake a brief interview by an official from the Office of the Superintendent of Immigration and in theory, at least, this would also entail a medical examination.

However, the steward confirmed that for a small "fee", they could be spared this aspect, especially given Lilian's condition. The requisite sum of money exchanged hands with little more than a nod and a wink, ensuring that their immigration would go unchallenged.

The newly created Mr and Mrs Tusker had a thirst for knowledge of their new homeland and Michael had explained that this was a great time for people who were not on the poverty line to make a new home in America. The economy was in decline with stocks and share prices plummeting and much political unrest had occurred after what had been labelled *The panic of 1893.*

The steward told them that unemployment had reached its highest level for many years and it was indeed fortunate that Theodore and

Lilian possessed sufficient funds so that he would have no need to look for a job.

In addition, falling prices and the general economic conditions meant that food, travel and living costs were lower than usual, meaning that the new arrivals would be able to operate on a relatively low budget. They would therefore have plenty of time in which they would be able to find a place to set up home whilst they awaited the arrival of the latest member of the family, who was expected the following January.

Thanks to their financial arrangement prior to arriving in Boston, they soon found themselves welcomed as immigrants and had been directed to the Omni Parker House, a well-established hotel in School Street, Boston. The hotel was ideal as still not wishing to draw too much unnecessary attention to themselves, the building was large enough for them to move around and be relatively unnoticed, especially if they stayed in their room or mingled in the crowded wood-panelled lobby, famous for its intricate carvings.

It was at this point that they realised they hadn't actually made any plans as to the next stage of their journey together.

In a little over four months, the birth of their baby was due and so they knew it was essential to find a home where the little Tusker could be raised.

Theodore ensured that he made the acquaintance of the concierge at the hotel and as he was generous in his tips, the man soon became a mine of suggestions as to various locations that would be considered but quickly dismissed. Not too cold, not too hot, not too wet as well as affordable property and land prices, were all important factors in their quest.

Eventually, on the recommendation of the concierge, the State of Georgia had been identified as falling within the criteria and

Theodore went into the commercial area of the city to seek advice from a real estate agent.

Back in the hotel room, it was an excited Theodore who was telling his wife that they were going to buy a small farmstead in Byron, Georgia where they would grow peaches and raise chickens.

'But Lilian, there is something else!' he added enthusiastically, 'not far from Byron, not more than about 30 miles in fact, is a community in a place called Forsyth County called….wait for it….Liverpool! It must be an omen.'

CHAPTER 33 – FINIS?

After Annie had finished her call to her partner at the office, she and Tom made their way down Marina Drive and after negotiating the lights by the CVS store, she parked directly behind Walgreens before turning off the engine.

After locking the car, the couple walked the short distance to Gulf Drive and crossed over the road, unaware that they were already under surveillance. 'Ok,' said Annie, 'the entrance to the preserve is just to the rear of the Mobil gas station,

Annie looked round, 'I can't see the Chief's car anywhere, can you, Tom?'

'No, but then if he's doing some undercover work to stamp out vandals and the like, he's not likely to park up in a police car with a flashing blue light!' he retorted.

As soon as they had exchanged the tarmac roadway for the extremely dry and sandy approach to the entrance of the nature reserve, unavoidably creating small dust clouds as they walked, they made their way towards the agreed meeting point. They were a little early, having agreed to meet up at 7pm but nevertheless, carried on along the boardwalk that circled the preserve, until they came first to a dense area of red and black mangrove forest, before reaching some strategically placed viewing platforms, designed to penetrate the open inlets of water.

Tom said ' You look a little distracted this evening, Annie. Is everything ok?'

Not wanting to alert him to her concerns, she nonchalantly answered in the negative, saying that she was just a little tired at the end of what had already been an emotional day for her.

They reached the tidal flats by the little creek and looked out with the slowly setting sun starting to cast shadows over the rooftop of a timber birdwatchers hide some 30 yards away and facing away from them, overlooking the intracoastal waterway.

'That was some walk,' said Annie as she sank down gratefully on one of the wooden benches facing in the direction from where visitors could see the sparkling waters of the bay.

Tom looked around quickly and sat down next to her, exhaling loudly as he did so.

'Did you bring the report with you, Tom?' asked Annie.

'Yes,' came the reply, 'but I have already emailed the bullet points to the chief and saved the full report onto my phone, so I can easily relay the main points from memory and then present the full report to him afterwards. It often helps to hear the headlines first and then the full facts are much easier to absorb and understand.'

'Hi, folks,' boomed out the loud voice of the chief as he appeared from out of the shadows of a large tree, 'thanks for stepping out to meet me here.'

The sun had dipped a little lower, casting long shadows across the wetland area and it was Tom who replied, 'You're sure cutting it fine, Chief. The light is starting to fade and the noseums will be coming out to play soon!'

'I don't think this will take long, Tom. I really did need to find the truth about my ancestry. I suspected that my forebears were not as honest as I would have liked them to be. I didn't tell you before but I had previously hired a researcher a few years ago and he drew a blank on establishing my lineage. When I heard of your genealogical abilities following your last adventure, I decided that I had to engineer you to take on my case. That's why when Annie was arrested following the shooting of her brother, I bribed the DA to drop all of the charges against you, so that the pair of you would be free to take on my Tusker research.'

He continued 'I found your summary report really interesting but I was concerned to find that my ancestors were basically thieves and murderers. If that came out into the public domain, I would be saying goodbye to any possible career development next year, when the County job will be open.'

His plan was simple: eliminate the only witnesses to his family's past crimes and make it look like an accident. He knew he had finally cornered Tom and Annie at the edge of the swamp and unholstered his gun before pointing the barrel of the police issue revolver in the direction of the couple.

The tension in the air was palpable but Tom and Annie had no option but to stand their ground as there was simply nowhere to run. The chief's plan was obvious and he sneered 'Sorry, but this is the end of the line for you two, I can't let anyone ever learn the truth about my ancestry.'

Just as he was about to squeeze the trigger, there was a splash to his right and although it was only a fiddler crab returning to the water, he glanced round, momentarily distracted by the noise which had seemed so loud in the heavy silence in the wooded area.

Taking advantage of the split-second hesitation, Tom lunged forward, knocking the gun from the policeman's hand and Annie watched as it skidded across the sandy ground before dropping into the salt water of the creek.

The two men were struggling and while Tom was the younger of the two men, the chief was taller and better built but then came the sound of running feet as five officers came running out of the bird hide where they had been concealed.

Reinforcements had arrived, summoned by Patrick Stringer, after Annie's last minute phone call to him before they had left the house. The other officers drew their guns, shouting orders to each other. The chief knew that he was outnumbered and tried to get away but tripped on a root of a cypress tree protruding from the ground, stumbled and went sprawling, nearly falling into the swamp.

His colleagues dragged him up and snapped the handcuffs on his wrists before leading him away.

"Don't forget to read him his *Miranda Rights!*" she yelled after the retreating figures, the sheer relief of the situation now coming to the fore.

Tom hugged Annie and they embraced, exhausted but safe. His threats towards the couple had been witnessed by the other officers, who had also heard his admission of corruption in his attempts to reduce the risk of losing his anticipated promotion. With his arrest, the truth would come out with justice being finally served.

'What I don't understand, though,' said Tom, 'is how the police came to be at the preserve to rescue us and make the arrest? Did you have something to do with it?'

'By Jove, I think he's got it,' she exclaimed, mimicking the events in Birmingham only a couple of weeks before but what already seemed like months ago. 'Yes, I thought it was odd, even if you believed the story about staking out the preserve to prevent anti-social behaviour, as it closes to the public at 5pm and so there wouldn't be many people, social or anti-social, around at the time we were scheduled to meet up. So, I rang Patrick and asked him to call his friend who runs the Bradenton Beach PD to set up a covert operation just in case. He cleared it with the Holmes Beach Mayor as technically they would have been operating out of their jurisdiction. I just had a bad feeling about the whole thing. The chief's demeanour just seemed to be different, somehow.'

The Holmes Beach community was shocked at the revelations and would no doubt ensure that the now ex-Chief of Police would soon be serving time.

The genealogy investigation by Tom and Annie had uncovered a web of crime, dating back generations. The chief had clearly seen the couple as a threat to his future security, as their findings would have exposed the dark family secrets of his criminal ancestors.

As they stood together, watching the sun set, Tom and Annie knew they had uncovered more than just family secrets —they had brought justice and peace to a community.

The past consists of provable facts but the future is always uncertain. However, Tom and Annie knew that they would be facing it together, their relationship bonded by the rigours of their shared ordeal.

One thing is sure, we haven't seen the last of Tom Harding and Annie Kane, genealogical investigators.

THE END

Printed in Great Britain
by Amazon